THE INSIDER

Reece Hirsch

BERKLEY BOOKS, NEW YORK

THE BERKLEY PUBLISHING GROUP
Published by the Penguin Group
Penguin Group (USA) Inc.
375 Hudson Street, New York, New York 10014, USA

Penguin Group (Canada), 90 Eglinton Avenue East, Suite 700, Toronto, Ontario M4P 2Y3, Canada (a division of Pearson Penguin Canada Inc.)
Penguin Books Ltd., 80 Strand, London WC2R 0RL, England
Penguin Group Ireland, 25 St. Stephen's Green, Dublin 2, Ireland (a division of Penguin Books Ltd.)
Penguin Group (Australia), 250 Camberwell Road, Camberwell, Victoria 3124, Australia (a division of Pearson Australia Group Pty. Ltd.)
Penguin Books India Pvt. Ltd., 11 Community Centre, Panchsheel Park, New Delhi—110 017, India
Penguin Group (NZ), 67 Apollo Drive, Rosedale, North Shore 0632, New Zealand (a division of Pearson New Zealand Ltd.)
Penguin Books (South Africa) (Pty.) Ltd., 24 Sturdee Avenue, Rosebank, Johannesburg 2196, South Africa

Penguin Books Ltd., Registered Offices: 80 Strand, London WC2R 0RL, England

This is a work of fiction. Names, characters, places, and incidents either are the product of the author's imagination or are used fictitiously, and any resemblance to actual persons, living or dead, business establishments, events, or locales is entirely coincidental. The publisher does not have any control over and does not assume any responsibility for author or third-party websites or their content.

THE INSIDER

A Berkley Book / published by arrangement with the author

PRINTING HISTORY
Berkley mass-market edition / May 2010

ISBN: 978-0-425-23462-4

BERKLEY®
Berkley Books are published by The Berkley Publishing Group,
a division of Penguin Group (USA) Inc.,
375 Hudson Street, New York, New York 10014.
BERKLEY® is a registered trademark of Penguin Group (USA) Inc.
The "B" design is a trademark of Penguin Group (USA) Inc.

PRINTED IN THE UNITED STATES OF AMERICA

10   9   8   7   6   5   4   3   2   1

For Kathy

ACKNOWLEDGMENTS

It takes a long time to write a novel, and even longer to write a first novel. Or maybe I'm just a slow learner. In any event, as I stopped, started, swerved and skidded down the long road from idea to publication, I have the following people to thank for helping me keep it between the lines.

First and foremost, my wife, Kathy, the love of my life and first and best reader. You read this manuscript more times than anyone should ever have to read anyone else's manuscript. Without your amazing patience and support, this book would never have been written.

Winifred Golden, my estimable agent, for rescuing me from the slush pile and providing unfailingly sound advice.

My wonderful editor, Natalee Rosenstein, as well as Michelle Vega, Caitlin Mulrooney-Lyski, and the entire team at Berkley Books and Penguin. I will be forever grateful for the way that you got behind this book.

Ed Radlo of Glenn Patent Group, who provided guidance on encryption matters. Any remaining inaccuracies are on me.

The writers groups that I have participated in over the years (the Rockridge gang and the San Francisco Writers Workshop) for telling me when I got it right and, more importantly, when I got it wrong.

Ed Stackler and Frank Baldwin, for helping me understand that there are rules.

My supportive colleagues at Morgan, Lewis & Bockius, a remarkable group of attorneys that (I'm very happy to say) bears no resemblance whatsoever to the fictional Reynolds, Fincher & McComb.

And finally, Donna Levin, who taught the UC Berkeley Extension Novel Writing Workshop where the first pages were written.

"San Francisco, the R... fine legal madness—... [who] is writing and n...
—John Lescroart, *New York Times* bestselling author

"Deftly plotted and filled with intricate twists and turns, Hirsch has written a terrific story that will keep you up late. We will be hearing more from this talented newcomer. Highly recommended."
—Sheldon Siegel, *New York Times* bestselling author

"An extraordinary, fast-paced thriller with compelling characters, understated humor, and a great story. It runs the gamut from national security issues to terrorism to the Russian mob . . . a cross between John Grisham and *Eastern Promises*." —Michelle Gagnon, author of *The Gatekeeper*

"Fresh and genuinely exciting . . . Hirsch manages to deftly combine a twisty plot involving Russian mobsters, insider trading, and a secret government surveillance program with a sly satire of life in a big law firm."
—Julia Scheeres, author of *Jesus Land*

"A big-time novel . . . fast, smart, and gripping. It hooked me on the first paragraph of page one and held me through to the end." —Frank Baldwin, author of *Jake & Mimi*

"Only a lawyer could have written a novel with so much deception and betrayal. I was hooked from page one."
—Tim Maleeny, bestselling author of *Jump*

"Reece Hirsch's *The Insider* is an absolutely stellar debut thriller, in which one tiny misstep lands us in a high-stakes mirror world of government subterfuge, terrorist plots, wannabe Russian mobsters, cutthroat white-shoe lawyers, and corporate double-dealing. What's not to like?"
—Cornelia Read, author of *Invisible Boy*

"Gripping and gritty, *The Insider* sizzles with tension and twists that both entertain and magnetize. All the danger, treachery, and action that make a reader clamor for more are there. Well done."

—Steve Berry, *New York Times* bestselling author

"Compelling in its intensity, and explosive with insider details, *The Insider* by Reece Hirsch introduces gifted young attorney Will Connelly, who is hurled on a pulse-pounding journey into the heart of one of the country's top law firms and San Francisco's powerful Russian mafia. This is a legal thriller sure to keep you up late into the night. Watch out, John Grisham!"

—Gayle Lynds, *New York Times* bestselling author

"Attorney Hirsch's debut thriller delivers on every front: a deft plot, blistering action, and plenty of unexpected twists. The finer points of the law are skillfully woven into a tale of insider trading that reaches all the way into the Russian *mafiya* and a terrorist cell. Hirsch brings San Francisco alive as the story unfolds in its famous streets and hidden alleys, its ethnic neighborhoods and corporate fortresses."

—Sophie Littlefield, author of *A Bad Day for Sorry*

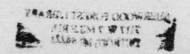

ONE

No matter how many times the police asked Will Connelly to recount the events of that morning, his story always began—and ended—with the same details. At six thirty A.M., he swiped his access card at the security desk in the lobby of his office building, then rode the elevator to the law firm's offices on the thirty-eighth floor. The hallways were empty, and he saw no signs that anyone had arrived at work yet. In his office, Will threw his suit jacket over the back of a chair, sat down at his desk, and began listening to the voice mails that had come in overnight from far-flung time zones.

Working on his first cup of coffee and first billable hour of the day, Will gazed out his window at San Francisco Bay, which was turning from black to Coke-bottle green as the sun rose through the mottled haze blanketing the Oakland Hills. The wind was already whipping up a light chop on the bay. There was a good chance that conditions would be right for windsurfing by late afternoon. Will had once been an avid windsurfer. He had even subscribed to a pager service that notified him when the conditions were right, but gave that up years ago. The beeping pager had only served to torment him while he was trapped in the office poring over contracts.

But he still kept a surf-shop sticker on the side of his computer monitor, the image of a great white cut through by a red line: NO SHARKS. An ironic motto for a guy striving to make partner in one of the world's largest law firms.

The phone on his desk rang, startlingly loud in the silent office. The Caller ID display flashed *Ben Fisher*, so he knew the call was coming from Ben's office one floor above him. Ben was a senior associate who was providing tax advice on a merger transaction that Will was running.

Will couldn't imagine what Ben might want from him at that hour, so he let the phone ring. He preferred to use these early-morning hours to work on projects that required some concentrated thought and a little quiet. Will needed every bit of concentration that he could muster because he was among the slate of proposed new partners that the executive committee of Reynolds, Fincher & McComb LLP was scheduled to vote on later that day. He had spent the past six years working toward the goal of partnership, and today his fate would be decided. It was more than a little distracting.

With his unlined face and longish brown hair, Will looked more like a law student dressed up for a job interview than someone on the verge of making partner. At thirty-two, he still didn't have the prematurely middle-aged look of many of his peers. In some quarters, looking like a kid was a disadvantage for an attorney, but Will's clients were mostly technology companies that seemed to like their lawyers young. Besides, it added to his reputation as a prodigy. He was two years younger than most of the other associates vying for partnership, a fact that could work against him when the partners' votes were counted.

The phone rang again, and once more the display showed that it was Ben Fisher. *If it's important,* Will thought, *he'll leave me a voice mail.* Anything Ben wanted to talk about could surely wait an hour or two. The phone stopped ringing, but Will continued staring at the console. Finally, the red message light blinked on. Will listened to Ben's message, which was nothing but dead air and the sound of breathing followed by a hang-up. If it didn't even merit a voice mail, then it really must not have been urgent.

Determined to find a quiet place to work and escape the phone, Will picked up a notepad and went down the hallway to the firm's law library to review some Delaware Chancery Court cases on fiduciary duty. Will doubted that Ben would find him there. In this age of online research, hardly anyone visited the law library.

He pulled a musty *Delaware Reporter* from the shelf and was halfway through *Axelrod v. Titanium Investments* when he heard a door slam on the other side of the floor. Will wasn't the only early riser today. Probably some first-year associate desperate to impress.

Will heard heavy footsteps, possibly more than one person. He tried craning his neck to peer down the hallway, but he didn't have the proper angle to see who it was.

A half hour later, Will went back to his office to locate some notes. After finding the notepad in one of the many piles of paper on the floor behind his desk, Will looked up and saw Ben Fisher.

Outside his window.

Thirty-eight floors up.

Plummeting.

He recognized Ben immediately by his lanky frame and close-cropped red hair. He even recognized the yellow striped tie that fluttered behind Ben like a cry for help.

The figure passed by the window so fast that he thought for a moment that he might have imagined it.

Will spun around reflexively in his desk chair, searching in vain for someone to confirm what he had just seen. Then he dashed out of the office, pausing only to fish the security card from his jacket pocket so that he could open the secure doors. Will ran through the empty lobby to the elevators. As the elevator descended, Will stared at the floor numbers as they ticked down like a launch sequence.

It didn't seem possible that Ben had committed suicide. After all, he was a tax attorney. Far too buttoned down for such a melodramatic gesture. On the other hand, it was difficult to erase the split-second image of Ben, like one of those Robert Longo paintings of men in business suits writhing in empty space, ripped out of context. The Falling Man.

But maybe he had not really seen Ben at all. Maybe his subconscious had taken a familiar image from that morning, prompted by the annoying phone calls, and slapped it on a bit of visual input that was otherwise incomprehensible. But even if it wasn't Ben, Will knew that he had seen someone falling past his window.

When he reached the lobby, a crowd had already gathered on the sidewalk around the splayed figure. His pants were shredded below the knee by fractured shinbones, which had torn through the fabric in sickening white and red. He must have hit the sidewalk feet first.

Ambulances arrived and the crowd was pushed back, widening the perimeter. A paramedic turned the body over, and before a blanket was drawn over the face, he saw smashed, bloodied features that were still recognizable. It was Ben.

The paramedic went through the motions of checking for a pulse. Heralded by the blurt of a siren, two uniformed policemen arrived.

Why aren't they taking away the body? Will thought. The paramedics and the police now seemed to be concentrating their energies on crowd control.

He heard people sobbing around him. A couple of secretaries from his firm were crying into their cell phones. Soon the crowd was filled with Reynolds Fincher attorneys and staff.

Someone touched him on the shoulder. "Are you okay?" Will snapped out of his daze to see Peggy Loo, who worked in the firm's Office Services department, standing next to him.

He then realized that three different people had asked him that question in the past ten minutes. Apparently, he looked like someone who was not okay.

"Yeah, I guess," Will replied. "Are you okay?"

Peggy nodded, a little uncertainly. "Did you know him very well?"

"Not really." Will knew only a few things about Ben, despite years of making small talk: he was single, a marathon runner, and a film buff.

"Why would he do this?" Peggy asked, as if she expected an answer.

"Just last week he told me that he was planning to run a marathon in Seattle. He was trying to break three hours," Will said.

"I saw him yesterday in the hallway," Peggy said, her voice starting to break. "I didn't even know him, really. He just . . . He just seemed . . ." Peggy started to cry.

Will put his arm around her as she sobbed. After a few minutes, a secretary who was one of Peggy's friends led her away, saying, "We should go. We need to go."

Will drew a little closer to the edge of the crowd around the body. Part of him wanted to run away from the crumpled man in the suit, from the bright red blood and the jagged shards of exposed bone. But he found himself staring nonetheless, trying to understand something that refused to be understood.

Then he saw it.

Next to Ben's bloodied right hand on the pavement lay a white plastic security access card for the office building. A cord woven with blue and green strands was threaded through a hole in the card. That was how Will knew that Ben had been holding Will's own access card. The blue and green cord had once held his name tag at a corporate law conference. The card was slightly warped—Will had once left it in a pants pocket and run it through a dryer.

Will had used the card that morning, swiping it on the pad at the front desk in the building's lobby. How could Ben have gotten it?

Then Will remembered that when he had gone to the library, he had left the card in the pocket of his suit jacket, hanging over a chair in his office. The blue and green cord had been dangling from the pocket.

As he stared at the access card, the full implications of what he was seeing came to him. Each access card was registered to an employee and created a record of where workers went in the building. Sooner or later, the police would figure out that Ben was using Will's access card as they attempted to track Ben's movements before his death. Will had clearly used that access card when he entered the building at six thirty—the guard at the front desk would verify that. Given those facts, anyone would assume that Will and Ben had met that morning in the office. If Will told the truth, that he had never seen Ben, no one would believe him. His story would seem even more implausible when the police learned that Ben had placed two calls to Will's office in the half hour before his death.

It dawned on Will that Ben's death might be a murder, not a suicide. Worse yet, someone seemed to be trying to cast suspicion on him.

As Will reached into his pants pocket, he already knew what he was going to find there. He removed the white plastic access card that he had used in his hurried exit from the building. There was no doubt in his mind that it had belonged to Ben Fisher.

TWO

When he returned to his office, Will placed a phone call to the police to report the switched access cards. The officer taking the call seemed distracted at first, but was quite attentive by the time Will had finished his story. "We'll send someone to your office to take your statement," the officer said. "Don't go anywhere."

Part of him had wanted to keep quiet because he knew that the police would immediately view him as a suspect. But he figured that they would eventually figure it out anyway, and, after all, he had done nothing wrong. While waiting for the police to arrive, Will tried to resume his work, hoping to put some psychic distance between himself and the events of the morning.

Within three hours of Ben's death, an e-mail appeared in his inbox from Don Rubinowski, the firm's managing partner:

Will—

What happened today with Ben was a terrible tragedy, and we all need time to grieve and mourn. But, unfortunately, there are matters that Ben was handling that will not wait. Ben was lead attorney on the Jupiter Software/ Pearl Systems merger, which must close very soon. I know I don't need to emphasize that this is a major transaction. Negotiations are at a particularly critical stage, and we need you to take the lead on this, effective immediately. You'll be receiving the files shortly. Claire Rowland will get you up to speed on the due diligence.

                                                         Don

Will replied that he would begin reviewing the files immediately. He was not about to say no to the managing partner when he was on the brink of partnership, especially not on a deal like this one. Jupiter Software was the world's leading encryption software company, and it was being acquired by Pearl Systems, the top maker of desktop computers, in a transaction that would change the landscape of the technology industry. It was the sort of deal that could make or break an attorney's career.

Around two P.M., he looked up from a conference call to see a tall man in a baggy blue-black sport coat standing in the doorway to his office. With a quizzical expression and a bit of sign language, the man asked if he could enter. Will nodded, and the visitor took a seat in front of his desk. Will gestured to indicate that the call was winding up.

If this was what a police detective looked like, it was not quite what he had been expecting. The stranger had a long, oval face, heavy eyelids, close-cropped black hair that was graying at the temples, and a mouth that seemed to naturally twist into a frown. He was unself-consciously examining the contents of Will's desk and bookshelves.

After waiting a couple of minutes for Will to extricate himself from his phone call, the visitor removed something from his jacket and slid it across Will's desk. It was the gold badge of a San Francisco Police Department detective.

"I'm sorry, but I'm going to have to call you back," Will said, hanging up without waiting for a response.

"Sorry for the interruption," the visitor said in a rumbling baritone that, if it were one octave lower, would have been subsonic. "Detective Lazlo Kovach, San Francisco Police Department."

Will hoped the panic didn't show on his face. "No problem, Detective. Sorry to keep you waiting."

"No problem." Detective Kovach once more glanced at the books on Will's shelves. "You're a corporate attorney?"

"Yes, that's right." Will braced for the next question, which he was certain would involve Ben Fisher.

"I have a question for you, if you don't mind. I have a little business I operate on the side, selling first-edition books on eBay. My specialty is crime and detective fiction."

"Very appropriate."

"I know, I know. I found a nearly pristine first edition of Ross McDonald's *The Galton Case* at a garage sale last month—you could have knocked me over. So, now my little business is starting to take off. I've even bought a climate-controlled storage locker for the books because there wasn't any more room in my house. So what I wanted to ask you is . . . do you think I should incorporate?"

"I wasn't expecting that one," Will said with a nervous laugh. "Incorporating is probably a good idea. It sounds like it's more than a hobby for you at this point. Having a corporation will protect your personal assets if there's a lawsuit or the business becomes insolvent."

"Thanks. I appreciate the free advice. It is free, right?"

"On the house," Will said, growing more comfortable, despite his knowledge that this was an obvious ploy to put him at ease.

"So we should probably get to it. My partner and I are here today talking to several of the people who worked with Ben Fisher. I understand that you called in."

"Yes. I actually saw him fall past my window."

"Horrible," Detective Kovach said with a shake of his head. "It must be hard to carry on with your day after something like that."

"Yes, it is. So what can I do to help?" He suddenly felt like one of those cheesily suave criminal masterminds in an episode of *Columbo*, a role that would be played by Jack Cassidy or perhaps Robert Culp. They always tried to appear so casual when Columbo arrived at their offices to ask a few questions, yet they all met the same fate by the final commercial break. He had to remind himself that he had no reason to feel guilty because he had not committed any crime.

"How long had you known Mr. Fisher?"

"About six years. We came up through the ranks together at the firm. Worked together pretty regularly."

"And you were both up for partner, weren't you? Were you competitive?"

"No. We were friends. Maybe not really close friends, but friends."

"But not everyone can make partner. That must have caused some tension."

"Not really. There are other associates here that are very

cutthroat about that sort of thing, but Ben wasn't one of them."

"Were you currently working on any projects together?"

"Ben was providing the tax advice on a merger transaction that I was working on."

"Which one?"

"I'd prefer not to say, if that's all right. The transaction involves a public company and it hasn't been announced."

"I understand, but this is a homicide investigation, so I'm afraid I'm going to have to insist. Don't worry, cops don't make enough money to invest anyway."

"It was the merger of Boston Technologies with Davionics. They make navigation systems for the aviation industry."

"And did you see Ben this morning?" The detective paused. "Other than when he was falling from the roof."

"No."

"Did you talk to him on the phone?"

"No, but he tried to call me twice this morning. He probably knew I was in the office early and wanted to talk about the Boston Technologies deal."

"How do you know it was Ben who called?"

Will pointed at his phone. "There's a display. I saw his name flash both times."

"Why didn't you answer?"

"I didn't want to be bothered. It was six thirty in the morning, and I wanted to concentrate on the project that I was working on. I figured that we could always talk later."

"And he didn't leave a message?"

"No. The second time there was a message, but he didn't say anything and hung up after a few seconds."

"Weren't you curious?"

"It was early, I hadn't had my coffee yet, and I wasn't ready to get my head around complicated tax issues."

"So you're sure you didn't meet with Ben at all this morning?"

"No." Will didn't like the way Detective Kovach had repeated the question.

"So how did Ben manage to have your card key to the office when he went off the roof?"

"I really don't know, but I suppose that Ben or someone else could have entered my office and taken it from my jacket pocket while I was in the library."

"But you didn't hear anyone else on the floor?"

"I heard a door shut around six forty-five or so, but I didn't see anyone."

"Tell me how you found the other access card."

"It was just there in my pocket."

"You told Lieutenant Morrison on the phone that you realized that Ben was using your access card because you recognized the blue and green cord that was attached."

"That's right."

"So why didn't you realize that the key you took with you to go downstairs wasn't yours? It didn't have a blue and green cord."

"I had just seen someone fall to his death. I was kind of freaked out at that point."

"So you have the other key with you right now?"

Will nodded and handed over the access card to the detective.

"Why don't you just set that on the desk," Detective Kovach said. He picked it up gingerly by its edges and dropped it into a plastic baggie that he removed from his jacket. "You know, Will, you have the right to have an attorney present while we have this discussion."

"Wait a second . . ."

"You know that you have the right to an attorney, right?"

"Yeah, sure. I know my story sounds odd, but I'm telling you the truth. I called you, remember?"

Detective Kovach examined the access card through the plastic bag. "What do you think the odds are that this belonged to Ben Fisher? Pretty good, I'd say, but we'll know soon enough. Or would you prefer to just tell me right now?"

The detective slipped the plastic bag into his jacket pocket. "I've got an idea. Why don't you just tell me the whole truth about what happened this morning?"

"I don't know what happened here, but I'm telling you the truth. I didn't meet with Ben Fisher this morning. And I have no idea how our access cards got switched."

"Now why would he sneak into your office and do that? What purpose could that possibly serve? He obviously had his own access card."

"I don't know. Maybe someone wanted to frame me for his murder."

"Frame you for his murder," the detective repeated softly. "And I thought I was the one who read too many crime novels. No one said that Ben Fisher's death was a murder. Did I say that?"

"No, but from the tone of your questions . . ."

"I'm sorry, did I have a tone?"

"Maybe I should have a lawyer."

"No, I think I'm done for right now. But the next time we talk, you'll want to bring a lawyer. And there will be a next time. In the meantime, I strongly recommend that you not tell anyone, other than your lawyer, about the access card thing. It will just make our job more difficult, and it could lead to some press coverage that I don't think you'd like."

Detective Kovach rose, unfolding himself slowly to his full height. "Oh, and thanks again for the legal advice."

Watching the detective leave, Will felt dazed, like the time he had cracked the windshield with his head after being struck in a rear-end collision. He had hoped that the police would appreciate the fact that he was coming forward voluntarily with useful information. Instead, Detective Kovach just seemed grateful to have a suspect. The fact that he was innocent should have been a comfort to him, but it wasn't. Innocent men were convicted of murder all the time—DNA evidence was freeing only the lucky ones. And even the rumor that he was a suspect in Ben's death would be enough to derail his partnership and perhaps his entire legal career.

Unable to concentrate on his work, Will kept turning the facts of that morning over in his head, but they refused to cohere. Why would anyone want to kill mild-mannered Ben Fisher? And if someone wanted to kill Ben, why would they do it at the office when they could have killed him someplace where there was less risk of discovery? Will thought he might know the answer to that one—whoever committed the murder wanted Will to be present so that suspicion could be cast on him. But why would anyone want to implicate him in Ben's death?

Will tried to dispel these disturbing questions by immersing himself in the details of the Jupiter-Pearl transaction. He had no choice if he was to be prepared to immediately step in as lead counsel.

Throughout the rest of the afternoon and a late night at the office, Will worked feverishly to get up to speed on the complex deal. He studied the latest draft of the merger agreement. Claire Rowland, a whip-smart young associate who was leading the team of attorneys conducting due diligence, briefed Will on the status of their review. When he was comfortable that he was conversant in the transaction, he called Jupiter CEO David Lathrop at home that evening to assure him that the transition would be seamless and the closing would not be delayed. Lathrop seemed satisfied that Will was being appropriately obsessive about his new responsibilities.

Will fell asleep at his desk sometime around three A.M. He started awake to find that the sun was coming up again over the Oakland hills, just as it had twenty-four hours before when Ben had plunged to his death. Will couldn't remember the dream that had awakened him so suddenly; he just knew that he'd had the sensation of falling from a great height.

THREE

The next morning, another visitor stood in the doorway of Will's office. This time it was Don Rubinowski, the firm's managing partner—and he wasn't smiling. Will immediately assumed that Don had spoken with Detective Kovach and learned that he was the prime suspect in Ben Fisher's death. If the firm didn't fire him on the spot, they would probably at least ask him to take a leave of absence until he was either exonerated or jailed.

"You okay?" Don asked, detecting Will's agitation.

"Not really," Will replied.

"Did you sleep here last night?"

"Yeah. Just trying to get my arms around the Jupiter Software merger."

"It's good to see that you appreciate what's at stake. But I would expect nothing less from you. That's why we gave you the assignment."

Don Rubinowski had been managing partner for twelve years, quite a run in the world of law firm management. In fact, he had come to be known as "Teflon Don," impervious to the vagaries of law firm politics and economic cycles. In a firm that was increasingly giving way to casual dress, one of the few lasting changes on law firm life wrought by the Internet boom, Don remained buttoned down and dapper. He wore a charcoal gray bespoke suit with a pocket handkerchief and suspenders. Like those children of the sixties who never quite moved on from that golden time, Don Rubinowski never really left the leveraged-buyout glory days of the late eighties.

"Awful thing with Ben. Just awful. No one seems to know why he did it." Don stepped into Will's office and shut the door behind him.

Will wanted to tell Don about the switched access cards and his interview with Detective Kovach, but he felt compelled to obey the detective's instruction to keep his mouth shut.

"But I'm not here to talk about Ben," Don added. "Or the Jupiter Software deal."

Will felt a sickening jolt, certain that he would soon be leaving the firm to pursue "other opportunities."

"Will, I'm here to inform you that the executive committee has voted to extend you an offer to join the partnership as an equity partner."

If he had heard this news yesterday, he would have been ecstatic. Today, he just felt numb. Detective Kovach obviously hadn't shared his suspicions with firm management. When Will realized that a response was expected, he said, "Thanks, Don. I've been looking forward to hearing that for a long time."

"I thought about waiting to tell you, given what's happened. But I figured the news of the vote would leak anyway. And a bit of good news can't hurt, right?"

Don clapped Will on the shoulder. "Over the years, we've all watched you develop into a superb attorney. You've earned this in spades, and we're all expecting more great things from you in the future. Harvey will provide a package of materials describing the terms of your equity contribution, the changes in your benefits. You know, you won't be an employee anymore. But listen to me, I'm talking like you've already accepted. I don't expect you to answer until you've reviewed the materials."

"I'll review the materials, but there's absolutely no question. Thank you."

"Enough with the thank-yous. We're not doing this just because you're a nice guy. You've made a hell of a lot of money for this firm. We want you here for the long haul . . . so you can put a bunch of associates to work and make even more money for all of us. Speaking of which, how's the Catalina Partners deal going?"

There was a limit to Don's supply of congratulatory chitchat, and, with that, it had been reached. Will proceeded to give Don a rote update on the progress of the Catalina deal.

Then it occurred to Will. "Did Ben make partner?"

Don scowled. "No, he didn't. I gave him the news the day before he died. It seemed like he was handling it just fine. He was kind of quiet, but Ben was always quiet. We have no reason to think that it was because of the partnership. I mean, elevation to partner is a great thing, but, c'mon, it's not life and death."

"No, it's not. Did anyone see him go off the roof? Were there any security cameras up there?"

"No. No cameras on the roof." Don let out an audible

sigh and continued. "Anyway, whatever happened with Ben, it doesn't change the fact that you've done a great job here."

Don shook Will's hand again, then hurried off down the hallway, clearly anxious to preempt any further conversation about Ben. Will returned to his desk and sank into his black leather chair.

Will tried to recall his most recent conversations with Ben. If Ben had been depressed, it had seemed to be the same low-grade depression that afflicted many of his colleagues. Will had never known anyone who had committed suicide, but he supposed that all such deaths must be, to some degree, inexplicable. He probably just didn't know Ben well enough to recognize his particular unhappiness.

Will found it difficult to imagine that someone would commit suicide over being passed over for partner, but he certainly understood how career goals could turn into obsessions. Will quickly dismissed the idea of suicide because it did not explain why Ben, or someone else, would have entered his office and swapped access cards with him. That action made sense only if someone wanted to frame him for Ben's death.

Besides, Ben couldn't have been that upset about being passed over for partner because he must have known that he was a long-shot candidate to begin with. Although Ben was a brilliant technician, he was a "service" attorney, advising on the tax aspects of mergers and acquisitions for the clients of corporate rainmakers like Sam Bowen and Richard Grogan. Will knew that Ben had missed out on at least one opportunity to land a client, Carlyle Industries, that would have surely propelled him to partnership. Like most legal careers, Ben's had probably turned on the outcome of a few critical moments when he had a shot at landing a franchise client, the kind that made careers and generated millions of dollars in billings. A partner's compensation is based largely on billing credit, and the assignment of billing credit often boils down to a negotiation among attorneys. Although Ben had received the initial call from Carlyle's CEO, Richard Grogan quickly asserted himself as Carlyle's primary contact at the firm, giving him leverage to demand most of the billing credit.

When a client like Carlyle Industries approaches a law firm for representation, it is like a gazelle wandering onto the African savanna within striking distance of a pride of lions. The dominant predators claim the largest portion of the kill. On the Discovery Channel, Richard Grogan would be classified as an apex predator. Richard was at the top of the law firm food chain—he eats others, but no one in his world eats him. Ben Fisher was not an apex predator, which explained why he did not receive credit for his role in bringing in Carlyle Industries and, later, why he did not make partner.

Will didn't consider himself much of a predator, either, and so he just felt lucky to have survived the partner selection process at a firm that one former colleague had likened to "a nest of tarantulas." Counting the three years of law school, he had spent the past nine years working toward the goal, nearly a third of his life. For Will, making partner meant that the financial gamble he had taken in borrowing more than $100,000 to go to law school had officially paid off. It also proved somehow that he was not like George, his father. When Will was young, George, an office supplies salesman, had been physically abusive to both Will and his mother. Now George was long gone and Will was paying for his mother's care in a nice, but very expensive, assisted-living facility. Making partner meant money, security, prestige, and never having to undergo another annual performance review. In the parlance of the gangster movies that he loved, Will was now a made guy.

Will wanted to call someone to pass along the good news, but he knew that he couldn't phone Anne, his mother, the one person in the world who might have taken the most pleasure in his accomplishment. Since the Alzheimer's had taken hold, the only way to really communicate with her was face-to-face, where he could see the flash of recognition and know that he had reached her. Talking to her over the phone was like trying to crack a safe without being able to listen to the tumblers turning.

Then there was his ex-girlfriend, Dana Houseman. Dana had made partner a year ago at the San Francisco office of Wickersham and Colbert, a white-shoe New York firm, and she dumped him shortly thereafter. There had been a time about four years ago when he had thought about leaving the law, and he had to admit that the main reason he had stayed was to maintain the necessary qualifications to remain Dana's boyfriend. When Dana made partner, she had apparently raised the bar another notch, and Will had failed to make the cut.

He had spent the past year trying to get over Dana by working obsessively, even by the firm's obsessive standards. Lately, though, it had become more difficult to blot Dana out because her picture kept appearing with alarming regularity in the local papers. She was dating James Pryce, a prosecutor in the district attorney's office who was the leading candidate to be the next mayor of San Francisco. The society pages never seemed to tire of running photos of the couple at various charity events. Nevertheless, Will knew that if he called Dana, she would meet him for a drink for old times' sake. The trouble was that he didn't think he could bear the pitying smile on her face as she reflected on the fact that he had resorted to calling her on his special occasion.

In any event, Ben's death and the meeting with Detective Kovach had cast a pall over what would have otherwise been a cause for serious celebration.

Perhaps it was best if he went out alone. Since there was no one in his life appropriate for sharing the moment, he would either mark it by himself—or find someone new. Will had never successfully picked up a woman in a bar, but that was his mission that night. He could start working on his defense strategy tomorrow—until the cops or a prosecutor made their next move, there was little to respond to.

Will had to admit that it was an unusual choice for him, but he was in an odd, untethered frame of mind. He felt numb and reckless, like a drunken mourner at a wake. Whether he categorized the evening as mourning or a celebration, it seemed that some combination of alcohol and sex was the most appropriate response. He had overheard a paralegal describing a place called the Whiskey Bar as "very cool, but a little bit of a meat market." It sounded perfect.

FOUR

As he stepped through the doorway of the Whiskey Bar, Will paused for a moment to allow his senses to adjust to the aqueous lighting, the pulsing techno beats, and the din of voices. He felt like a deep-sea diver who had just touched down on the ocean floor.

The Whiskey Bar was a new club on Fillmore enjoying its evanescent moment of unassailable hipness. The place was a perfect specimen of the latest trend in post-postmodern clubs: the bizarro hunting lodge theme. The high-ceilinged room was steeped in dark wood paneling and murky, recessed lighting. Faux antlers and animal hides were everywhere. Behind a couch and some low-slung velvet chairs, backlit panels on the wall displayed line drawings of an emu, a water buffalo, a python, and other exotic animals. Somewhere a team of designers and architects had spent a great deal of time formulating some crypto-ironic message that the room was intended to convey, but all he really wanted at the moment was a drink.

He found a seat at the bar and, after several attempts, managed to hail a bartender and order a beer. On either side of him were rival hunting parties of young men in business suits, each braying at the top of their lungs to be heard above the Thievery Corporation track throbbing over the club's sound system.

Going to a club alone usually made Will uncomfortable. But now he was a partner, and that was supposed to change things, right? With bitter irony, he noted that things had changed, all right—now he was both a partner and a murder suspect.

The group on his left got up and was quickly replaced by a woman with shoulder-length blond hair wearing a cream-colored skirt and violet blouse. Judging by her clothes, Will guessed that she might work in advertising, maybe public relations.

The woman ordered a pomegranate Cosmopolitan and removed a BlackBerry from her purse, placing it on the bar. The BlackBerry immediately began thrumming excitedly. She picked it up and tilted the screen at various angles, trying to read her messages in the dim light.

"Is that the new BlackBerry?" Will asked, pointing at the device.

BlackBerry Girl looked back at him quizzically. She had not understood what he had said, but she took him in with a glance that made Will feel like he had just had one of those full-body MRI scans, the kind that find more things wrong with you than you ever could have imagined.

"Is that the new BlackBerry?" Will repeated. The noise level made every statement sound like an exclamation. Even the simplest communications required the concentration of a lip reader.

"Yeah!" she said.

Will reached into his suit pocket and pulled out his own BlackBerry. "Ever since I got this thing, I can't stop checking my e-mail. I'm addicted."

"You're addicted to what?" she shouted back.

The music seemed to grow louder, or maybe it was just his social anxiety ratcheting up a notch as he watched the tenuous connection unravel. He ran his hand through his hair and forged ahead, already wincing at the obviousness of it all. "My name's Will! What's yours?"

The woman seemed to recognize that she had a rapidly narrowing window of escape. She picked up her Black-Berry again and pointed to it, acting as if she hadn't heard him, but this time he felt certain that she had.

"Sorry, but I need to go someplace quiet to make a call. It was nice talking to you!"

She sipped the last of her drink and slid off the stool. Will didn't blame her a bit. He gave her points for the effective use of the BlackBerry in her exit strategy.

Will turned away to order another beer and noticed a woman several stools down the zinc-topped bar regarding him with an amused, knowing smile. She had short, black hair framing a pale face. She had obviously been observing Will's exchange with BlackBerry Girl. She couldn't have heard what they were saying, but she probably didn't need to.

Will drank another beer and began to relax a bit. During the years of struggling to make partner, he had sometimes entertained the comical notion that making partner would imbue him with new powers, like a budding superhero who had been bitten by a radioactive insect. It appeared that any superpowers that he had gained did not include the ability to pick up women in bars. He began to suspect that his new power might be something disappointingly mundane, like the ability to calculate the tip on a large restaurant tab.

He turned to survey the room. No one was dancing, but everyone's movements seemed to twitch to the pulse of the thudding beat. It crept into the earnest nodding of a young man at the bar listening to a girl he was trying to pick up. It insinuated itself into the stride of an attractive woman walking across the room, conscious of the eyes on her.

Will sipped his beer and, out of simple curiosity, continued to watch the reflection of the dark-haired woman in the mirror behind the bar. She was perhaps five feet four, in her late twenties, dressed in a chocolate-brown, slightly low-cut blouse. Will guessed that she might be a clerk in an expensive clothing store, with her full lips and high cheekbones lending the right note of fashionable exoticism. She finished her drink, then began rummaging in her purse.

The woman examined the contents of the purse with increasing frustration, then placed it on the bar so that she could excavate its depths. She glanced about the club, as if she were looking for someone. Finally, she called the bartender over and they launched into an extended dialogue, which she punctuated with some pleading hand gestures.

Will flagged the bartender and told him that he would pay the woman's bar tab. This was a bold move for him, and a sure sign that four beers had impaired his usually all-too-efficient impulse-control mechanisms.

When the bartender passed along the message, the woman gave a reluctant smile. She looked down at her purse again, probably deciding whether she should come over and thank him or simply leave and cut her losses.

After a final appraising look, she stood up from the bar and approached. She sat down on the stool next to him. They leaned in close to one another to be heard, their faces inches apart.

"Thank you," she said, with what sounded like a Russian accent. "My friend she walked out on me without paying for her drinks. And she'd been sitting here for hours! I only had twenty dollars in my purse. Do you know how much you just agreed to pay?"

"Actually, I don't."

"Thirty-five dollars. See, that's what happens when you agree to buy a Russian's drinks. It can get very expensive. Let me at least give you ten."

"No, no, it's fine. You looked like you could use some help."

"So is that what you do? Go around helping women in distress?"

"No, not usually."

"So you made an exception in my case?"

"Yes, that's right."

"Hmm," she said with mock suspicion.

"My name's Will Connelly."

"Katya Belyshev."

Will took a moment to study Katya. Her dark brown blouse accentuated her Eastern European pallor. She brushed her long fingernails against a charm bracelet that she jingled on her wrist, the only indication that she might be uneasy. The silver bracelet's charms were in the shapes of Cyrillic letters.

"What do you do?" he asked.

"I'm a receptionist at a securities firm."

"Oh? Which one?"

"Not one of the big ones. You've probably never heard of it—Equilon Securities."

"No, I haven't." To avert a lull in the conversation, he added, "Can I buy you a drink?"

"You want to buy me *another* drink? But okay. Stoli martini. Two olives."

"Is your friend coming back? I noticed you've been sitting alone over there by yourself for a while."

"Were you spying on me?"

"No . . . Well, maybe just a little bit. Sorry, old habit from the cold war."

"Funny. You are a funny guy, Will." She nodded, appreciating the joke rather than laughing at it, like a professional comic.

Will ordered, and they sat at the bar struggling to hear one another as the music enveloped them. When Will was in his early twenties, he had spent many nights in clubs like this one. Now he wasn't sure whether it was his hearing that had deteriorated or simply his tolerance for crowds, loud music, and people who drink mojitos, but he knew that he needed to find a better place to talk.

Finally, Katya stood and said, "Follow me."

Will trailed Katya up some stairs to a loft in the back of the club. The room, which was arranged with deep sofas, was quieter, out of the crossfire of the club's speakers. On each sofa were young couples groping one another.

Katya pointed to a couch in the corner. "You wanted a quiet place, right?" On the next couch, a man with a shark fin of spiked-up blond hair was fondling his girlfriend's breasts underneath her glittering chemise. Glancing at the couple, Katya added, "It is not required, you know."

Will burst out with a nervous laugh, and they settled on the couch.

He took a swallow of his Johnnie Walker Black and exhaled. "How long have you been in the U.S.?" His eyes fell on the outline of Katya's breasts beneath her blouse, and he forced them away, not wanting to be caught staring.

"About two years."

"Your English is very good." He glanced again.

"Thank you. I started learning when I worked for U.S. company in Russia."

"Where did you grow up?"

"A town called Kharkiv, which is in Ukraine."

"What was that like?"

"Kharkiv is a farming town. I have a friend who lives in Fresno and it is a little like that. Just take away movie theaters, shops, and most of the things that make life bearable . . . then add some more crime."

"I don't even like our version of Fresno. Is that why you came to the U.S.?"

"Partly. I also want to go into business for myself some day. Run a restaurant. In Russia, that is not possible. To start a business over there, you must deal with *avtoritet*."

"What's that?"

"It is organized crime, but very out in the open. It's hard enough for a man to start a legitimate business in Russia today, but it is almost impossible for a woman. A woman does not get the necessary respect. And if you don't get respect, you can't buy the produce and supplies to run a restaurant. You can't even hire dishwashers." Katya took a long sip of her martini.

"That must not be easy, picking up and moving to the U.S."

"No, not easy. I was working as office manager for a U.S. oil company. They agreed to hire me for their San Francisco office if I paid my own travel expenses. It took two years, but I saved the money and got my visa."

"How did you end up at the securities firm?"

"I left the oil company for an office manager job at an Internet company called CatsPajamas.com."

"What did they sell?"

"What else? Pajamas for the cats."

"Really?"

"No, not really." She giggled. "They sold women's clothing. The company went bankrupt after about six months when the bubble burst, and I ended up at Equilon. Familiar story, eh?"

"The last part is certainly familiar. But it looks like you landed on your feet."

"Yes, I landed on my feet," she said, appreciating the American expression. "No place else to land."

"You'd never go back to Russia?"

"It is my home, but no, I think I will never go back."

"So how did you wind up working at a securities firm?"

"Things were hard for me after CPJ went out of business. My stock options were worthless. Too many people looking for work in the city. Very scary. I was afraid I was going to get evicted from my apartment, not have money for groceries. I called everyone I knew from Russia who was over here. Finally, I found out that my second cousin Irina was living in Brighton Beach. Irina knew someone in San Francisco who knew this guy Yuri. Yuri helped me get the receptionist job at Equilon. Being a receptionist is a step down from my last job, but it is only temporary."

Will sipped his drink, searching for something encouraging to say about her job search that didn't sound patronizing.

"So now you know everything about me and I know nothing about you," Katya said. "What about you? What do you do?"

"I'm an attorney," Will said, somewhat reluctantly. Will knew from experience that things could take a turn for the worse at this point.

"I knew it," she said, pleased with herself.

"It was the suit, right?"

"No, it was the way you talk," she said. "Like someone who is used to having people pay attention. If I were on jury, you'd get my vote."

"Thanks, but I'm not that kind of attorney. I don't go to court. I'm a corporate lawyer. I negotiate deals."

"So how long have you been a lawyer?"

"Almost seven years. As a matter of fact, I just made partner today."

"Today? That is amazing, Will! Congratulations!" Will had been congratulated many times that day, but this was the one that made him feel the best because there was no qualifier, no personal history to take into account.

"Thanks. So, I hope you don't mind me asking, but what are you doing hitting the clubs alone?" Will surprised himself with his liquored directness. "Don't you have a boyfriend?"

She noted his forwardness with an arched eyebrow. "No, not really. There was a guy back in Moscow, but that ended when I came here. So what about you?"

"I have a few friends I can call up for dinner or a movie, but nothing to get excited about."

"Well, if you can't get excited, there is no point, right?" Katya tried to be deadpan, but she couldn't suppress a crooked little smile. At that moment, Will knew how the evening had to end.

Will looked around the room at the couples wrestling on the adjoining couches. "Would you like to get out of here?"

Katya lifted herself out of the couch. "I must get home. Securities dealers start early. Markets open at six thirty and I have to be in by eight thirty."

"Where do you live?"

"Not far from here. I've got an apartment off Polk Street on Russian Hill. And no Russian Hill jokes, please."

"I didn't say anything."

"It's not too far. I can catch a cab outside."

"I'm headed that way. How about if we share a cab? I can see you to your door."

"That is very sweet of you. Sure." Will felt that he and Katya were like chess players, both looking several moves ahead, barely concentrating on the current maneuvers.

It was eleven thirty and the club was shifting into high gear as Will and Katya made their way through the bar, heading for the door. The suit-and-tie crowd from the financial district was now gone, replaced by resplendently funky club kids.

The city seemed unnaturally quiet when they emerged onto Fillmore Street from the noisy club. Accustomed to shouting to be heard, Will felt tentative now, not wanting to say the wrong thing.

They walked quickly down Fillmore to California Street and caught a cab. During the short taxi ride, they filled the pauses with the smallest of talk, comparing the weather in the Bay Area and Ukraine. As they drew closer to Russian Hill, the silences grew longer.

Finally, the cab stopped in front of a three-story Victorian on Pacific Street. It was simultaneously charming and a bit run-down, like so many San Francisco apartment buildings where the landlord knows that he has an inexhaustible supply of young tenants.

Katya twirled and pointed to the building like a game show hostess revealing a prize. "What do you think?"

"Very nice."

Katya gave him a quick kiss on the cheek.

"Can I come up?" he asked.

She paused. "Not tonight. Too soon. But I hope you'll give me a call. Equilon Securities. It's in the book. You were very sweet to see me home."

They said good night, and he watched her enter the building. He kept the cabbie waiting for a moment as she made her way to her apartment, and he watched the light come on in a second-floor window.

Then the curtains opened to reveal Katya, who saw him standing on the lawn looking up at her. It was hard to tell because she was in silhouette, but he sensed that she was smiling.

After a moment, she pushed the window open and leaned out, tossing her key chain at his feet. Marveling at his good fortune, he dispatched the cabdriver and picked up the keys.

He climbed the stairs and the door opened before he could knock.

"I just want you to know that I am breaking rules for you," she said.

The shortcomings of Katya's small studio apartment were gamely overcome by a coat of yellow paint and her decorating efforts. Glancing around at the white, pressed-wood chairs and other Ikea-style furnishings, Will noted that he'd probably spent thousands of dollars more in furnishing his condo in the marina, with results that resembled a high-tech dorm room. Katya's apartment, and the way she had made something warm and homey out of what was essentially a dump, told him more about her than any single thing that she had said to him that night.

Will studied the Matisse and Moscow Ballet posters on the walls as Katya hurried about picking up a bra and a few other stray items of clothing and tossing them in a closet.

"Please, sit . . . sit," she said as she returned to him. "Can I get you a drink?"

Katya stepped past Will to turn the dead bolt. Will moved aside to make room, and they were only a few inches apart, both radiating heat in the cold apartment.

Katya looked up at Will and brushed a lock of black hair out of her eyes. Will bent down and kissed her, inhaling the metallic aftertaste of vodka. Katya pushed Will back against the door of the apartment. They took each other's clothes off like two kids unwrapping Christmas presents. Her fingers felt cold as she unbuckled his belt.

After they struggled out of their clothes, Will was naked in the bed. Katya returned from the bathroom wearing a black bra and panties. She had two tattoos: a tribal design around her ankle and a star on her right shoulder blade. Her navel was pierced by a small silver ring. Will had never slept with a woman with tattoos or piercings before and decided that, for reasons he could not begin to fathom, he liked the idea. Dana, his ex, certainly had not borne tribal markings of any kind. In fact, Will did not know of an attorney with tattoos or piercings. Of course, he had not seen that many attorneys with their clothes off.

Without saying a word, Katya jumped into bed and straddled him. Her dark hair hung straight down around her face like a curtain. Looking up at her, he found himself unable to resist the urge to touch her navel ring, examining the surface tension of skin where the silver band disappeared to complete its circle inside her. As he drew a circle around her navel with his index finger, her stomach muscles trembled.

Okay, Will thought. *I guess the superpowers have kicked in now.*

FIVE

Will awoke in the morning, hung over, in Katya's bed with her arm draped across his chest. His head felt like a railroad car in which heavy crates had not been properly secured. He reconstructed the events that had led him to the apartment on Pacific Street, trying to decide whether this was something he was going to regret. The sunlight shone with depressing clarity on the tiny apartment, with its threadbare sofa and flaking paint. But, then again, it also revealed Katya.

She was breathing softly into her pillow next to him. He admired the white-on-white of her skin against the sheets. The downy black hair on her forearm. The curve of her back as it dipped beneath the sheet. There was really no telling who she was or what her reaction to him might be when she awoke. Better to lie very still and let this pleasingly strange moment linger.

He noticed a small stack of CDs next to the bed. Atop the stack was a CD from some Russian rock band with an unpronounceable name. The Slavic fellows on the cover all had shoulder-length hair and some wore headbands, suggesting that somewhere in the Commonwealth of Independent States was a land where eighties hair-metal bands still roamed the earth. Will decided to chalk that one up to cultural differences. Next was a Dave Matthews Band CD (a little pedestrian, but not a deal breaker). At the bottom of the stack was *I'm Your Man* by Leonard Cohen.

"Good morning," Katya said, rolling over in bed. Her eyes followed his over to the stack of CDs. She ran her hands through her hair. "So . . . what am I supposed to do with you now?" she asked.

"Anything you like."

"Okay, then, I'd like you to feed my cat."

"Is that some kind of Russian euphemism?"

Katya's face went blank for a moment as she checked her mental English-Russian dictionary. If her face were a computer screen, it would have displayed a tiny hourglass icon. Then she laughed, apparently deciding that she got the joke, and made an expression of mock disapproval.

Will scanned the small apartment. "You have a cat?"

"He's under the bed. That's where he goes when I have company."

"What's his name?"

"Ron."

"Ron? I would have thought Vlad or Ivan or something."

"He is American cat, so he should have proper American name," she declared. "Where do you come up with these names? . . . Bill, Frank, Dave, Mike . . . " she said, mimicking a flat Midwestern accent.

"How about Will?"

"Will is a sweet name. And William . . . I think I like that even better."

Katya simultaneously rolled onto her back, stretched, and pulled up the covers. She scratched her finger across the comforter several times. Ron the cat, a stocky white shorthair, responded to the summons, bounding heavily onto the bed. Ron studied Will with a mixture of fear and contempt as Katya massaged the furry slope of his forehead with her index finger.

"I saw you looking at my CDs. I hope you are not music snob."

"Uh, no. Well, I mean . . . okay, yes, some of my friends have said that."

"So, do you have problem with my musical taste, Will?"

"No, not at all. I noticed you listen to Leonard Cohen."

"Yes. Very popular in Russia. I think we relate to his . . . pessimism."

"What time is it?" Will asked.

Katya glanced at the bedside alarm clock. "Seven fifteen. What time do you have to be at work?"

"No later than nine. I have a meeting at the office."

"If you need to go now, I understand," Katya said. "I have to get ready for work, too."

"No, I have some time. I'll need to stop by my place to change into some fresh clothes before I head over to the office."

To Will's disappointment, Katya put on some clothes, slipping on an oversized Giants T-shirt. She made coffee in the corner of the apartment that served as a kitchen. Will rummaged in the sheets at the foot of the bed, looking for his boxer shorts.

Along the wall next to the bed was a low shelf filled

with cookbooks, including several by Alice Waters of Chez Panisse.

"You sure have a lot of cookbooks," Will observed.

"Like I told you, I plan to open restaurant someday. Maybe I'll call it Katya's. It would be a California twist on Russian cooking. I've already got the menu all worked out; all I need is the money. Every other cuisine has gotten an Alice Waters makeover, why not Russian?"

"Why not?" Will said. "Sounds like a great idea."

Katya poured orange juice into two glasses. "So, what is your day going to be like? Some big deal, right?"

"As a matter of fact, yes. A merger."

"Oh, really? What kind of business?"

Will considered his next words carefully. He knew that he really shouldn't say anything, but he wanted to impress Katya and figured there could be no harm if he kept the details sketchy. "Encryption software."

"I just read something about a company like that. What was the name? Jupiter something. Right?"

There was no mistaking the surprised look that crossed Will's face.

"It *is* Jupiter, isn't it?"

He could have lied to Katya (there were certainly plenty of other encryption software companies), but he knew that his expression had given him away. Blatantly lying would only create awkwardness between them, so he tried evasion.

"I'm afraid I really can't talk about deals that I'm working on."

"So I was right!" Katya exclaimed. "But we've just met and you don't trust me enough yet to talk about it."

"It's not about whether I trust you."

Katya simply stared at him, unconvinced.

Finally, Will gave in. "How did you know about that, anyway?"

"I work at a securities firm, remember?" Katya replied, mildly annoyed. "And there was an article about Jupiter last week in the *Chronicle*. It said they were the biggest en-cryption company. You know, Will, sometimes I even read the *Wall Street Journal*. What I want to know is, were you surprised that I guessed, or surprised that I knew it?"

In his pre-coffee stupor, it took a few seconds for him to fully grasp the potential consequences of what had just happened. He had, however inadvertently, disclosed the pending merger of a publicly traded company, violating about a dozen securities laws in the process. If Katya went to work at her securities firm and told one of the dealers about this, or if she bought Jupiter stock herself, then he would be guilty of insider trading. Attorneys had lost their jobs and their licenses and sometimes even gone to jail for similar offenses. Since he was already the suspect in a mur-der investigation, this was the last thing that he needed.

For a moment, he considered whether Katya might have sought him out at the club for just this purpose—to extract insider information. He promptly dismissed the notion as paranoid, concluding that he had enough worries and didn't need to invent new ones.

Will pulled on his boxer shorts and slid out of bed, wide-awake now. He had to make sure that Katya did not do or say anything about the Jupiter deal. But he didn't want to mention it at that moment, while she was still furrowing her brow at him. From the annoyed look on her face, he could see that he was not going to get very far with her if she thought that he was being condescending.

"Forgive me," he said, beaming his most ingratiating smile.

Katya made a show of judging him, her arms crossed. "Okay."

Covering the three paces that separated the bedroom from the kitchen, he studied Katya's face, as he had been doing ever since they had met the night before. He kept thinking that he detected the flicker of a smile in her dark eyes or at the corners of her mouth.

Katya and Will sipped coffee and watched Ron bask in the sunlight that streamed through the blinds. Will was surprised that he didn't feel the need to fill the silence with small talk.

A pounding at the door shattered the quiet.

"Hey, Katya! *Otkroi!* It's Yuri!"

"Oh shit," Katya said, putting down her coffee. "I'm not going to answer it."

"Yuri? Who's Yuri?"

"I told you about him. The guy who got me the job at the securities firm. A friend of a friend of my second cousin Irina."

"What does he want?"

Katya fluttered her hand at him, indicating that there was no time for that story.

The pounding continued and grew louder. Yuri was hammering his fists on the door, rattling it on its hinges. "*Ya znaiu, chto ty tam!* Don't make me break this fucking door down!"

Katya and Will both retreated to the far wall of the apartment and stared at the door as if it were about to explode into splinters. Will felt Katya's long nails dig into his arm. It made him feel protective of her, but he wasn't yet sure what it was she might need protecting from.

The pounding stopped. "Listen, Katya," Yuri said, calmer this time, a skewed voice of reason. "I could kick this door in. You know that. But if I do, who is going to pay for it? You are. And your landlord, oh he will have many questions." Yuri slammed his fist into the door to punctuate his point.

Katya whispered, "Get your clothes and hide in the bathroom. I'm going to have to let him in."

Will shook his head. "Just wait for him to leave."

"You don't know him. He'll either kick in the door or stay out there all day till we come out. If he thinks I am avoiding him, it will only make things worse."

"I'm not hiding in the bathroom from this guy. What is he, your boyfriend?"

"No, but there's no time to explain. You just don't want Yuri to find you here. Trust me on this."

Gathering up his clothes, Will went into the bathroom and shut the door. He tried to lock the bathroom door, but it was broken. He stood with his back against the sink in his boxer shorts, his suit wadded into a ball in his arms. Will examined the image of himself in the oval mirror hanging on the bathroom door. His eyes were bloodshot from the hangover. He looked pale, and his jaw was clenched with fear. His fingers gripped his pinstripe suit as if someone was about to tear it from him.

He heard the front door open, then the footsteps of more than one person on the hardwood floor. Something was said that he couldn't understand, or perhaps it was in Russian. More rapid footsteps. It sounded like the apartment was being searched.

Then the bathroom door swung open to reveal a tall man in a leather jacket. His sharp, narrow face seemed to consist of two planes that met in a long, aquiline nose. Yuri.

A feral smile spread across Yuri's face at the sight of Will in his boxer shorts. "Hello, asshole," he said.

SIX

Still grinning malevolently, Yuri motioned for Will to step out of the bathroom.

"Look, she doesn't want you here," Will said. "If you don't get out right now, we're going to call the cops!"

Despite his bluster, Will didn't feel very bold as he stepped into the room. The apartment, which had seemed so warm and comforting a moment ago, was now freezing. The front door was wide open and he was standing in the center of the room in his bare feet and boxer shorts.

By the doorway stood a heavyset man in a gray wool overcoat. He was nearly bald except for a few wisps of dark hair that clung to his scalp in damp strands. With his aero-dynamic head and massive build encased in the overcoat, the man resembled some kind of lethal, heavy-gauge armament. His face was broad and flat, with dark, deep-set eyes that darted furtively in the shadows of a protruding brow.

"This guy . . . " Yuri said to his companion, wagging a finger at Will. "You ever see someone and just want to beat the crap out of them?"

"All the time," the heavyset man responded in a thick Russian accent.

Katya, wearing only her Giants T-shirt and underwear, stood at the kitchen counter looking scared. "Nikolai . . . Yuri . . . why don't we just talk later after he's gone," Katya said, nodding at Will. "I'll come and see you. I promise."

Nikolai pondered for a moment, the gears seeming to turn slowly but with reasonable precision. *"Postoi, Yura! On nam mozhet prigoditsia."*

"What do they want?" Will asked Katya.

Katya simply shook her head.

"Don't talk to her," said Nikolai in his labored English. "You talk to me. Who are you?"

"I met Katya at the Whiskey Bar last night. That's all."

Nikolai's tone was calm, patient, and only mildly amused. "Just answer questions. What is your name?"

"Will."

"Full name, please."

"Will Connelly." Although Will's voice was steady, his hands were trembling, fear coursing through him like a low-voltage electrical current. For someone who had always resolved his conflicts through thoughtful discourse, the idea of real physical violence was strangely difficult to comprehend. The situation made him recall the moment when he had stood up to his wife-beating father when he was fifteen. He had faced down George late one night in the front yard of their house, wielding a driver from his bag of golf clubs. Will still vividly recalled that moment, the feel of his bare feet in the wet grass and the surging anger that almost caused him to swing the club. But instead, after some blustering and shouting, George had walked off down the dark suburban street, never to return. Anne had joked later that he should have used a nine iron.

"And what do you do, Will Connelly?"

"I'm an attorney."

Nikolai extended a meaty hand and said, "Your card. Please."

"Yeah," Yuri added, "you guys always carry cards, don't you?"

"I don't think I have one with me." Will was still hoping that he could avoid giving them too much information.

"Yura, posmotri u nego v pidzhake," said Nikolai, pointing to Will's suit.

"Use your English," Yuri responded testily. "How else are you going to get any better?"

Yuri grabbed Will's jacket and pants out of his arms and fished in the suit pocket. After a few seconds, he produced a business card, then threw the clothes back at Will.

Yuri handed the card to Nikolai, who studied it as if it were written in Phoenician cuneiform.

Will, in turn, studied Yuri and Nikolai. Although he could have sized up a lawyer he was negotiating with in ten seconds flat, Yuri and Nikolai weren't nearly so easy to read. All he was able to conjure up was a long line of fictional gangsters from movies, television, and books. Were they members of a Russian organized-crime family or just garden-variety bullies?

"You do criminal work?" Nikolai asked, perhaps contemplating his own affairs.

"No. Corporate law. Mergers and acquisitions."

"M&A, huh?" Yuri added, determined to be part of the conversation.

"Will works on big-time deals. He is way out of your league," Katya goaded.

"Then that means he's out of your league, too, doesn't it?" Yuri countered, with a vindictive rise in his voice that made Will wonder again if they had ever been a couple. "You think Will here is going to take you away from all this? He's just here to get laid. Isn't that right, Will?"

"Shut the fuck up, Yuri." Nikolai said it as if it were all one word and one of the few English phrases that seemed to roll trippingly off his tongue.

Nikolai and Yuri conferred in Russian, with Nikolai doing most of the talking. When they finished, Yuri walked up to Will. "You know, Will, I have never had much luck in the stock market. I was heavy into tech stocks. You being such a smart guy and all, I bet you got out of the market in time."

Yuri's glare seemed to demand a response. "No, I got burned, too," Will offered. "Just about everyone did."

"But if you are such a big fucking deal, like Katya says, then you probably know some things."

"No, not really."

"But even if you did know something, something profitable, you wouldn't tell me, would you?"

Will could not think of a safe answer to that question, so he remained silent.

"Nikolai and I are entrepreneurs. We are always looking for business opportunities. We think maybe we see an opportunity in you, Will."

"I think you've got the wrong idea about me."

"We'll see."

Yuri stepped behind the kitchen counter and examined some dirty dishes in the sink. "She is not much of a housekeeper, is she?" He picked up a dirty wineglass from the counter. He held it up to the light and examined the fingerprint smudges.

"Now I'm sure that if you really tried, you could think

of something," Yuri said. He wrapped his fingers around the base of the glass and let it dangle at his side.

"I really can't help you," Will said.

"I don't think you're trying hard enough."

"I don't know anything, and even if I did—"

"Take a moment," Yuri said. "Think about it."

"You really should think about it," Nikolai added, with a note of what could almost pass for concern.

Will paused, making a show of giving it some thought, then tried again. "Attorney-client privilege prevents me—"

Yuri swung quickly, smashing the wineglass into Will's temple. Will collapsed to the floor. Blood flowed warm into his eyes. He watched in stunned fascination as drops of his blood formed a small, dark puddle on the floor.

Yuri stood over him. "Fuck attorney-client privilege."

Katya came out from behind the kitchen counter, but Nikolai stepped forward to block her advance. "Animals! Leave him alone!" Katya punched Nikolai in the bicep, producing the dull, unyielding thud of someone striking a stack of phone books. With little effort, Nikolai grabbed Katya by the shoulders and hurled her onto the bed.

Yuri motioned to Nikolai. "It's your turn, big man."

Nikolai removed his overcoat and laid it carefully over a chair. He resembled a retired football player going to seed, with his hard, protuberant belly and pectorals like balloons the day after a party.

Yuri pulled Will up off the floor, twisting his arms behind his back. Will struggled, but Yuri's grip held firm. He seemed to have done this before.

Will blinked to clear his vision. With his hands pinned, he was unable to wipe the blood from his eyes or probe his throbbing temple. He shook his head like a dog to get the blood off his face.

"Cocksucker!" Yuri shouted. "You get blood on this shirt and I'll really go to work on you."

Nikolai slowly advanced toward Will, giving him time to contemplate what was coming. Will twisted in Yuri's grip, attempting to free his hands.

Nikolai had dark rings under his armpits, and as he stood before Will he smelled of damp wool, sweat, and cologne.

"This is crazy," Will said. "I really don't . . ."

Nikolai put his finger to his lips. "Please," he said, before slamming a fat fist into Will's stomach. Katya shrieked.

Will slumped in Yuri's grip, gasping for air with a thin, wet wheezing sound.

"Come on, Will, don't be a pussy," Yuri said as he straightened Will up. Nikolai approached again.

"Stop it! He told me something!" It was Katya, who was crouched on the bed on her hands and knees.

Nikolai turned to her. "What did you say?"

"He told me something about a deal he's working on. Just stop hitting him."

"Go on," Nikolai said.

"Don't . . . " Will managed to gasp.

Katya sat up on her knees on the bed. "Will, I'm sorry." Then, to Nikolai: "He told me that he's working on a big deal. A company called Jupiter. Jupiter Software. They're going to be bought."

Yuri released Will, and he slumped to the floor.

"Good," Nikolai said, with a smile that revealed a set of square, gray teeth like cinder blocks.

Will slowly rose to his feet. Nikolai and Yuri now focused on Katya, who was sitting on the side of the bed, pulling her long T-shirt down over her knees.

"We will talk to Katya alone now," said Yuri, addressing Will.

Katya's eyes were on the floor. Will couldn't tell what she was thinking.

"So you can get the fuck out of here," Yuri continued. "We know where to find you. We've got your card." He snapped the card with his index finger for emphasis.

For the second time in the past twenty-four hours, Will surprised himself. "I'm not leaving her alone with you two."

Yuri slapped his forehead with his palm in sheer incomprehension. "The ingratitude of the fucker! *Kaifu*."

"What?" Will said, reflexively.

"You must be high!" Yuri exclaimed. *"Kaifu!"*

Nikolai smiled dimly at Will's foolishness, but decided to humor him. "Okay. Yuri, take him out in hall while I talk to Katya." Nikolai grabbed a dish towel from the kitchen counter and threw it at Will. "For your head."

"It's okay," Katya said to Will. "I'll be fine."

Yuri took Will by the arm and led him to the open door. "See? She is going to be fine. You, I am not so sure about."

Nikolai pulled the door shut, leaving Will standing in his boxer shorts with Yuri in a dingy hallway dappled with shafts of morning sunlight. Will mopped the blood from his face with the towel and attempted to locate the cut on his temple with his fingers, the pain sharpening as he got closer. The bleeding had slowed. Three quarters of an inch to the right, though, and he might have lost an eye. He began to sort out the bundle of clothes in his arms and get dressed.

Will strained to hear what was being said inside the apartment, but all he could make out was the vague rumble of Nikolai's voice.

A woman emerged from an apartment a few doors

down, hair still damp, with a coffee mug in hand. As she locked her door, she looked up to observe Will holding a bloody towel and doing a one-legged dance as he pulled on his pants.

Yuri stared at the woman with an unblinking gaze that could be read as a threat.

The woman locked her door and walked briskly away, apparently deciding that she wanted no part of whatever was going on.

Yuri stared at Will as he got dressed, and he wondered if he was about to get punched again.

Finally, Yuri spoke. "Is that wool?"

"Yeah," Will said, curious where the conversation was headed.

"Looks a little heavy for spring."

"Not in San Francisco."

"Where'd you get it?"

"Brooks Brothers."

"That's what I thought. Not bad," Yuri conceded. "But I like something a little more tailored. Hugo Boss."

Yuri had nothing else to say to Will as they waited in the hallway. Yuri removed a small plastic bottle of hand sanitizer from his jacket and rubbed some in his hands, giving off the smell of alcohol. When Will had put on the clothes, he was left without shoes, socks, or a tie, which had all been kicked under the bed in Katya's apartment before he hid in the bathroom.

After about ten minutes, the door to Katya's apartment opened and Nikolai emerged. Katya stood behind him in the doorway, holding the rest of Will's clothes. Her eyes were red, but she appeared unharmed. Her face seemed unsettled.

Nikolai said to Katya, "Give him his things."

"I'm not leaving yet." Will wanted to talk with Katya out of the presence of Yuri and Nikolai.

"It's okay," Katya said. "You should go. We can talk later."

He studied her, then Yuri and Nikolai, and concluded from everyone's demeanor that the incident was over. "Okay. I'll see you soon."

Yuri rolled his eyes at Nikolai, seemingly exasperated by Will's belief that he had a choice in the matter.

Katya closed the door, which was followed by the sound of two locks and a chain being hastily secured.

Will put on his shoes and socks and shoved the tie into his jacket pocket.

Nikolai patted Will on the shoulder. "I know you don't think so right now, but you are going to like doing business with us. You will see. We are not bad guys. We will talk again soon."

Yuri and Nikolai walked with Will down the worn stairs, emerging on Pacific Street, blinking in the bright morning light like three businessmen commencing their workday. Yuri pointed up the street. "We're parked up this way," he said matter-of-factly. "Which way are you headed?"

Without hesitation, Will pointed in the opposite direction. As he walked away, he had the growing realization that he had been had.

SEVEN

It was one of those crisp, perfect mornings that San Francisco produces so effortlessly in the spring. Will watched the drivers on their way to work, hands on the wheel and eyes fixed on the middle distance, gliding through the comforting autopilot of the daily routine, just as Will usually did on a Tuesday morning.

But this was not a typical Tuesday morning. It was eight thirty. Will was standing on the corner of Polk and Broadway waiting for a taxi to pass, rumpled and unshaven. As he dabbed at his forehead with a bloody dish towel, he had the inescapable sense that all of the terrible things that had happened to him in the past forty-eight hours were somehow connected.

Being framed for Ben's murder. Taking over the Jupiter transaction from Ben. Picking up Katya in the club and her "guess" that he was working on the Jupiter deal. The inopportune appearance of Yuri and Nikolai and their interest in Jupiter. Following this reasoning to its logical conclusion, it seemed likely that Yuri, Nikolai, and Katya had played some part in Ben's death.

He needed time to think, to shuffle these facts until he could discern more of the pattern. But there was no time for that. He had to be at his office in Embarcadero Center by nine, looking sharp, to negotiate the merger of Jupiter Software and Pearl Systems. After the meeting, he would have time to consider whether he should report Yuri, Nikolai, and the whole bizarre series of events to Detective Kovach, Don Rubinowski, and perhaps even the SEC.

Across the street was a drugstore. He rushed in and bought toothpaste, a toothbrush, shaving cream, a comb, bandages, and a disposable razor.

With his purchases in a paper bag, he flagged down a taxi. The cabbie was a sun-baked, bearded man who appeared to be made out of the same faded, dirty material as the taxi's upholstery. Will asked to be taken to the Hyatt Regency, which was across the street from his office building. The cabbie glanced at his bleeding head but was undeterred; he had clearly seen worse.

Will pulled out his phone and dialed the cell number of David Lathrop, the CEO of Jupiter Software. They had spoken only once before, when Will had called to inform him that he would be taking over as lead counsel on the deal.

"David? Hi, this is Will Connelly."

"I hope you're a quick study, Will," David said.

"I've done my homework. I've been through all of Ben's files and notes. Any final thoughts before our meeting?"

"Not really. I was just about to walk over to your offices. I had a breakfast meeting with the bankers." Will read David's terseness as nerves.

"I have a little point of strategy I want to discuss with you."

"What do you have in mind?"

"You said that when you and Ben were over at their attorneys' offices, they kept you waiting for nearly a half hour while they talked."

"That's right," David said. "What a chickenshit little maneuver that was."

"Well, I think we should let them sit for about that long in our conference room before we make our entrance. I know it sounds petty, but you have to set a tone with these guys. Every time they push us, we have to push back. They want this deal to close as badly as you do."

The cell phone signal wavered as faint street sounds cut in and out. If David decided that they should arrive at nine sharp, he knew there was no way he could be there in time. That would not make much of a first impression.

"I like it," David said. Will could almost hear him grinning on the other end of the line. "I knew there was a reason why I pay your firm so much money."

"When they arrive, I'll have my secretary take them into the conference room and tell them we're in a meeting. You can take your time getting over here. We can meet up at around nine twenty-five or nine thirty."

"See you then."

The taxi pulled into the driveway of the Hyatt. Will handed the driver some bills and hit the ground running.

He did not want to use the restroom in the firm's offices to clean himself up. They would immediately assume that he had gone on some kind of postpartnership bender, which, admittedly, was not far from the truth.

Will entered the hotel's soaring atrium lobby and ducked into the restroom, which was empty. He assessed his appearance in the mirror. The cut on his temple was actually fairly small and no longer bleeding. Nikolai's punch hadn't left any bruising, and as far as he could tell, none of his ribs were cracked. Will quickly brushed his teeth, shaved, combed his hair, straightened his tie, and dusted himself off.

He reviewed the results in the mirror. His suit was still a little wrinkled, his eyes were bloodshot, and he was certain to get some questions about the bandage, but he was presentable. Now if he could only calm his nerves. His hand trembled slightly from residual adrenaline and he gripped the sink to make it stop. He checked his watch: nine twenty.

Leaving the Hyatt, he crossed Sacramento Street to Embarcadero Center. The four massive, white towers of Embarcadero Center lined up like dominoes. It seemed that nearly every law firm in San Francisco had an office somewhere within the complex. Will dashed up the steps and pushed through the revolving door into the stark lobby, which was composed of large blocks of white stone that made the place look like some kind of twenty-first-century version of a Mayan temple.

Riding the elevator up to the firm's offices, Will took a deep breath and composed himself. He strode purposefully through the hallways, avoiding eye contact. The last thing he wanted right now was to be waylaid by some partner who hadn't gotten around to congratulating him yet. In the unspoken language of law firms, it was understood that when someone was power-walking through the hallways, it meant that they were under a deadline and not to be interrupted.

Will arrived at the desk of his secretary, Maggie Boze-man, a plump woman in her early fifties with a tumbleweed frizz of light brown hair. She wore granny glasses and a parachute-sized paisley skirt. Maggie was a former flower child who had miraculously managed to maintain both her job and her idiosyncratic ways through fifteen years at the firm. Maggie's longevity was attributable in part to the fact that she was smarter and more capable than most of the firm's paralegals. It also didn't hurt that the office administrative staff zealously protected the jobs of senior secretaries. Will had developed a grudging appreciation of Maggie's talents as a merciless grammarian.

Maggie looked up from her computer, revealing an upper lip coated with cranberry-colored Jamba Juice. "The group from Pearl has been in the conference room for twenty-five minutes. Didn't seem too happy to be kept waiting," she noted, with a hint of reproach.

"Good," Will said.

"Oh, and David Lathrop just arrived. He's in the soft seating area," Maggie added. She looked Will over, noticing the bandage on his forehead. "Have fun last night?" she added blithely.

Will shot a look at Maggie that was intended to have the devastating intensity of an industrial-grade laser. As usual, Maggie remained impervious, so he entered his office to gather his papers for the meeting.

Whenever visitors entered his office for the first time, they found it difficult to take their eyes off the windows, which offered a magnificent view of the utilitarian gray spires of the Bay Bridge. Will was usually too busy to even notice whether the sun was shining.

Will's files for the merger transaction were labeled "Project Zeus," the firm's code name for the Jupiter deal. He always joked about the code names that were given to M&A deals involving the firm's publicly traded clients—it all seemed just a little too much like a bad spy novel. In any event, the secretaries, office staff, and anyone else who was remotely interested could easily figure out what deals were in the works. Today, the use of code names didn't seem like a joke.

With his draft agreements and negotiation notes in hand, Will went to the reception area to greet Jupiter's CEO. Given the way things were going, Will viewed the negotiation session as just another opportunity for the next unpleasant surprise. Someone was trying to ruin his life and he couldn't rule anyone out at this point, including his own client and opposing counsel.

He found David Lathrop in the reception area halfheartedly thumbing a copy of *Forbes*. David was a small man with lank, brown hair who looked unassuming enough in his olive khakis and black-framed nerd chic glasses. But if the industry press were to be believed, David was fluent in the languages of both the Wall Street analyst and the programming geek. He was touted as a true scientist-businessman—a hybrid as rare as the minotaur or the gryphon.

"Well, there he is, the master of psychological warfare," David said, rising and shaking his hand. "What happened to your head?" he asked, pointing at the bandage.

"It's nothing. I was working out and got a little clumsy."

"Hey, you're not in your twenties anymore. At our age, everything comes with a price."

Will fingered the bandage and winced. "I think I'm figuring that out."

"So, do you think they've stewed long enough?"

"I suppose so," Will said. "I get the impression that you're going to enjoy seeing them pissed off."

"As long as it doesn't look like I'm the one being the jerk," David said.

"They won't blame you." Will smiled. "They'll just assume that your new lawyer's an asshole."

David was walking a fine line between sticking up for the interests of his company and avoiding antagonizing his possible future employer. The proposed merger would make Jupiter a wholly owned subsidiary of Pearl. After the deal closed, it was still uncertain whether Pearl would allow David to remain as the CEO of the company that he had founded twelve years ago in a student apartment in Palo Alto.

Will and David entered the conference room to be greeted by the cool stares of the three Pearl representatives and their two attorneys. The wait had extended long enough that four of the five were making calls on their cell phones. Two against five, Will thought as he placed his papers on the conference room table. He liked the odds.

———

After the negotiation session, which turned out to be fairly routine, Will returned to his office. Most of the day's discussions had revolved around the rate at which Jupiter shares would be converted into Pearl shares. Based on new but contested data produced by the valuation consultants, it now appeared that each Jupiter share would be converted into 0.27 of a Pearl share, up from the prior figure of 0.22. This fractional difference would add more than fifteen million dollars to the purchase price.

Finally, he had an opportunity to catch his breath and consider his own legal problems. As an attorney, he had advised his clients as they faced some of the biggest crises of their personal and professional lives. Will resolved to approach his own predicament with the same dispassionate logic that he brought to his work. At least that was the plan.

There was really nothing he could do about the investigation into Ben's death but wait to see if Detective Kovach and the DA's office took the next step by charging him with murder. Based on what he knew so far, the evidence linking him to Ben's death seemed insufficient. But then again, since he had forgotten most of what he learned in his first-year criminal procedure class, most of his knowledge of this area derived from watching TV dramas. It was also quite possible that whoever had switched the access cards had set other traps for him.

Although he was familiar with the basics of insider trading law, he thought a refresher was in order now that those statutes might be turned against him personally. He already knew the black letter law: the antifraud prohibitions of Section 10b-5 of the Securities and Exchange Act of 1934 held an insider liable for purchasing or selling securities of a corporation at a time when he or she knew material information about the issuer that would significantly affect the market price of the securities.

As Jupiter's attorney, Will was definitely an insider, and his knowledge of the Pearl merger was certainly material information. When the pending merger was announced, the price of Jupiter stock was expected to skyrocket. Will scanned the *CCH Federal Securities Law Reporter* for a "good faith" defense that might help him. He had hoped that he might find a court case holding, more or less, that if a horny idiot stupidly disclosed insider information to a girl that he'd slept with, then the horny idiot was not liable. Instead, he found cases holding that no "evil motive" was necessary to be guilty of insider trading.

On a more positive note, Will knew that he couldn't be guilty of insider trading until someone actually purchased or sold Jupiter stock based on his disclosure. It was unlikely that the two Russian thugs had purchased the stock yet, because they still knew very little about the company and the merger. Nikolai and Yuri were looking for a sure thing, and how could they be sure of anything with the little information they had?

Although they might not have done so yet, it was fairly certain that Nikolai and Yuri were going to buy Jupiter stock. But how would the SEC or anyone else ever link them to Will? He could scarcely believe himself that Yuri and Nikolai had entered his life. He considered reporting his indiscretion to the SEC. That would probably preempt any prosecution for securities law violations. However, if he went to the SEC, then his firm would find out about the incident. They would take a very dim view of the lapse in judgment that had led to the disclosure, particularly if it brought them negative press or SEC scrutiny. His partnership offer would be revoked. In fact, that was probably a best-case scenario. It was likely that he would be fired. And if he was fired for this sort of breach, he would never work in a major law firm again.

Forty-eight hours ago, the primary concern in Will's life had been whether he would make partner. Now he was facing the possibility of not one, but two, criminal prosecutions, one of them for murder. And he knew that Yuri, Nikolai, Katya, and whoever else was involved were just getting started.

Will knew that he must speak with Katya as soon as possible. He didn't trust her, but she seemed to be the best available source of information if he hoped to understand what was happening to him. If Katya was conning him and wanted to maintain the charade, then she would talk to him. He also needed to find out everything that Katya knew, and was willing to tell, about Nikolai and Yuri. Will pulled out a San Francisco phone book and looked up Equilon Securities. He began to dial the number, then stopped.

If Will ever became the focus of an insider trading investigation, the first thing the SEC would do is subpoena his office and home telephone records. The record of a phone call from Will's office to Katya at Equilon Securities on the day that Nikolai and Yuri (or maybe even Katya) traded Jupiter stock would make the SEC's case. Will gingerly placed the phone receiver back in its cradle as if it were a loaded gun.

Will went downstairs to a pay phone in the back of a Burger King. Above the din of children's voices reverberating off the tile floor, Will again dialed the number for Equilon.

"Equilon Securities." For a second, Will didn't recognize Katya's voice because she had almost completely excised her Russian accent.

"Katya?" In a spasm of paranoia, he wondered if Equilon tape-recorded its calls, then quickly dismissed the thought.

"Will?" The Russian accent returned. "I am so sorry. I never meant to get you involved in all this." There was a tremor in Katya's voice. She sounded rattled.

"Katya, did Nikolai hurt you this morning?"

"I can't talk right now. Not here." In the background, Will heard the sounds of phone lines pinging and bleeping like a well-played video game.

"Then how soon can you get off work? Can you meet me at Justin Herman Plaza in a half hour? This can't wait."

"Make it an hour and I can do it," Katya said. "Look, I've got to go. My lines are lighting up."

"Just tell me one thing. How dangerous are those guys?"

She sighed wearily, in the Russian manner. "Oh, Will. You have no idea."

EIGHT

Across from Justin Herman Plaza, the clock tower of the Ferry Building showed twelve thirty. *Katya should be here by now*, Will thought. He watched office workers unpacking their lunches on concrete benches. Now that the ice-skating rink had been removed, the square was an arena for skateboarders, who clattered off the concrete ramps and unoccupied benches.

Then he spotted Katya making her way through the crowd. He scanned the crowds for a glimpse of Yuri, Nikolai, or anyone else who might be accompanying Katya. She was wearing black—a long, sleek black jacket, black turtleneck, black skirt, and long black boots. He watched her intently as she came toward him, admiring the geometry of her walk, the sway of her hips. He knew that she was probably untrustworthy and he needed to focus, but when he saw her all he could think of was lying in bed with her that morning.

Katya looked just as worried and tense as she had sounded on the phone. If she was trying to deceive him, she was a good actress.

"Hi," Will said. Katya paused and looked around to see if anyone could overhear them. Nearby, a solitary man in a Windbreaker was feeding bits of his sandwich to a congregation of pigeons.

"It's too crowded here," she said. "Let's go for a walk."

They crossed the plaza, stopping in front of Vaillancourt Fountain, which always reminded Will of rusted ventilation ducts.

When they were standing before the fountain in the hiss of its waterfall, she continued. "I had to do it—tell Nikolai about Jupiter. You don't know what they are like. They could have killed you."

"If they're so bad, then how do you know them?"

A hurt look crossed Katya's face. "It's like I told you at the club. Yuri helped me get the receptionist job." After a reluctant pause, she added, "We were together for a while."

"Why didn't you tell me that before? You said he was just someone you knew from work."

"I didn't tell you everything because I wanted you to like me, okay? I'm telling you now."

"Is it over between the two of you?"

"Yes, yes, it's over."

"When did the thing with Yuri end?"

"He took me to dinner about a month ago and all he wanted to talk about was how he was going to join *mafiya*. I wanted no part of that, so I told him not to call me again."

"Wait a second." Will took a long, queasy moment to replay her pronunciation of the Russian word, which sounded disturbingly familiar. "Did you just say that Yuri is connected with the mafia?"

"Not mafia. *Mafiya*. Russian, not Italian."

"Okay, *mafiya*," Will said, imitating her pronunciation. "It's still organized crime, right?"

"Yes."

Will took Katya by the hand so that she was looking directly into his eyes. "Katya, I need you to tell me everything that you know about them." A pool of acid had begun to form in the pit of Will's stomach. "Who is Nikolai?"

She turned to him and squinted in the sun, her eyes narrowed to slits. "Nikolai is someone that Yuri met a few weeks ago. Yuri looks up to him because they say he was known as some kind of tough guy in Moscow."

"A tough guy? What does that mean?"

"He owned a grocery store in the Arbat." She said this with a wave of her hand, as if the meaning were apparent.

"A grocer? How tough can a grocer be?"

"You don't understand the way things are over there. Nikolai started his own business, an American-style supermarket. It wasn't Safeway, but pretty good for Moscow. Lots of American brands. Very profitable."

"So?"

"In Moscow, it is not an easy thing to run a profitable business without paying the *mafiya*'s tax collectors. Also not easy to get the suppliers to sell to you without paying big kickbacks. Yuri told me that Nikolai hired his own army of goons and refused to pay the *mafiya*'s taxes, the *dan*."

"So what happened?"

"*Mafiya* burned down the store. No one can stand against them for long. That's when Nikolai came to U.S."

"So he wanted to open a grocery store here in this country?"

"No, no. Yuri says now he just wants to become a criminal. He was afraid that he'd made too many enemies in

Moscow. With his business gone, Nikolai was vulnerable and thought he wouldn't live long if he stayed."

Will hoped that this part of Katya's story was a lie, but unfortunately it had the ring of truth.

Two young boys passed by, following a walkway through the fountain. They became small, dark shapes behind the curtain of water. Katya and Will fell silent until the boys sprinted across the plaza in an impromptu footrace.

"So is Nikolai in the *mafiya* or not?"

"He isn't, but he wants to be. Ever since he got to U.S., he's been hanging around with the *sportsmeny* in restaurants and bars, hoping to catch on."

"Sports what?"

"*Sportsmeny*. Sportsmen. They work for the *mafiya* as bodyguards or enforcers. They're usually former athletes or bodybuilders. It's easy to spot them because they wear these tracksuits that are . . . foolish? . . . No, that is not it. . . ."

"Dorky?"

"Dorky! Yes, that sounds right." Katya's face brightened for a moment at the new addition to her English vocabulary.

Will could not share her enthusiasm. "Tell me about Yuri."

"Yuri is just a stupid young man with big mouth. He has no connection to *mafiya*. Yuri is hoping that Nikolai will bring him along."

"What were they doing at your apartment this morning? Did they know that I was there?"

"No. They came to see me because I want to quit my job at Equilon. Yuri had recommended me, and he thought it would make him look bad if I quit. That was one of the things that Nikolai and I talked about when you were outside."

"Should I be afraid of them?"

"Yes, if they think that you have something that will help them. They would do anything to prove themselves to the lowlifes that they hang out with."

"What else did Nikolai say to you this morning when I was out in the hall?"

A few yards away, a skater's board shot out from under him, and he landed with a thump on the concrete.

"He asked me if I knew anything else about your 'big-time deals.' I told him that you had just mentioned Jupiter and that was it." She paused and frowned.

Will waited for her to continue.

"He said he didn't believe me," Katya said flatly. "He punched me in the stomach. And he wouldn't stop. He pulled me up by my hair and started twisting my wrist." She paused and looked around the plaza, as if for help.

Will wondered why he hadn't heard her scream when Nikolai struck her. The only thing that had separated them had been a thin wooden door.

"We need to go to the police. Next time, he could kill you."

"Don't worry about me. I don't have anything that they want now. It's you we should be worrying about. Nikolai and Yuri will want more information about Jupiter. I am afraid of what might happen if you don't give it to them."

"Yeah, me, too."

She jingled her bracelet with the charms shaped like Cyrillic letters. "How bad can it be for you to tell them a few things?"

Here it comes, Will thought, but he continued to play along. "Katya, when I told you this morning about Jupiter, I made a very big mistake. I'm not supposed to share that information with anyone. First, it violates attorney-client privilege. Second, it's insider trading if anyone buys Jupiter stock based on what I said." He paused. "If you buy Jupiter stock, it's insider trading and you could go to jail."

"Yes, I understand."

"And if anyone, an agent from the SEC or anywhere else, asks you about what happened, you will have to tell them the truth about everything. If you don't, you could go to jail for that, too."

Katya crossed her arms on her chest, as if she were trying to muffle an explosion.

"Did Nikolai say anything about what he intended to do with the information?"

Katya pulled a pair of sunglasses out of her purse and put them on. "He let go of my wrist and smiled. Then he said, 'I told Yuri that you were a worthless bitch, but perhaps you are not so worthless after all.'"

"That sounds pretty articulate for Nikolai."

"He said it in Russian."

"Was that it?"

"He wanted to know if that was everything I knew about Jupiter. Then he asked me if he needed to 'hold my hand' again. I said that I'd told him everything. He seemed satisfied and said that he'd get the rest of the information from you. That's when he opened the door."

Katya and Will walked slowly across the plaza to the busy thoroughfare of the Embarcadero. They crossed the Embarcadero in front of the Ferry Building and went past the hangarlike pier buildings. A family of tourists emerged from the shadows of a pier, fresh from their cruise ship, and huddled on the sidewalk with their roller bags, squinting at them from under baseball caps.

After walking in silence for a while, Will and Katya arrived at Pier 39, which had more to do with tourism than shipping. The wooden pier was jammed with T-shirt shops, ice cream stands, and video arcades. Will detested tourist traps, but it was comforting to be absorbed into the sneakered, T-shirted throng.

A rank, fishy smell grew stronger as they reached the end of the pier and the spot for viewing the sea lions. Dozens of them were lying on abandoned docks beside the pier. They came in every shade of brown, from the mud brown of the sleepers that scratched themselves with webbed flippers to the dark chocolate of the ones that emerged, dripping and indignant, from the water to bark and bump chests in territorial scuffles.

"You know," Will said, "they're all males."

"This does not surprise me," Katya replied.

"They should be off mating somewhere. But instead they come here for the food. It's one big, stinky bachelor pad."

"What is bachelor pad?"

"Never mind."

Will studied Katya as she leaned on the wooden railing, surrounded by tourists snapping photos. She still wore her dark glasses, her face impassive.

It was likely that Katya was lying to him. There were still too many questions, too many of what the litigators at his firm would call "bad facts." She had already admitted to dating, and accepting a job recommendation from, a would-be Russian gangster. If she was working with Yuri and Nikolai, then that would explain the appearance of the two thugs at her apartment that morning. It would also provide a plausible explanation for why she was so quick to volunteer the information about the Jupiter deal. And he still had to believe that Nikolai, Yuri, and perhaps Katya had some connection to Ben's death, which had led them to him when he took over the Jupiter negotiations from Ben. On the other hand, if Katya was telling the truth about the pummeling she had received from Nikolai, then he felt like a jerk for doubting her.

Katya looked up at Will as she made room for two little girls crowding to the railing to get a better look at the sea lions. She extended her hand, and he took it.

Then Will lifted Katya's hand and examined her wrist where Nikolai had grabbed her. There was no bruising, no marks at all. By itself, it was not decisive, but it was enough to tip the scales.

"I think you've been lying to me," he said.

"Why would you say that?"

"There are no bruises on your wrist."

"Maybe I don't bruise so easy."

"No, it's not just that. It's everything. I just don't buy it. I think you're working with Yuri and Nikolai. I think you knew they were coming to your apartment this morning. It was all an act for my benefit."

"So it's all about you, is it?" Katya said. "That sounds a little paranoid, doesn't it?"

Will simply stared at her. Katya stared back at him from behind her sunglasses for a long moment.

"Okay, you're right," she finally said with a shrug of her shoulders. "I do work with Nikolai and Yuri. But everything that I told you about them is true."

"Why should I believe a word that you say? You want me to be scared of them."

"Obviously, it's your decision, Will."

Still adjusting to his newly revised vision of Katya, Will was silent.

"I may not be your friend, but I'm not your enemy, either," Katya added. "Not really. I think you're a sweet guy—and a good lay. I'll try to help you if I can." Katya turned and began to walk away.

Will grabbed her arm and turned her around. "Then I need you to tell me more. What do Nikolai and Yuri want from me?"

"Let go of my arm, Will. Yuri is following us, you know. Don't make me call him over here." She pointed down the pier to an ice cream stand, where Yuri was eating an ice cream cone. Displeased at being discovered, Yuri tossed his ice cream into a trash can.

Will released Katya's arm, and she strode away through the crowd of tourists, leaving him standing at the railing as the sea lions filled the air with their groaning cries. Will realized that when Katya played with her bracelet, it had indeed been a tell, but not for nervousness. It meant she was lying.

Will's cell phone rang. It was a law firm extension, so he answered.

"Will, where are you?" It was Don, sounding impatient.

"I went out to get some fresh air. I'm just a couple of blocks from the office."

"Well, get back here right now, will you? There are some people here to see you. It's important."

Before Will could ask who the visitors were, Don hung up.

NINE

When Will returned to the office, he was greeted by Don, who was standing waiting for him in the lobby.

Will immediately suspected the worst. Was it possible that Nikolai had already purchased Jupiter stock and been linked to Will by the SEC? Or maybe Detective Kovach was waiting to escort him to a cell.

"There are some people in conference room C that I'd like you to meet."

"Clients?"

"Something like that."

Will followed Don down the hallway and past the reception desk. He noticed that the receptionist and office staff eyed them knowingly as they passed. Clearly, something was up.

Don held open the door to the conference room and motioned for Will to enter. Will put on his game face and stepped inside, ready for anything, even handcuffs.

In the conference room, the twenty-two San Francisco partners were clustered around the conference table, drinks in hand. A mild cheer went up, mingled with scattered exclamations of "Congratulations, partner!"

Will smiled with relief as a glass of champagne was thrust into his hand. "I could tell you bought it," Don said, patting him on the back. "There's a career in acting for me yet."

Will lifted his glass to the room and was relieved to see that no speech was expected of him. Everyone promptly resumed their conversations.

The office's other new partners were already there: Jay Spencer, his former classmate at Boalt Hall, UC Berkeley's law school; Jill Lewis, a litigator; Marc Tucci, a copyright attorney; and Norm Reynolds, a corporate attorney and grandson of one of the firm's venerable founders, Stewart Reynolds.

Will immediately realized that Rob Kramer, a senior associate in the technology group, was not among the new partners. Not so long ago, before the Internet bubble burst, he had appeared to be a shoo-in for partnership. During the dot-com mania, a kind of struggle had taken place for the soul of the law firm. Some partners wanted the firm to concentrate on the big money to be made taking Internet and tech companies public. Another faction felt that the firm was expanding too fast and ignoring its traditional mainstay practice areas, such as business litigation. Now that the technology sector had tanked, the old guard of the firm was once more in ascendancy, and the technology attorneys were like the zealots of a failed revolution, forced to bite their tongues and suffer the tired jokes about "dot bombs," waiting until times changed or their penance was complete. Rob Kramer was a casualty of this internecine war, his principal sin that of being championed by the wrong people at the wrong time.

Will made a little small talk with Don about the Niners' chances for next season, then turned to the subject that he was really interested in.

"Don, I don't mean to spoil the party here, but I've got a question for you about Ben."

Don's expression darkened. "Okay, if you must. Ask."

"Was there any indication that he was suicidal?" Will still believed that Ben had been murdered, but he was hoping that something interesting might have come to light now that everyone in the firm had spent two days scouring their memories for anything out of the ordinary.

"No, no one could see it coming, even in hindsight. I hope you aren't thinking that there's something that we could have done."

"No, that's not what I meant. I was just wondering if anyone saw any signs, or if there was a reason. . . . "

"There's no understanding this thing with Ben, so you shouldn't even try. But something one of the detectives said gave me pause. When they examined Ben's body, there were burns on his chest and upper arms. Probably about a week or two old. Maybe it was some kinky sexual stuff, maybe someone tortured him. The police don't know . . . and I don't think I want to know."

"Do the police have a theory?"

"How should I know?" Don snapped. "Take my advice, Will. Enjoy this moment. It's a milestone. It only comes around once. Now, pardon me, but I'm going to go find out where they're keeping the single malts around here."

As Don walked away, Will speculated that the burns were probably administered by Yuri, Nikolai, or some other Russian thug—the same bunch that had now turned their attentions to him. But how did Katya know that he was the new lead attorney on the Jupiter merger? She must have been informed by someone at the firm, probably someone in the room at that moment. Will scanned the faces of the attorneys as they chattered over their drinks, trying to guess who might have betrayed him. Will's thoughts were interrupted when he saw Jay Spencer making his way across the room toward him, wiseguy smile firmly in place.

Jay was tall and loose-limbed, with a tan and a smile both a few shades too vivid to be real. He resembled a young golf pro who had been cut from the tour and found his true calling hustling duffers at the country club. Jay had one of the most facile minds in their law school class, but he never became the attorney he might have been because his moral flexibility was always just a little too apparent.

Will and Jay had been competing ever since they both ran for editor-in-chief of the *Boalt Law Review*. Jay had won the election and never ceased to amaze Will with the creative ways he found to introduce that fact into conversation. As they raced neck and neck toward partnership, it was clear that their competition was not going to end anytime soon.

Jay extended his hand. "Congratulations, man. You earned it. Not as much as me, but you earned it."

"I think I'll take that as a compliment. Congratulations to you, too."

Jay leaned in to examine the bandage on Will's head. "That looks painful. Must have been some celebration."

"Racquetball injury. Got smacked with a backhand." Will had prepared his story in advance, concluding that a racquetball injury struck the proper note: suitably preppy and virile, but not too klutzy.

Jay put his arm conspiratorially around Will. "Come on,

Will," he said in a stage whisper. "That crack habit was okay when you were an associate, but now that you're a partner, it's time to lay down the pipe."

Will laughed in spite of himself. Jay was the Eddie Haskell of Reynolds Fincher. He adopted a serious, regular-guy persona with everyone else at the firm, but with Will, who had had his number since law school, Jay gave free and unapologetic rein to his inner Machiavelli.

"Excuse me," Will said, removing Jay's arm from around his shoulder. "But it's that sulfur smell. It's hell getting it out of the clothes."

Jay smiled. "Hey, don't be that way. You know, ten years from now, we're going to be running this place, you and me."

"What's with this 'we' business? That doesn't sound like you, Jay."

"I'm using the word loosely . . . to mean 'me.'"

"That's the guy I know." Tiring of the banter, Will changed the subject. "Have you heard anything more about Ben?"

Even Jay was sobered by this turn in the conversation. "The funeral service is Saturday."

"Is anyone from the firm going to speak?"

"I don't think so. I hear that the family somehow blames the firm for the suicide. What can you say? The guy just didn't make the cut."

Will shot Jay a disgusted look.

"You know, Will, you've gotta stop treating me like I'm the recruiting director for the forces of darkness. Look around. We're on the same team."

Before Will could field a retort, Jay headed off to join a group of corporate partners who were listening attentively as Don Rubinowski regaled them with tales of his last

quail-hunting trip to Mexico. Will wondered how long he
had to stay before he could slip out.

Just as Will inched toward the door, he spotted Richard
Grogan approaching from across the room, a tumbler of
scotch in hand. Richard, the co-chair of the firm's corporate
department, had a client list that included a host of publicly
traded companies. With his immaculate gray suit and perfectly coiffed salt-and-pepper hair, he looked as if he had
been genetically engineered to make board presentations.

Richard was the ultimate anal retentive; he even had a
policy regarding the correct positioning of binder clips on
documents. Jay Spencer was Richard's right hand, sitting
in the second chair on a number of transactions for Richard's clients. It was widely known within the firm that he
had taken up smoking just so that he would have an excuse
to join Richard on his regular cigarette breaks outside the
building. Will had never become one of Richard's "team"
of associates, not because he wasn't talented enough, but
because he was unwilling to join the cult of personality that
Richard cultivated.

Will realized that his failure to suck up to Richard
could have compromised his chances of making partner.
Fortunately, he had found an ally in Sam Bowen, the other
co-chair of the corporate department. Sam's style could
not have been more different from Richard's. He seldom
wore a suit, favoring khakis and rumpled button-down
shirts. While Richard was five feet six and tightly wound,
Sam was six feet two and gangly, with an unflappable
calm. Although he could match Richard in his grasp of
every facet of a transaction, Sam always treated his associates with respect, even when they made mistakes, and
that was enough to inspire Will's loyalty. Sam's specialty
was international mergers and acquisitions. He spoke

five languages fluently and, Will suspected, with a north Florida drawl.

When Sam noticed that Richard was coming over to greet Will, he broke away from his group to perform a rescue.

"Congratulations, Will," Richard said, extending a hand. Richard noted Will's wrinkled suit and the bandage on his forehead with an arched eyebrow. "It's great to have you in the partnership. You know, we haven't worked together enough lately. When the Jupiter deal closes, you should come around and see me about tackling a project together."

Will performed a rough translation of Richard's statement. Richard had probably tried to sabotage his partnership candidacy because Will was not among his cadre of associates. Since that effort had clearly failed, Richard wanted to align Will with his faction within the corporate department.

"I'll definitely do that, Richard. Right now Jupiter's keeping me pretty busy. Taking over for Ben at a moment's notice has been challenging, to say the least."

Sam joined them and raised a bottle of beer. "Welcome to the old bastards club, Will."

"Thanks, Sam, but I still like to think of myself as a young bastard."

"I stand corrected." Sam laughed. "You are a young and vigorous bastard. A bastard in the very prime of life. Richard, this young man is going to be the future of our department," he proclaimed.

"Will has certainly done a great job here over the past few years," Richard said coolly. Will knew that the quickest way to turn Richard against him was to be seen being chummy with Sam. As he sipped his champagne, Will took comfort in the thought that, as a partner, he no longer had to be as concerned about Richard's temperament.

"Will, once again, congratulations," Richard said. "See you at your first partnership meeting on Thursday. I'm afraid it's going to be a tough one."

Will nodded his thanks as Richard left, limboing through an obstacle course of wineglasses.

"What's so tough about this meeting?" Will asked.

"We have a difficult personnel decision to make," said Sam, looking uncharacteristically grim. "There's some talk about reducing our associate leverage to increase profits per partner. In English, that means laying people off. But it looks like the process is going to start with a termination."

"Who's getting fired?"

"C'mon, it's a party. You'll hear about all of this soon enough."

"Please, Sam. I really want to know. Who is it?"

"Claire Rowland."

"Not Claire! She's always done great work for me, and she really seems to have a handle on the Jupiter due diligence. . . ."

"Whoa, there. This is not my idea. She got on Richard's bad side somehow. I don't think there's much we can do for her. . . ."

"What do you mean, 'there's not much we can do for her'? It's not like she has cancer!"

Sam shook his head. "Sometimes you've got to know which battles to fight. Besides, if Claire doesn't get nailed this month, she'll probably get sent packing when the associate layoffs hit. She'll get more severance pay this way." Sam took a long swig of beer. "Shit, did I just say that? I really am becoming an old bastard. You should have another drink and enjoy yourself. It's your party, pard. Now I've got to get home before my wife murders me."

Claire Rowland was a talented young Stanford graduate who was heading up the team of associates conducting the due diligence review of Jupiter. He could imagine how upset she would be if she was fired from her first law firm job. Claire's work for him had been consistently excellent, and he resolved to speak up for her at the partners' meeting.

But Will had more pressing concerns at the moment. The burns on Ben's body demonstrated what Yuri and Nikolai were capable of. Once they had taken their profits from insider trading, they probably planned to bring their talents to bear on Will. He figured that he would be safe in the short run if he could prevent them from getting what they wanted—the closing of the Jupiter merger. In the meantime, he would try to find out who at the firm might be in league with the Russians.

As Will looked around for a place to set his empty glass, he noticed Annette, a plump, redheaded receptionist, waving to him through the glass door of the conference room. Annette was training to be a paralegal; she read her night school course books behind the reception desk when the phones were quiet.

When Will reached the entrance to the conference room, Annette pointed to the reception area.

"Two gentlemen are here to see you."

"Who are they?"

"They said they had an appointment and that you'd know."

Will hoped this was not another surprise partnership celebration.

Will saw Yuri and Nikolai sitting in the reception area, making themselves at home. Nikolai was trying to read a copy of *BusinessWeek*, his lips moving slightly as he sounded out the English words. Yuri had his feet up on the spindly wooden table in the center of the room, which looked as if it could barely support a newspaper and a couple of magazines.

"Great," Will muttered.

Will glanced at Annette, who wasn't even pretending to be doing anything other than watching them.

Will strode toward the pair. Nikolai stood up and put down his magazine. Yuri brought his feet down from the tiny table with exaggerated ease.

Will knew that if a scene ensued, Annette would make sure that the entire office staff of the firm knew about it by the time they'd finished their first cup of coffee the next day. He needed to get them out of the building as quickly and quietly as possible.

"Good to see you again," Will said, extending his hand to Nikolai. "Are you all ready to go? I made dinner reservations."

Nikolai glanced at Annette, leaving Will's hand hanging long enough to create an awkward moment. Then he gave Will's hand a perfunctory shake.

"You are having a party, but you did not invite us? Very rude."

"Fucking rude," Yuri affirmed.

"It's a firm party. Attorneys only."

"Then we will have party of our own," Nikolai said.

TEN

Yuri and Nikolai shoved Will inside the elevator, and they rode down to the parking garage in silence. Yuri was carrying a small brown paper bag. A video screen in the elevator flashed CNN news. President Bush was speaking from the White House Rose Garden, squinting into the camera with a gaze that was intended to read as steely-eyed confidence but came off as something more tentative. Yuri and Nikolai watched the news without glancing at Will. They exchanged a couple of terse sentences in Russian about "Boosh."

"Where are we going?" Will asked.

No response from the Russians.

"I'd rather talk in a public place," Will said, feeling less in control of the situation by the moment.

The elevator doors opened on an empty parking garage. The Russians walked on either side of Will, their steps echoing on the concrete floor. Will looked around for someone who might at least serve as a witness to his abduction, but he saw no one.

They stopped in front of a black Lincoln Town Car, and Yuri entered the backseat. Nikolai motioned for Will to get in the front passenger seat. Will considered running, but Nikolai was standing too close. Will climbed in, and Nikolai slammed the door shut behind him. Nikolai walked around the car, opened the driver's-side door, and got behind the wheel.

Nikolai turned the key in the ignition and the pale green dashboard lights came on, but he did not start the engine.

Yuri reached around beside Will's seat. With an electrical whirr, Will's seat slid forward until his knees were pressed against the dashboard. *Zzzzzzzzz.*

"Tell us about Jupiter," Nikolai said. "We need to know that this is investment that we can recommend."

"Anything I do for my clients is privileged. I can't talk to you about it. And besides, Katya misunderstood. There's no deal."

"I am pretending that I am not hearing this shit," Nikolai said, shaking his head in disappointment. He pushed a button, and the electric door locks clicked.

"I don't know what you think you know, but you've got it wrong."

Yuri reached around beside the seat again. *Zzzzzzzzzz.* Will's seat tilted backward. For a moment, he had the sickening sensation that he was reclining in a dentist's chair. He leaned forward uncomfortably so that he could remain upright.

Yuri grabbed Will's shoulders and jerked him back down into the seat.

Yuri's hands were on either side of the headrest, and

he was speaking almost directly into Will's ear. Will could smell onions on his breath. "We need to know that you are a team player, Will. You know what it means to be team player?"

"Yeah."

"When you have shown us that you are a team player, then we can bring this opportunity to some friends of ours. Serious men. Men who are not to be fucked with. Once they become involved, any bullshit from you will reflect badly on us. And we will not allow that to happen." Yuri's measured statements reinforced Will's feeling that he was in the middle of a dental examination, one that was not going well.

"We'll need more information on the deal," Yuri continued. "Who is the buyer, when it is scheduled to close, everything. Then we're going to need regular reports from you on how it is going."

"I told you, I can't do that. I could be disbarred. I could go to jail."

"There are worse things, my friend," Nikolai said.

Yuri adjusted the seat again, and Will was now almost flat on his back, staring up at the sunroof. He incongruously wished that his own car had a sunroof.

Nikolai and Yuri spoke to each other in Russian. From the tone, it sounded like they were bickering over something mundane. As their exchange became more heated, it slowly dawned on Will that they were working themselves up, stoking their aggression like football players slamming each other's shoulder pads before a game.

Nikolai and Yuri stopped talking. Nikolai reached into the pocket of his coat and withdrew a box cutter with an exposed razor blade. He heard the rustling of a paper bag in the backseat, but he couldn't turn around to see what

Yuri was up to. He couldn't turn around because that would mean looking away from the dull gray edge of the blade. If he looked away, there was no telling what might happen.

"Take off your jacket," Nikolai said.

"Look, this isn't going to accomplish anything," Will said.

"Take off your fucking jacket!" Nikolai shouted, raising the box cutter.

Will slowly removed his jacket, his mind racing. Everything seemed too close and too vivid. The stench of Nikolai's perspiration, which was staining the underarms of his shirt. The sound of Yuri mouth-breathing a few inches behind him, clearly excited by what was coming next.

Will noticed the button on the dashboard that released the electric door locks. Placing the jacket in his lap, Will felt his breathing grow shallow as he prepared himself.

Will slammed his elbow backward between the seats, aiming for the spot where he thought Yuri's face would be. His elbow connected with Yuri's forehead with a thud, and a Russian curse issued from the backseat.

Will reached for the button on the dash to unlock the doors. Before he could reach it, Nikolai pressed the blade against Will's throat. Will's eyes darted, searching for someone outside the window, but the garage was still deserted.

"If you touch that, I'm going to make a mess in here," Nikolai said. Will withdrew his hand and faced forward. To the backseat, Nikolai added, "You okay?"

"*Pohsol na khuy!* You stupid, fucking asshole!" Yuri spat, again yanking Will's arms behind the seat. "Nikolai, hand me the blade. This is taking too long."

"In a minute," said Nikolai, shifting the box cutter from one hand to the other, watching Will's eyes follow.

"Look, this is a mistake," Will said. "There is no deal! Katya got it wrong!"

"Don't worry, Will," Nikolai said reassuringly. "We won't touch your face or your hands. No one at work will be able to tell how fucked up you are." To Yuri, Nikolai added, "Roll up his sleeve."

Yuri loosened his grip on Will's shoulders and pulled up Will's shirtsleeve to expose the forearm.

Nikolai's hand shot forward, leaving a long, bright red gash about an inch below Will's elbow. Pain and shock scrambled his thoughts like a bad radio signal. There was a sound echoing in the car's confined space. It took him a moment to realize that he had shouted.

"You know, every animal responds the same way to pain," Yuri said. "You could be Albert fucking Einstein. Doesn't matter."

More rustling of the paper bag, then Yuri's hand emerged from the backseat holding a Band-Aid and a dish towel with the price tag still on it. "Use these," Yuri said.

Will's hands were shaking a little as he applied the bandage. The cotton pad went red instantly, and blood oozed out the sides.

"Talk to us, Will," Nikolai said. But before he could respond, Nikolai lunged again. This time, he buried the short blade in Will's upper forearm and ripped downward.

Will thrashed to release himself from Yuri's grip. He was shaken by the pain, by the sight of his blood, and most of all by the realization that Nikolai and Yuri were just warming to their work. He examined his arm; it looked like he was wearing a red elbow-length glove.

"Use the towel," Yuri said. "You better put some pressure on that."

"It hurts, doesn't it?" Nikolai asked.

"He made more noise than I thought he would," Yuri said. "You think we should be doing this in a parking garage? Somebody could hear."

"I was thinking same thing," Nikolai said. "Maybe we should go outside." Nikolai turned again to face Will. "I'm going to give you a few seconds to think about this before we continue."

Will desperately searched for something that he could say that might make them stop.

"You know, you're going to get caught. You can't pull this off," Will gasped, as he applied a second towel proffered by Yuri.

"Oh, yeah? And why is that?" Yuri asked.

"The SEC has systems that detect unusual trading activity, particularly when a public company is acquired."

"Yes, we know," Nikolai said.

"The first people that the SEC looks at when there's a leak of inside information are the attorneys. And if they find me, it's going to lead them to you."

"You're not leading anybody anywhere," Yuri said. "You're not going to talk to anyone about this because if you do, we're going to kill you."

"Time to decide," Nikolai added.

As he pressed the dish towel to his arm, he still couldn't stop looking at the blade of the box cutter, which was now smeared with blood. Suddenly there seemed to be so many reasons why he should talk to them. And insider trading was just about money, after all. What was money compared to the blade of that box cutter?

He tried to wipe his nose, but the movement sent a shooting pain through his arm.

Nikolai watched him expectantly, tightening his grip on the box cutter.

"Okay," Will said. As soon as he said the word, he felt a wave of relief, quickly followed by sickening guilt. He had to admit, though, that as he watched Nikolai put away the box cutter, the relief was stronger.

Yuri released his grip on Will's arms and raised the seat to a sitting position.

"Good," Nikolai said. "Then we are going to need to get a few facts straight. First, who is buying Jupiter?"

"Pearl Systems."

"Really? I have one of their computers at home. They are publicly traded, yes?"

"They're on the New York Stock Exchange."

"And this deal makes the price go up?"

Will pressed the dish towel to his arm. "I don't really know."

"I think that you do. Please, no bullshit."

"Yeah, the market is probably going to like the deal. Jupiter's encryption software is a natural fit with some of the new business applications that Pearl is developing."

"And when is deal going to close?"

"We don't know for sure, but we're aiming for May first."

"Just two weeks away."

"Yeah, but a million things could still go wrong. It could take much longer. It might not close at all."

"You will see that it does," Nikolai said.

"If you think that I control this process, you're mistaken. If either party gets cold feet, I can't be responsible for that."

"Oh, but you can. We are making you responsible," Yuri said.

"But what's so special about this deal?" Will asked. "Surely there are easier ways to make some quick money. And there are plenty of other public-company transactions you could have chosen."

Yuri leaned forward from the backseat, already snickering at his own joke. "We could tell you that, Will . . . BUT THEN WE'D HAVE TO KILL YOU!"

Nikolai removed a cell phone from his pocket. "There's something else that you need to see, just in case you're thinking of going to the SEC or some stupid shit like that."

Nikolai switched on the phone and played a video clip that was recorded on the phone's camera. He held the small screen inches from Will's face.

An out-of-focus, color-saturated image appeared on the phone's video display. At first, all he could see was a blue, carpeted floor, which Will immediately guessed was the blue carpeting of the Lincoln Town Car that he was sitting in. The picture showed a portion of a man's face—a nose and an eye. The soundtrack consisted of static and a series of thumps as someone adjusted the camera in their hand, brushing the speaker with their fingers.

Then the camera pulled back to show Ben Fisher, who looked more upset than Will had ever seen him. His eyes were moist and bloodshot, and it looked like he had been crying.

The sound crackled through the tinny speaker. "This is Ben Fisher. I want whoever is watching this to know that Will Connelly has been threatening to kill me for the past week and I know now that he intends to do it. I know that Will committed malpractice on a deal that we're working on. He's afraid I'm going to tell the firm and spoil his chances of making partner. If I die, I want whoever finds this to know that it was him." The clip abruptly ended.

"That's Ben's cell phone," Yuri said. "All we have to do is give it to the police and you'll be arrested for his murder."

"You forced Ben to say that. No one will believe it," Will said.

"Oh, I think the police will find it interesting," Yuri responded.

"You murdered Ben," Will said.

"What's important for you to know," Nikolai said, "is that you belong to us, just like Ben Fisher belonged to us."

"When you put the video together with the security card thing," Yuri added, "it's more than enough to get you convicted for Ben's murder."

"So you switched the access cards. How did you get into the office to do that?"

"It doesn't matter," Nikolai said.

"Ben made us a lot of money," Yuri said. "We aren't about to walk away just because he had an accident. You're our new guy, Will."

"Let him out, Yuri," Nikolai said.

Will's knees were still jammed against the dashboard. He opened the door and climbed out, his legs numb from the cramped quarters. Still woozy from the pain, he placed his hand on the roof of the Town Car to steady himself.

Yuri got out and took his spot in the front passenger seat. "Hey, Will! You messed with my seat! I had it just the way I like it." *Zzzzzzzzzzzzzzzzzzz.*

ELEVEN

Still clutching the blood-soaked dish towel to his arm, Will managed to make it upstairs to his condo without being seen by any neighbors.

Once inside, he unwrapped his arm and rushed to the sink, wincing as the cold water rinsed away the blood to reveal two long, ugly gashes down his left forearm, blackening at the edges where the blood had dried. He felt nauseated watching the pinkish water slosh in the basin.

Nikolai had been right—no one at work would be able to tell what had happened to him. Unless, of course, his frayed nerves gave him away. Ben must have gotten the burns on his chest and upper arms during a similar encounter with the Russians. Will imagined that Nikolai and Yuri had probably used the Lincoln Town Car's cigarette lighter to coerce Ben into making the statements on the cell phone video.

He felt light-headed, but it wasn't from blood loss. The adrenaline that had started pumping the moment the Russians greeted him at the elevators had taken its toll. Will slumped onto the couch, feeling both leaden and weightless, like someone running a high fever.

Will's apartment made up for what it lacked in domestic niceties with enough gadgetry to outfit an electronics showroom. A seventy-inch flat-screen plasma TV with home theater speakers, a coffee table littered with Xbox games, a Bang & Olufsen stereo, and a StairMaster occupied the places of honor in his living room. A couple of windsurfing boards and sails were stacked in one corner, gathering dust. No woman who entered the place failed to note that it was a perfect example of a single thirtysomething male's impaired notions of interior decorating.

The phone rang, and he picked it up. "Congratulations on making partner!"

"Hi, Dana." It was his ex-girlfriend. Her tone was easy and light, as if it were a year ago and they were still a couple. "I saw the item in the *Daily Journal*. I just had to call when I heard."

Six months ago, a call from Dana would have been a major event, cause for hope of reconciliation. But now that she was very publicly dating the odds-on favorite in the San Francisco mayoral race, he knew that he had no shot.

Will, still dazed from his encounter with Yuri and Nikolai, was having difficulty generating banter. "So . . . congratulations!" she added again in an ebullient tone. "You so deserved it. Remember all those Sunday afternoons we sat around drinking beer at the Grove, planning our careers?"

"Back then, you were the one who was really into the career planning. I was just trying to figure out what I had to say to sleep with you."

"Well," she said with a sharp laugh, "you figured it out, didn't you?"

"That I did." He recalled her long, elegant body, which looked wonderful in a black cocktail dress. She'd get plenty of opportunities to wear one on the political fund-raising circuit.

"There's actually something else I wanted to talk to you about," Dana said, sounding a little uncomfortable. "I guess you probably know that I've been dating Jamie Pryce."

"Yeah, I was at the dentist's office and saw the *San Francisco* magazine piece. Nice photo." *I'd rather not talk about your new politico boyfriend*, he thought. And did she have to call him Jamie?

"Thanks. It's so ridiculous all the attention we've been getting," she said, unconvincingly.

"Wait until he gets elected mayor. You might even graduate to the *Star*."

"Actually, that sort of thing has been worrying us a little."

"Really? Isn't it a little early for that?"

"Maybe not. See, I have some news of my own. Jamie and I are getting married."

Although he liked to think that he was over Dana, he found this news surprisingly depressing. It underlined the fact that she'd moved on and he hadn't. "That's great," he managed. "Congratulations to you, too. Have you set a date?"

"June. Call me a traditionalist." Another awkward pause. "We plan on making an announcement in the next week or so. When we do, you may get some calls from reporters."

"What would they want with me?"

"Well, we dated for so long, they'll probably be hoping you'll say something nasty about me."

"I can't think of any skeletons in the closet . . . except maybe that time you shot a man in Reno just to watch him die."

"Cut it out," she said. He could picture her tight-lipped smile on the other end of the line.

"Or the night in Cabo when you ate the mescal worm. . . ."

"You may think things like that are funny—"

"As I recall, you did, too."

"Okay, it was funny—but please be careful. They may not even identify themselves as reporters."

"You don't have to worry about me. I get it." *I'll bet some media relations consultant told her to make this call,* he thought.

"Thanks, Will. I knew I could count on you, but I just thought I'd call anyway."

"I understand. By the way, the number on Caller ID is different. Did you move?"

"Uh, not yet, no. I'm over at Jamie's place right now."

He was tempted to ask if Jamie was in the room with her, listening to their conversation, but decided that he already knew the answer. The real question was how many media advisers and campaign managers were there. They were probably planning their marriage announcement like it was a product launch. And maybe it was. He vowed to go nowhere near the *Chronicle*'s society pages for the foreseeable future. National news, business, then straight to sports, no detours in between.

After hanging up the phone, Will sat on the couch trying to study his notes for the next day's meeting at Jupiter's offices in Palo Alto to negotiate the terms of the merger. Pressing a towel to his wounds to stanch the bleeding, his thoughts turned to his predicament. If he helped the transaction move toward closing, then he was doing exactly what Yuri and Nikolai wanted. The sooner the deal closed, the sooner they could take their profits from insider trading. On the other hand, if he reported Nikolai and Yuri to the SEC, his legal career was probably over. His life would probably be over, too, if he made himself a witness against the *mafiya*. And, last but not least, if he didn't cooperate with the Russians, they would release the video of Ben Fisher that would put him in jail for Ben's murder.

Everything was happening too fast. He needed time. Time to figure out who at the firm might have helped set him up. Time to find a way out of this trap before the merger closed. The deal was probably less than a week away from closing and he needed to find a way to stop it.

TWELVE

Driving south to Silicon Valley, Will contemplated the inauspicious office parks that dotted the rolling hills of Palo Alto and Menlo Park. A few years ago, before the bubble burst, he would have been thinking of the new technologies and wealth that were being created behind the glinting, mirrored windows. Now his speculation turned to how much of the office space was vacant.

Weaving his black BMW through traffic on the 101, Will struggled with how he should approach the day's negotiations. He decided that his best strategy was to stall, finding issues that would temporarily sidetrack the negotiations while he searched for a way to extricate himself. But didn't that in itself compromise the interests of his client? Will had assembled a list of points that Ben had put forward for Jupiter that Pearl had refused to budge on. He was prepared to revisit those issues today, a tactic certain to infuriate the Pearl team. He told himself that if he won any of these concessions, then he had served his client's interests. Of course, there was always the possibility that the stunt could blow up the entire deal.

Will pulled into the parking lot of the Palo Alto offices of Jupiter Software. It was a standard-issue Silicon Valley office park: a three-story box encased in mirrored glass and surrounded by a moat of black asphalt, dotted with a few well-manicured trees. Atop the building was the Jupiter logo, a stylized representation of a padlock.

As he walked quickly across the parking lot, Will could already feel his crisp white shirt dampening and sticking to his ribs under his jacket. That morning, he had passed from one of the Bay Area's microclimates into another, leaving fog-shrouded San Francisco for the sweltering summer heat of the Valley.

Will entered Jupiter's generic reception area, where he signed in and picked up his security pass. You would never know it by the bland offices, but Jupiter was a high-tech fortress guarding the nation's most valuable secrets. Jupiter's leading encryption software program, Paragon, was used by banks, credit card companies, HMOs, hospitals, government agencies, and countless other businesses to protect the sensitive personal information of millions of Americans.

The hallway was lined with framed color photographs of vintage padlocks, the rust and corrosion rendered in loving close-up. He passed a closed doorway secured by a card key pad, which led to the room that housed Jupiter's most precious trade secret—the encryption algorithm at the heart of the Paragon program. The algorithm generated an eighty-bit encryption key. An eighty-bit key meant that more than one trillion trillion possible key combinations were necessary to arrive at a correct encryption key through an exhaustive search. Put another way, if the eight processors of a Cray supercomputer (each performing about eighty-nine thousand encryptions per second) were all dedicated twenty-four hours a day, seven days a week, to the task in a so-called "brute force" attack, it would still take a billion years to produce a single correct encryption key.

Will knew that the card key pad on the doorway was just the beginning of the security measures used to safeguard the Paragon algorithm. To reach the room at the end of the hallway where the algorithm was stored, he would have to pass a security guard and two biometric scanners (one fingerprint and one retinal). Jupiter's engineers referred to the room as the SCIF, or Sensitive Compartmentalized Information Facility. Although the offices of Jupiter Software were far less imposing than the Pentagon, they were nearly as secure.

At the end of the hallway, Will arrived at a room that was filled with boxes of paper and four young attorneys— the due diligence crew. Like supply lines in a military campaign, due diligence was the most mundane but indispensable element of a successful acquisition. In a merger like the Jupiter deal, the disappearing corporation (Jupiter) would be merged into the surviving corporation (Pearl Systems) through the filing of a merger agreement with the Delaware Division of Corporations (both Jupiter and Pearl were Delaware corporations). Because Jupiter would be absorbed into Pearl, Pearl would automatically assume Jupiter's corporate liabilities and obligations. As a result, Pearl was keenly interested in understanding the nature and extent of those liabilities and obligations. Assembling that information and making it available to Pearl was Jupiter's primary task in the due diligence process, which brought the four young associates to a stuffy room filled with boxes containing the history of Jupiter's short but eventful corporate life.

Once all of this data had been reviewed and organized by Jupiter, it would be pored over by Pearl's team of attorneys. If a particularly alarming fact was discovered—such as the possibility that one of Jupiter's encryption program patents might be vulnerable to challenge—then it could sink the deal or substantially lower Jupiter's selling price. Although Will had given each of the associates the standard speech about the vital importance of their task, that did not make it any easier to read six software license agreements in two hours.

Josh Stanton, a hyperactive first-year associate from USC, was holding forth to his colleagues. His back was turned so that he couldn't see Will standing in the doorway. "You've all seen *The Matrix*, right? Remember the pods that the robots used to keep the people on life support and harvest the energy of their brains? Well, that's exactly what the firm needs for these big due diligence projects. See, if we were being fed nutrients and stuff, then we'd never have to leave this room. No coffee breaks. No bathroom breaks. Increases productivity, right? And here's the beauty part . . . when Keanu was in the pod, he was given the *illusion* that he was living a full, normal life. When you bill as many hours as we do, you don't really have a life, right? But with the pod, you would at least *think* you had a life."

The other three associates struggled to maintain deadpan expressions.

Claire Rowland, who was leading the due diligence team, at last mercifully interceded. "That's a very interesting theory, Josh. I, for one, would like to hear Will's take on it."

Josh turned to face Will, mortified.

"Ah, yes, the pods." Will nodded meaningfully. "You're not supposed to know about them yet. They're actually still in demo. But, Josh, I'm sure you'll be happy to hear that you've been selected for beta testing."

It's nine A.M. and they're already punchy, Will thought. With most partners, the associates maintained the party line that due diligence work was a fascinating and highly educational process that taught them "how a company works." With Will, however, they often felt free to acknowledge due diligence for what it really was: well-paid but mind-numbing drudgery. Each of the associates was nursing an extra-tall latte. A molar-grinding caffeine buzz was a necessity to maintain focus during document review.

"What brings you down here? A negotiating session?" Claire asked.

"Yeah, we're scheduled to start in a few minutes."

Will could not be sure whether Claire had gotten her morning coffee yet because she came naturally caffeinated—her motor always seemed to be turning a few RPMs faster than everyone else's. Some considered her high-strung, but Will found it kind of endearing. She was tall and slender, with shoulder-length blond hair that she tied up in a ponytail. Claire was twenty-nine, slightly older than the other associates. She had worked with the Electronic Privacy Information Center, a consumer privacy rights organization, before Stanford Law. Even though Claire was only a few years older than her cohorts, they deferred to her as the natural leader of the project. Will hated the idea that Claire was going to be fired. She deserved better.

"If you need anyone to second-chair for you in there,

you know any of us would be happy to help," Claire offered. Occasionally Will brought an associate in to a negotiation, particularly if he or she had assisted in drafting the provisions that were being discussed. Claire and the other associates regularly lobbied for the opportunity to sit in.

"Thanks, Claire, but this isn't going to be a good day for that. Maybe next time." He did not want any of them to witness what he had planned for that day's session.

Will turned to leave, but Claire followed him into the hallway.

"Do you have a second for a couple of questions?" she asked. "There are some things I've been running across in the due diligence that don't make sense to me."

"Sure. What's up?"

They were interrupted when a young man with shaggy blond hair approached down the hallway, smiling nervously at them. He was in his late twenties, wearing jeans and a black shirt; he looked like he belonged in a rock club, not a software company.

"Hey, Claire," he said. "I realized that I have yet to introduce you guys to the best coffee shop in Palo Alto. You're a macchiato person, right?"

"You're good," Claire said. "Will, this is Riley Boldin, one of the top programmers here at Jupiter."

"Assistant VP, software development," Riley added, with a quick glance at Claire. "You've got a bunch of hard workers here. Laser-focused. I've been trying to play host a little bit, but they hardly ever break from reviewing those documents."

"You've been a great host," Claire said.

"It's nice to meet you, Riley," Will added, extending his hand with an air of finality.

Riley took the hint. "Oh, you guys have work to do. I

didn't mean to interrupt." To Claire, he added, "I'll stop by later to give you the directions to that coffee shop. Hey, I can even walk you over there."

"Thanks, Riley. See you later."

When Riley walked off down the hallway, Will said, vaguely jealous, "I think Riley likes you."

"Stop it."

"So what was it you wanted to talk about?"

Claire stopped smiling. "There's a set of files that Jupiter is not producing in the diligence. I haven't actually seen them, but I found an internal memo mentioning them. That memo also contains some cryptic references to the NSA—"

"The National Security Agency?"

"And there was also something called 'Clipper.' Is there anything we should know here? Just so we understand what we're looking at."

"I don't know what that memo refers to, but I don't think it's anything you need to bother with. I'm sure the NSA has regular dealings with companies like Jupiter. You have to figure that the use of encryption in the private sector is something the NSA would take an interest in."

"If it's standard procedure, why isn't Jupiter disclosing it in the due diligence? Doesn't that seem a little suspicious?"

"Well, *suspicious* is a little strong. But I will look into it."

"Thanks, Will. Sorry if I'm being nosy."

"In due diligence, nosy is good," Will said as he headed down the hall.

When Will entered the corner conference room, everyone was on time for once. No more gamesmanship over who could keep whom waiting the longest. Perfect, he thought. *Now* they want to get down to business.

Today the Pearl team consisted of two attorneys from the New York firm Davidoff & Perkins and Clive Shusett, the vice president of operations. David Lathrop was already there, picking at a fruit plate.

"Hello, gentlemen," Will said, shaking hands with the three Pearl representatives. "Hi, David."

Will leaned in to whisper to David, "I'm going to yank their chain a little today. Just go with me, okay?"

David nodded. "You want to discuss this outside?"

Will shook his head. He didn't want to give David the opportunity to stop him.

Clive interrupted with a tight, perfunctory smile. "Okay, let's get down to business, shall we?" Because Pearl was a much larger company than Jupiter, Pearl's CEO made only a few token appearances during the course of the negotiations. Instead, Clive's responsibility was to ride herd on the transaction and see that it closed promptly and on terms favorable to Pearl. Because Will had negotiated a deal opposite Clive several years ago, he knew that Clive's negotiating style was schizophrenic, which allowed Clive to play bad cop to his own good cop.

In his guise as good cop, Clive was disarmingly chummy, telling stories about his seven-year-old daughter's piano recital, laced with discreet references to the other globe-straddling deal that he was closing for Pearl. Good Cop Clive wanted to welcome you to the big leagues and allow you to bask in the attention that international giant Pearl was bestowing upon the somewhat thinly capitalized niche player that was Jupiter Software.

Bad Cop Clive began to emerge as soon as you began to push for terms that differed from those Pearl was accustomed to ramming down the throats of acquisition targets. First, he greeted the introduction of a new issue with mild surprise, followed by a brief explanation of how customary the particular provision was and how no one had ever asked them to alter it before. If that approach was unsuccessful, Bad Cop Clive escalated to questioning opposing counsel's experience in handling major transactions. Finally, Clive would try going over the attorney's head by asking the client to overrule, expressing doubts as to whether Pearl would proceed with the deal. When he was really pissed off, a submerged Scottish accent surfaced—Clive's nastiest and most elemental incarnation. It took a skilled negotiator to get Clive that agitated—it was akin to reaching level four of Donkey Kong.

Will had seen similar tactics work on midlevel associates who were negotiating their first deal, but he was too experienced to roll over.

Will took a deep breath and began. "Clive, there are a few points I'd like to revisit before we move on." Around the conference room table, the scribbling of notes, the shuffling of papers, and the surreptitious checking of Black-Berrys stopped. Everyone's attention focused on Will.

Clive's smile froze. "Revisit? You've only been on this transaction for a couple of days."

"I've been studying the file and some of the points that Ben had made previously."

"So we're going back to square one just because there's a new lawyer at the table?"

"Why don't you just let me get through the issues?"

"Okay," Clive said. "Let's hear them."

"We want the sandbagging clause deleted."

Carl Sutro, diminutive and fierce, was the lead attorney for Pearl on the deal. "First, I don't like the term *sandbagging*," Carl interjected. "That clause just ensures that Pearl gets the benefit of the bargain."

"A provision like that allows you to close the deal, then turn right around and seek damages for breach," Will shot back. "If you think you've discovered a significant problem during due diligence, then we should have the opportunity to address the issue preclosing."

The so-called sandbagging clause stated that Pearl could hold Jupiter liable for a breach of its representations and warranties under the merger agreement, even if Pearl gained knowledge of the breach in the course of its due diligence review and failed to speak up.

"Will, you know that issue was settled," Clive said. "If we have to backtrack at this point, I question whether we'll be able to meet our closing date. But go ahead, you look like you have more." The two Pearl attorneys took their cue from Clive and settled back in their chairs.

"Second, we don't like the scope of the covenant not to compete that you're holding David to. Under these terms, David would basically have to retire if he doesn't remain with Jupiter. He couldn't be involved in any business related to data security. We think the scope of the noncompete should be limited to businesses directly involved in the development of encryption software. And it should only last for two years."

David was staring at Will in bewilderment, wondering what game he was playing and why he hadn't been informed of the rules.

Will waited for a reaction, but Clive, furiously taking notes, refused to look up. "Also, I'd like to remind you that you still haven't responded to our information requests. We've certainly been responding to yours."

Clive made another note, then looked at Will across the conference room table as if he were a dog that had just crapped on the carpet. "Is that all?"

"Yes, that's what I've got today."

"So—wait a minute—are you saying that you might be asking us to revisit other deal points later?"

"No, that's not what I'm saying. What I'm saying is that you aren't going to tell me what issues I can and can't raise."

"Frankly, I am very surprised by what I'm hearing."

"These are all points that have been discussed before. Maybe not with me, but they've been discussed. Just because you haven't responded and we've agreed to push forward on other issues doesn't mean we've forgotten about them."

"Look, Will, we've done many deals similar to this one," Clive said, gesturing to include his team of attorneys. "Those deals have included the same benefit-of-the-bargain and covenant-not-to-compete provisions that you're balking at. As for the information request, we're publicly traded just like you are. What's the point? Everything you need to know about us is in our 10-Q."

"Don't tell me we should agree to something just because you've been able to get someone else to agree to it. That's just not very persuasive. As for our information request, take another look. We're not concerned about Pearl's finances. What we want to know is how you plan to integrate Jupiter into your suite of desktop products. Jupiter shareholders are going to become Pearl shareholders. They want to know that this operation is going to be a success when the deal is closed."

"With requests like this, it may never close. You follow?"

Will pressed on. "The Jupiter board has a fiduciary duty to make sure that this transaction will work over the long haul and provide long-term value to shareholders, not just a good stock price at closing."

As he was speaking, Will felt a throbbing pain from his wounds, as if Yuri and Nikolai were there in the conference room with him, bullying and cajoling. Will even found himself breaking away from Clive's glare to look at his forearm, half expecting to see a bloodstain blossoming across his starched white shirt.

Now Clive turned to David. Will noticed David tense slightly, as if he had just waded into a cold lake. "David, I can't tell you how many times I've seen deals go south because a lawyer or a CEO let things get out of hand. I suggest you take a few minutes and talk this over with your new attorney. Clearly he doesn't have a handle yet on where we're at in this negotiation. Let's not turn this into a dick-measuring contest because, I'll tell you right now, Pearl is an international company with fifty billion dollars in annual revenues. Ours is bigger."

"We don't need to step outside. Will speaks for me on this," David said without a pause.

Will felt like hugging David. The gambit was working.

"Okay. But you know the key terms of this deal have already been approved. If we reopen these issues, I'm going to have to take all of this back to senior management and the board. And they're going to ask me what the fuck is going on. There's always the possibility that they could just say fuck all and move on to the next deal. You know, David, they're already looking forward to having you as part of the Pearl management team."

The temperature of the room seemed to drop as David, who did not like being threatened, returned Clive's stare. "Tell them that I'm grateful for their confidence in me, but that right now my first responsibility is to the shareholders of Jupiter. I'm sure they can appreciate that."

"Oh, I know you're just thinkin' of the shareholders,"

Clive said, a hint of Scotland creeping into his voice. "I'm sure your shareholders are going to be real happy if Pearl walks away from this deal and leaves you bright boys twisting in the wind."

"Let's keep this civil, Clive," Will said. "These are valid concerns that were never fully addressed. I'm sure your board won't be pleased to learn that you represented these points as nailed down when they really weren't."

Clive stared down at his notes, clearly struggling to contain a Vesuvius of invective. He slowly closed his leather notebook and nodded to his two attorneys, who, after exchanging arched eyebrows, gathered their papers. The three members of the Pearl negotiating team stood, walked around the conference table, and strode out of the room without another word.

When the conference room door swung shut, David spoke in a clenched voice. "Will, you were way out of line just now. Don't ever do something like that again without talking to me first. I know every attorney has their own negotiating style, but that was not the way I do things."

"It won't happen again." Will felt ashamed that he had let his personal problems affect his representation.

"I do agree with your points, though, and I think I'm basically glad you did what you did. But I just don't like being blindsided like that. I hope it didn't show."

"No. You kept your poker face on. If you want to go directly to Clive and tell him that I exceeded my authority, I understand."

"No, it's okay. I certainly don't like being threatened by a midlevel deal jockey like Clive. Besides, if I cut you off at the knees like that, I might as well negotiate the deal myself. They'll just start looking to me on everything."

"I understand."

"You know what? Let's not worry about this too much," David said. "I've got a feeling Clive has more room to move on these points than he lets on."

"That was my thinking, too. These aren't really the kinds of issues that he would take back to his board. I expect that he'll be back with a counterproposal within twenty-four hours, forty-eight if he wants to let us dangle a bit."

Will was consumed by recriminations as he crossed the parking lot at the end of the day, worried that he had compromised the negotiations. But his stunt had bought him a few days, and now he needed to figure out a way to put that time to good use by getting to the bottom of the conspiracy against him.

He had nearly reached his car when he realized that something didn't fit the surroundings. A maroon Lincoln Town Car was parked among the BMWs, Saabs, Audis, and Jettas in the Jupiter parking lot—it didn't match the employee profile. He could see the outline of two figures in the front seat, but couldn't make out their faces.

Will felt a chill despite the sweltering heat, which was rising from the asphalt and penetrating the soles of his shoes. He quickly unlocked the door and started the engine.

Will could not take his eyes off the rearview mirror, nearly colliding with another car as he lurched into traffic. Okay, the Lincoln Town Car was still parked in its spot under a tree. He changed lanes to turn the corner and again searched in the mirror for a view of the Town Car. Still there.

As he waited at a red light, he adjusted his mirror so that he could continue to watch the Town Car. When he found the tree again, there was an empty parking space beneath it. Will jerked around in his seat and saw the Town Car pulling out of the parking lot and taking up a spot in the stream of traffic about twenty-five yards behind him, waiting for the light to change. Two figures warped and shapeshifted behind the glare of the windshield, but became no more recognizable.

Will watched helplessly as the Town Car slowly rolled up alongside his BMW on the right. In the front seat were Nikolai and Yuri. On the passenger side, Yuri smiled crazily and motioned for Will to pull over.

THIRTEEN

Will pretended that he didn't see the Russians and inched forward another few feet, waiting for the light to change.

He heard a tapping and looked over to see that Yuri was standing in the stalled traffic peering through the passenger-side window, still beaming a twisted grin. He opened his jacket to reveal a pistol tucked into his pants. Will unlocked the door, and Yuri slid into the passenger seat.

"I hope you weren't trying to run from us, Will. That would not be wise."

"Stay the fuck away from me."

"What's wrong? Tough meeting?"

"Fuck you."

"You did see the gun, right? You want me to pull it out again? You want me to put the barrel in your mouth? Turn off here," Yuri said, pointing.

Will pulled into the parking lot of a convenience store, and the Town Car followed.

"You could have just stopped me in the Jupiter parking lot," Will said.

"It wouldn't look good for us to be seen with you there after a meeting. You're a smart guy, Will, you should know that."

"I'm new at this."

"It's okay. We were all beginners once. Now get out of the car. You're coming with us."

"What about my car?"

"Leave it."

Will climbed into the backseat of the Town Car. It was not the one that had been the setting for his inquisition.

"What's with you guys and Lincoln Town Cars?"

Yuri responded, "Nikolai likes the leg room. Not exactly my taste, but what can you do?"

"Town Car is a good ride," Nikolai grunted over his shoulder. "So you can all shut the fuck up."

They rode in silence up the 101 into San Francisco, past the anonymous airport hotels of Burlingame, past the working-class homes of South San Francisco crowding the hillsides. In the dusk, a stream of white-hot headlights and red-ember taillights poured over the hillside from the city like a lava flow.

"Can you tell me where we're going?" Will asked.

No response from the front seat.

"I'm going to have to go back to get my car. That's going to be a pain in the ass." Will was hoping for a response that might provide some confirmation that he was going to return from the trip.

Nikolai and Yuri continued to ignore him as the car curled off the Civic Center exit into the city. Soon they were cruising through the Tenderloin, where the streets became an obstacle course of people who were either too drunk, high, mentally unstable, or generally belligerent to observe pedestrian etiquette.

Kaifu, Will thought. *We all must be high.*

The Town Car came to a stop in front of a small restaurant on Geary Street that was sandwiched between a Russian grocery and a Russian deli. A tiny, faded sign over the door read, "Dacha Restaurant."

Inside, the place was poorly lit, cramped, and smoky (in blatant contravention of San Francisco's no-smoking law). Will imagined that this must be what a working-class Moscow dive looked like. There were only three customers in the place, each over seventy years old and indistinguishable from the others to Will's untrained eye. Observing the cloud of smoke pooled against the ceiling, Will could only conclude that the kitchen staff must be smoking like chimneys.

Nikolai and Yuri claimed a circular booth in the corner. They sat on either side of Will, blocking him in. No one seemed to take any notice of them.

A waitress with a pinched face emerged from the back room, tossed smudged, laminated menus on the table, and exchanged a few laconic words in Russian with Nikolai.

A few minutes later, three plates of pirozhki arrived at the table, along with three glasses of water and three shots of vodka. Although, on second thought, Will wasn't sure that the tall glasses didn't hold vodka and the short ones water.

"Is there something you want to talk about?" Will asked.

"Not now. I'm eating," Nikolai said.

After picking at the greasy pirozhki, Will looked up at the sound of the front door slamming. A compact man in a glossy, black leather jacket approached their table. He wore his hair slicked back, and his dark, deep-set eyes were accentuated by a bushy unibrow. He was trailed by a tall, dark-skinned Arab man who was dressed nondescriptly in khakis and a blue Ralph Lauren button-down shirt.

The man in the leather jacket, whom Nikolai and Yuri referred to as Valter, greeted them in Russian and gave each a curt, professional handshake.

"This is our new friend Aashif," Valter said. "He and I will be doing some business later, so he is going to sit in on our meeting."

Nikolai and Yuri nodded respectfully.

Aashif had the slightly unfocused, myopic gaze of a scholar, and it was difficult to tell whether his reserved demeanor signaled disdain or social awkwardness. Aashif barely looked at Nikolai and Yuri as he shook their hands. Instead, he kept staring at Will.

Valter and Aashif slid into the booth next to Nikolai.

"So, Nikolai, Yuri. What have you brought me today?" Valter asked. "Something better than last time, I hope." He made a quick gesture with his hand, as if to dismiss their previous proposal. Everything about Valter moved a little too fast, from his speech to his darting eyes, like a mechanical toy that had been wound a few times too many.

"This is Will Connelly," Nikolai said carefully, as if he were reciting from a script. "He's a partner at a law firm . . ." Nikolai glanced down at the business card in his hand. "Reynolds, Fincher and McComb."

"So I am guessing that Will has fucked up in some way, yes?"

"Very much so, Valter. Will picked up Katya Belyshev in a club. Do you know Katya? She's the new receptionist at Equilon."

Valter seemed to think for a moment, then said, "Oh, yeah, Katya. Sure. Good worker."

"Will is a lawyer. He wanted to impress the girl and told her that he was working on the sale of a publicly traded company, Jupiter Software."

Valter smiled sagely and shook his head. "A man should never tell his business to a woman."

"I'll try to remember that," Will said.

Nikolai continued: "Jupiter is going to be acquired by Pearl Systems. Will says everyone is expecting the stock price of Pearl to go up when the deal is announced."

"I never said that about the price," Will interrupted.

Valter disregarded Will's comment. "How do we know that Will is telling us the truth?"

"We cut him a few times . . . by the time we were done, he would have given up his mother."

"But how do we know he will stay cooperative?"

"We're in a position to send him away for the murder of that other attorney, Ben Fisher. We could also turn the SEC on him for disclosing insider information. He's ours."

Valter nodded. "You know that the SEC will spot unusual trading activity," he said. "Their computers pick that shit up."

"That's what I was telling them," Will said.

Valter gazed at him with a blank, affectless stare usually reserved for lifeless objects. Will decided that he should not interrupt again.

"We could purchase the Jupiter stock through shell companies or through people we control who would turn over their profits."

"And the SEC wouldn't see through that?" Nikolai asked.

"Not if it is handled correctly. We've done this type of

deal before," Valter said, working through the possibilities. "We'd need to muddy the waters a little, spread the tip around. If you have a few people trading, it is much harder for the SEC to find the connection."

Nikolai leaned forward, looking to close the deal. "So do you think this is something that your people would be interested in?"

"Maybe," Valter said. He reached across the table for Will's glass of vodka and tossed it down. "But it would take some real money to make it worthwhile. I recommend this to Boka, and it is my ass on the line. And I have not done business with you before. No offense."

"None taken," Nikolai said. "We want to work with you, so when we see opportunities, we bring them here. . . ."

"If you take a chance on this, you won't regret it. This is a sure thing," Yuri said. Nikolai threw him a glance that, if they were not in Valter's presence, Will felt certain would have been accompanied by his patented *Shut the fuck up, Yuri.*

"I think I'm going to recommend that we put a little money in as a test," Valter said. "If the *vory* like the idea, we'll see how it does. If it works out, maybe we'll go again."

"Thank you, Valter. We appreciate this."

"I hope that you do. If it turns out that your shit is fucked up, we all have a problem. But for you two, it would be much worse. Much worse."

Nikolai and Yuri nodded solemnly.

"You said that if this goes well, you could do it again. I just want you to know that I don't get involved with mergers of publicly traded companies very often," Will said. "I don't think I'd be of much use to you after this."

"I think you'd be surprised how helpful you can be," Valter said. "Your firm is big, isn't it?"

"Yeah."

"They represent big companies, wealthy individuals, yes?"

"Yes."

"Even if you are not working on a deal, someone else is. You can find out what is going on with your other publicly traded clients. With the individuals, maybe you might know something that we could use against them."

Maybe the pirozhki and the smoke-filled room had something to do with it, but Will suddenly felt queasy. He had an image of himself going from office to office at the firm late at night, digging through other attorneys' trash cans and client files.

"Stay close to this one for a while," Valter said to Nikolai and Yuri. Will looked up to see Valter examining him. "It usually takes time for them to get used to what they have to do. It's like a fish when you set the hook. At first he struggles, does things that make his situation worse. After a while, struggling stops."

"You think he might kill himself?" Yuri asked.

"Maybe. Or worse."

Will considered what to them could be worse than killing himself. There were many things that probably fit into that category, he decided, such as talking to the FBI or the SEC.

"Will, I want you to know that we don't want something for nothing," Valter said, adding a smile for his benefit. "If we make money, you'll make money. Who knows? Soon you might be making as much from your dealings with us as you do from your law firm job. Not a bad sideline, huh?"

Will declined to respond, staring at the table.

"I mean it. Watch this one," Valter said to Nikolai and

Yuri. Then to Aashif, "So, Aashif, you are a good judge of character. What do you think of our friend Will? Do you think we can trust him to do what we ask?"

Aashif, who was still staring at Will, responded, "Trust him? No. But he doesn't seem like the sort to take his own life. And I suspect that he's capable, if properly motivated." Aashif had what sounded like a North London accent. Given the company that he was keeping, Will wondered if the serious young man was connected to a terrorist organization.

Valter put his elbows on the table and leaned forward. "One more question, Will. Is there anything else that you know about Jupiter that might be of value to us?"

"No, I don't think so."

"No need to answer so fast. Jupiter is an encryption company. A copy of their encryption algorithm . . . wouldn't that be valuable?"

"I suppose so," Will said, surprised that Valter knew enough to throw around a word like *algorithm*. "But it's kept under tight security. I don't have that level of access."

"Why don't you think about how you might get access," Valter said. "We will ask you again later."

Valter and Aashif rose from the booth. Nikolai and Yuri stood quickly to join them, shaking hands with Aashif and exchanging embraces and slaps on the back with Valter. As Valter and Aashif left the restaurant, the three old men in the dining room studied their plates.

Instead of leaving by the front door, Valter entered a room at the rear of the restaurant. Before the door closed, Will saw lights filtered through a haze of cigarette smoke. Apparently, it wasn't the kitchen staff that was smoking up the place after all.

When the door swung shut behind Valter, Nikolai and

Yuri beamed at each other. Yuri hollered for the waitress, "More vodka!"

When the waitress brought the vodkas, her pinched face was further contorted by a scowl. Their little celebration was disrupting the dour atmosphere that the restaurant seemed to cultivate.

"Who is Valter?" Will asked.

"A true criminal," Nikolai said. "An associate of Boka, who is the top *vor* in the *mafiya* here in San Francisco."

"Valter doesn't sound like a Russian name."

"It is his *klichki*, his nickname. He is named after the Walther pistol."

"It also comes from a character from an old Soviet TV movie, *Variant Omega*," Yuri added. "Valter was this bad-ass Gestapo, a real killer."

"I loved that movie," Nikolai said warmly. "Must have come out around seventy-five. Takes me back to my childhood."

"Yeah," Yuri said. Nikolai and Yuri were silent for a moment, contemplating the innocent days of their youth.

Nikolai raised his glass and proposed a toast. *"Vorovskoi mir."*

Yuri followed. *"Vorovskoi mir."* He nudged Will to down his vodka.

Will didn't need any encouragement. Maybe the shot would calm his nerves.

"What was the toast?" he asked.

"To the thieves' world," Nikolai replied. *"Vorovskoi mir."*

FOURTEEN

The phone on Will's desk was ringing, and the number on the Caller ID screen told him that it was Clive Shusett of Pearl Systems. Clive had no doubt prepared his response to the demands that Will had made in their last negotiating session.

Will let the phone ring until voice mail picked up. He was still tired from his adventures the night before. After Nikolai and Yuri had finally allowed him to leave the restaurant, he had taken a cab back to Palo Alto to retrieve his car where he had been forced to leave it.

From her desk outside, Maggie craned her neck to confirm that Will was in. He usually picked up his phone immediately, but Maggie knew better than to answer the call herself, which would have violated their protocol.

Will listened to Clive's message. "Will, this is Clive Shusett." He could hear car horns in the background. Clive was probably calling from his cell in a taxi. "We'd like to schedule another meeting with you and David to go over the points you raised. I think we have a bit of room for discussion. I'd like to schedule a meeting on April twenty-fourth, either in Palo Alto or at your offices. That's the one day that I can be in the Bay Area. I hope you appreciate that this is an accommodation."

The Jupiter deal was only a meeting or two away from being finalized, so a meeting with Clive Shusett did not fit with Will's stalling tactics.

Will dialed Clive's office immediately because he knew from the cell phone static that he would not be there. "Clive, this is Will Connelly. I got your message, but I'm afraid the twenty-fourth is bad for me. I've got an all-day meeting scheduled. Do you have another date that we can try for? Let me know. Thanks."

Once again, Maggie peered into his office. She had access to Will's schedule, so she knew his calendar was clear on the twenty-fourth.

"Hi. I couldn't help overhearing," Maggie said, entering the office. "I show no appointments for you on the twenty-fourth. Just wanted to make sure that I had your calendar straight."

"You got me, Maggie. It's called strategy."

"Okay. I just hate it when you start keeping your own calendar and not entering your appointments. It makes it so much harder for me to schedule things for you."

"I would never do that to you, Maggie. I live to make your life easier."

"If only it were so," Maggie said, returning to her desk.

Will hoped that he had assuaged Maggie's curiosity. He did not want anyone getting the impression that he was delaying the closing of the Jupiter deal, especially Maggie, who frequently swapped gossip with the other secretaries in the corporate department.

An electronic reminder popped up on his computer screen: "Partners' meeting." Will rose from his desk and headed for the main conference room to attend his first meeting of the San Francisco partners, a little curious as to what the view was going to be like from the other side of the great divide.

When he reached the conference room, everyone was gathered around the table or serving themselves dim sum.

Managing partner Don Rubinowski led the meetings. "All right, folks, we'd better get started," he said. "The first order of business is welcoming our new partners."

A smattering of applause and lame kidding greeted the newcomers, as Will and the other four smiled dutifully.

As the meeting progressed through an agenda that included the status of billings and collections and a lateral partner candidate, Will grew bored.

Then Don's voice went somber. It was probably the same tone he employed when advising a white-collar-crime client who was going to be trading in his pinstripes for an orange jumpsuit. "Now we have some more serious business to attend to. Claire Rowland."

Don recapped the situation for the newcomers. "Claire got mixed reviews last year. A handful of you identified problems in her work. Now we have another set of reviews in front of us, and it looks as if those problems have, if anything, worsened."

Don nodded at Richard Grogan. "Richard, would you like to say anything for the benefit of those who weren't at the last meeting? You seem to have particular issues with Claire's performance."

"It's regrettable that Claire isn't measuring up, but I

don't think we're doing her or us any favors by keeping her on when it's not working out," Richard said.

Apparently, the process was further along than Will had realized, because no one else was saying anything.

Will saw that the other new partners were obviously fascinated by this discussion, but none of them were about to open their mouths. It seemed that Claire's termination was a done deal, and Don wasn't exactly inviting an open debate of the matter. Will turned his gaze to Sam Bowen, who was concentrating resolutely on his moo shu pork—he would be of no assistance.

Will thought Claire had done a great job on due diligence for the Jupiter deal and other transactions. In his opinion, she was smart, creative, and responsible. He felt certain that there was nothing in her job performance that could possibly justify firing.

Don droned toward a conclusion. "This is certainly an unfortunate situation, but Richard's right, it's better not to let these kinds of problems fester. Now, before we vote, does anyone have any final comments?"

Will knew that it was in his best interests to just shut up and let the vote proceed. Nevertheless, he spoke up. "I was just wondering, who else has given Claire bad reviews? I had no idea that there were such serious concerns about her work. Frankly, she's done a great job for me on my projects."

Three hands went up. Jay Spencer, Daria Finotti, and Jim Hugasian, all members of Richard's deal team. Will instantly recognized the dynamic that was at work. Jay, Daria, and Jim would follow any lead set by Richard. From personal experience, Will knew that associates who worked with Richard were expected to become his fawning disciples, swearing allegiance to Richard and his transactions to the exclusion of all others. Those who did not, such as Will and, he suspected, Claire, did so at their peril. Although he had no evidence, he was certain that Claire was being fired because she was simply too independent-minded to kiss Richard's ring.

"Claire really dropped the ball on the due diligence for the Kamen deal," Jay offered. "The work was sloppy, there were key issues that were missed. It nearly jeopardized our representation. The problems were substantial enough that I simply don't think I could trust her to work on one of my projects again."

"I have a very different perspective on Claire's work," Will said.

"Please, Will, go ahead," said Don, clearly surprised to be hearing from him.

"Claire's currently heading up the due diligence team on the Jupiter deal, and I'd really hate to lose her. Her work has been excellent. I think it's important that we have a tolerance for the learning curve. We have to allow young attorneys like Claire the room to make a few mistakes. I'm sure we've all had at least one project from hell as an associate, or a partner that you just didn't click with."

Will waited for a moment to see if anyone else would rally to Claire's defense, but no one spoke.

"Thank you for your input," Don said coolly. "But it appears that this was more than just a failure to 'click,' as you say, with a particular partner."

Scanning the conference room table, Will noted a few faint smiles beginning to appear. Unsurprisingly, Jay Spencer was already in full smirk.

"In the absence of further comments, I think it's time to call the vote," Don said. "Who's for termination?"

Everyone around the table raised their hands, except

Will. As a token of sensitivity, the hands did not shoot up like the class know-it-all. Rather, the hands went up slowly, reluctantly, rising barely above the shoulder, as if to signify, *This hurts me as much as it hurts her*.

"Okay," Don said. "I'll meet with Claire to deliver the news, and we'll put together a severance package. Looks like we're adjourned."

As soon as the vote was cast, Richard was immersed in conversation with Jay, Daria, and Jim, already back to the day's business. Will contemplated Richard and wondered, with genuine curiosity, how someone could do such damage to the life of another person without thinking twice. Will had once been on the receiving end of Richard's sniping when he was a second-year associate, and the only thing that had saved him from Claire's fate had been the support of Sam Bowen. Unfortunately, because Will was a new partner, his opinion did not carry the same weight as Sam's when it came to swaying votes.

Don stopped on his way out the door and put his hand on Will's shoulder. "These decisions are always tough, but you have to start thinking like a partner now."

Will nodded, then waited for Don to remove his hand.

Don studied him for a moment, then clapped him on the shoulder and walked away.

Jay Spencer approached, smirk still firmly in place. "Will, I must say I was touched by the speech." He tapped his fist to his chest. "Got me right here, buddy. Right here."

"You're all heart," he responded.

"We've got to maintain our standards," Jay said, heading for the door. "It's what separates us from those PI lawyers who advertise on TV and the *abogados* on Mission Street."

Will hoped that he hadn't just made an enemy of Richard Grogan. Did being a partner really provide him with immunity from Richard's machinations? He knew that his new status provided some measure of protection, but he didn't want to test its limits so soon.

But perhaps Richard had been his enemy all along. Someone within the firm seemed to be involved with the Russians, and Richard was as good a candidate as any. As a chair of the corporate department, Richard was privy to what was happening in the Jupiter transaction. Will wondered if Richard might have already learned of Claire's discovery of Jupiter's NSA connection, and whether that had played a role in his decision to have her fired.

Will resolved that if it was Richard who had framed him for Ben's death and brought the Russians into his life, then he would find a way to bring him down. Richard was not untouchable. But then again, neither was Will.

FIFTEEN

The first thing that Will noticed when he returned to his condo was the insistent red light of his answering machine flashing in the dark.

"You have two new messages," intoned the gender-neutral, synthesized voice.

The first message was from Katya. "Hello, Will." She pronounced it *Weel*. "Are you still mad at me? I hope not. I really did have fun that night, and I'd like to see you again. I'm free tonight if you are. You don't have to trust me if you don't want to. Just call me."

So now Will was getting booty calls from a Russian gangster's moll. How his life had changed in the past four days.

The second message was from Claire, left at ten thirty that night. "I guess you've heard the news by now. Actually, I suppose you must have been at the meeting where it was decided." Her tone of voice wavered as she tried to apply a forced cheerfulness that wouldn't stick. "You're probably the last person I should be calling right now—but I've really enjoyed working with you—and I don't really have anyone else to talk to about this tonight—and—I can't get fired twice! And there's something else that we really need to discuss. I'm going to have a drink at Lefty's. Make that a couple. I'll be over there by about eleven. If you can make it, that's great. If you can't, it's no problem and I understand. I think I'd better stop now. Bye."

He had to go. Will knew from personal experience how devastating the loss of a job was for careerists like himself and Claire.

When a Reynolds associate was fired, he or she was regarded during the notice period much like a zombie—dead, yet still inexplicably roaming the hallways in a Thorazine shuffle. In contrast, a departing partner was usually ejected from the offices in short order because he or she usually had clients that the firm was hoping to retain. The partners viewed a terminated associate as an unwelcome reminder to the other associates that although Reynolds Fincher might be a family, it was a family where love was not unconditional. For their part, the associates treated their soon-to-be-departed colleague with the cool sympathy usually reserved for someone who had contracted a disease brought about by a perceived moral weakness, like an alcoholic suffering from liver failure. They had to believe that it was a fate that could not befall them.

Even though Claire was usually more than capable of looking out for herself, a depressed woman drinking alone in a bar like Lefty's was a recipe for disaster. He checked his watch. Eleven thirty P.M. She'd probably already been hit on at least five times by now.

But Will also had more self-serving reasons for rushing to offer solace to Claire. Her discovery of Jupiter's links with the NSA was just the kind of information that, if leaked to the press, might bring the merger process to a halt. If Grogan was working with the Russians and had gone to the trouble of having Claire fired, then it was also possible that Claire knew something that might help him penetrate the conspiracy.

Will took a taxi to Lefty's, a marina district bar frequented by boisterous ex–fraternity brothers in their midtwenties. Claire's choice of venue was ill-advised because of the predatory male clientele, but he could understand the appeal. Everyone was so intent on having a good time, and loudly broadcasting that fact, that it was difficult to think, much less brood.

Will found Claire seated at the corner of the bar, shielded on one side by the wait stand, leaving her with only one border to defend. She was wearing jeans and a white cotton shirt open at the collar. On the stool next to Claire was a callow young man with short black hair wearing a Radiohead T-shirt. He was glancing up from his beer at regular intervals, trying to catch Claire's eye to restart a failed conversation. Claire was leaning slightly forward over her martini glass, eyes determinedly fixed on the television set above the bar, which was tuned to a Giants game.

Will couldn't really blame the poor bastard. If they hadn't been co-workers, Will might have approached Claire in a bar. When they first began working together, he had allowed himself to think about what it would be like to go out with her, even though that was a practical impossibility because she was a subordinate. Largely to console himself, he had concluded that Claire was just a little too intense for him. Like living in a house next to a power line, he decided that long-term exposure to Claire would probably not be good for him, although he couldn't pinpoint exactly why that was so.

Will tapped Claire on the shoulder, and she turned slowly, braced to repel another onslaught. When she saw that it was Will, her defenses went down and she managed a small, taut smile.

"Hi, Will. Thanks for coming."

"I couldn't let you drink alone. Not tonight."

The guy on the next stool cast a sullen glance at Will and returned to his beer.

"What happened today really sucks." Will didn't want to say *fired* because he didn't want their neighbor, who was clearly listening in, to know the story.

"It's okay to say it, Will," Claire said, taking a long sip of her martini. "I was fired. And it's going to be okay. Not tonight, but it will be."

"I'm glad to hear you say that."

Giving up, Radiohead slapped some bills on the bar and vacated the stool. Will slipped in beside Claire and ordered a beer.

"So do you want to talk about it? Or just drink?"

In response, Claire raised her martini glass to him.

They sat for a while, drinking and watching the Giants game, each lost in their thoughts. Claire finally broke the silence. "That conversation from this afternoon just keeps playing on a loop in my head."

"So who gave you the news?"

"Teflon Don. The bastard."

"Yeah."

"Hey, you're a partner now, you're not supposed to be agreeing with me."

"He's a dick."

"I'll bet you stuck up for me in that partners' meeting, didn't you?"

Will dismissed the question with a wave of his hand.

"You did, didn't you?"

"I wasn't the only one," he lied.

Claire squinted at him shrewdly. "See, now I think you're lying."

With her instincts for cross-examination, she should have been a litigator, he thought.

"I understand that you don't want to talk about what happened in the meeting. That's okay. They're probably afraid I'm going to file a gender discrimination suit or something."

Will wondered if she might actually file a lawsuit. He thought of a time last week when he had touched Claire on the shoulder to get her attention as she was reviewing documents at Jupiter's offices. Were there the stirrings of a sexual harassment lawsuit in the startled look she gave him as she looked up from her papers?

With an effort, Will resisted the lawyer's instinct to prepare for every situation as potentially adversarial. Claire twisted her feet under the rungs of the bar stool like a kid, bumping her boots on the bottom rung and concentrating on her martini, clearly waiting for Will to offer some words of comfort.

"You're going to find another great job," he said. "In today's market, hardly anyone spends their entire career at one firm. Everyone hits a few bumps in the road."

"Yeah, but not everyone keeps going. And this feels more like a wall."

"Are you thinking about leaving the law?"

"I'm thinking about just about everything tonight."

"Look, you're a good attorney. You're going to have a great career. Just hang in there."

"You know you're not supposed to be telling me stuff like that, that I'm a good attorney. It muddies the record when someone's getting terminated for cause."

"I'm here tonight as your friend. Nothing else."

"I'm glad. 'Cause what I need tonight is a friend."

They sat in silence for a moment, and then she added, "I really am trying to get some perspective on this. I've been thinking a lot about Ben Fisher. Now I know we don't know what really happened with him, but my guess is that he was someone who let his job become this all-consuming thing in his life. I've certainly been that way, but I want to change. That sounds very twelve-step of me, doesn't it?"

"It sounds healthy," Will said.

"I think that, in a way, lawyers at firms like Reynolds almost have to be obsessed. I mean, if you're going to devote twenty-two hundred hours per year to a job—and that's just the billable hours—well, you can't turn your life over like that without convincing yourself that it's worth the effort. You have to buy in. Which means that you look absolutely crazed to anyone who's outside that environment."

"Did you know Ben very well?" Will asked.

"I knew he was working on the Jupiter deal, but I never dealt with him directly. He didn't seem to socialize much. How about you?"

"We made small talk. The last time I saw him we were at the gym. It was the evening before he died. I remember we were running on treadmills next to each other. It got a little competitive."

"What was the last thing he said to you?"

"Nothing much. He'd lost the key to his gym locker and asked if I'd seen it. That was it."

On the television set above the bar, a Giants player launched a home run over the right field wall into McCovey Cove, drawing applause and hooting from the crowd. They both smiled a bit as they surveyed the raucous scene. Then, as Claire took another sip of her drink, he could almost pinpoint the instant when her eyes lost focus and she returned to replaying her meeting with Don.

Will nudged her with his elbow. "C'mon. Stop thinking about it."

"I just can't decide whether I'm glad this happened or not. I've worked really hard to become a lawyer, and I feel like I have to follow through now. Particularly with the student loans I've got. But part of me, and maybe it's just a total rationalization, says that this is for the best. A last chance to do whatever it is that I'm really supposed to be doing."

"If you don't stick with the law, what would you do?"

"You know, I feel like I should be able to answer that question, but I have no idea. I know that I want to stop *becoming* something and start *being* something. You know what I mean?"

"I think so. Yeah."

"It just seems like no one grows up anymore. We're always on our way to becoming something else, and we never quite get there. High school, college, law school, associate, non-equity partner. You can get to be thirty-five or forty years old without ever feeling like you've graduated."

"A legal career is what happens to smart people who don't know what to do with their lives. And once you start down that road, it's hard to walk away."

"Right. The money's too good. But you can always spot the ones who are really into it. Like you."

"You think so? Believe me, I never thought I was going to end up as a lawyer."

"Well, it suits you, anyway."

"I guess so. Probably because I don't have any other talents to distract me. But listen, about those student loans. The first thing you need to do is get a deferral on payments for a few months. They'll give you that if you're out of work."

"Thanks. I really appreciate that, but I'd rather not deal with reality right now. Maybe tomorrow. Tonight, it's martooni time."

Claire set down her glass and flagged down the bartender.

"You sure that's a good idea?" Will asked. "You're okay, right?"

"Absolutely. This is the most okay I've been all day. One more drink and I will be totally okay."

"Maybe it would be best to call it a night."

"No way. If there's one time when a person is entitled to get sloppy drunk, it's the night they get fired." She held up her martini glass and let the last drops, oily with vermouth, slide onto her tongue. "It's just hitting me a little harder than I thought."

The waiter brought another round of drinks. They leaned together to be heard over the noise of the crowd.

"After a while, you're going to reach a point and suddenly it won't bother you anymore," Will said. "It'll be just like you turned a corner."

"I know you're probably right. But not everyone is as well adjusted as you. You may find this hard to believe,

Will, but some people think I'm a little high-strung."
Claire was self-aware enough to know how the other associates perceived her, so this was meant to be a joke, but
she seemed unable to add the smile that might have put
it over.

"Actually, there's something else that we need to talk
about." She removed a couple of folded sheets of paper
from the pocket of her jeans and smoothed them out on
the bar.

"What's this?" Will said as he examined the papers.

"The minutes of a Jupiter board meeting. It wasn't included in the corporate minutes book." She pointed to a
paragraph halfway down the page. "See this? This is what
I was telling you about. Jupiter is submitting reports to the
NSA about something called the Clipper Chip."

"You're not supposed to bring stuff out of the due diligence room. Especially after you've been fired from the
firm. And how did you get this, anyway, if it wasn't in the
due diligence materials?"

"I did a little due diligence of my own, poked around in
a few file cabinets."

"This just gets better and better."

"I've been talking to my old boss at EPIC, and I think I
know what's going on—"

"Wait a minute. You mean that you're discussing confidential trade secrets of a client with a consumer privacy
rights organization? Are you insane?"

"This is something that needs to be public. Just listen
to me for a minute. Have you ever heard of the Clipper
Chip?"

"No," Will said. Giving in to his curiosity, he added,
"What's that?"

"In 1993, President Clinton announced that the NSA

had developed a new superstrong form of encryption, based on an algorithm called Skipjack. The program began development under the first Bush administration. Skipjack was going to be made available to the public and would probably have become the predominant encryption method in the U.S. But there was a catch."

"And I'm guessing that would be the Clipper Chip?"

"Exactly. Every device that used the encryption method was going to contain a tamperproof computer chip, which would allow law enforcement authorities to decrypt the data."

"So the chip generated some sort of key?"

"Right. The key was going to be split into two parts. Two separate government or private entities would act as custodians of the key. The custodians would provide law enforcement with the two parts of the key only if a court order had been obtained or if the requirements of federal electronic surveillance laws had been satisfied."

"So what became of this brilliant plan?"

"Groups like EPIC raised privacy concerns in congressional hearings, and several major tech companies finally joined in, sensing that this was not going to be popular with their customers. The Clipper Chip was perceived as being too Big Brotherish, and the plan was abandoned."

"But you think that it was never really abandoned."

"I think the reason that Jupiter has been so successful is because the NSA gave them the Skipjack encryption algorithm. In return, the NSA must have required Jupiter to include the Clipper Chip in the installation of devices that used their encryption."

"Wouldn't the manufacturers of the telephones and computers be able to tell that the chip was there?"

"Not necessarily. It could have been baked into the hardware supplied by Jupiter for installation of the encryption application."

"So each computer using Jupiter's encryption program generates a secret key, a back door, and Jupiter supplies those keys to the NSA?"

"That must be how it works. The list of chip keys would provide access to all devices using Clipper encryption."

"Then an enormous amount of damage could be done if those keys fell into the wrong hands."

Claire took a large gulp of her martini. "Some would say that it already *is* in the wrong hands."

Claire continued. "From the NSA's point of view, doing it this way is probably much more effective in fighting terrorism. Under the original Clipper Chip program, the public would have known that law enforcement could access their encrypted communications. So terrorists would have been pretty stupid to use those encryption products. Now, no one knows they're being spied on, including the general public."

Will took a sip of his drink, trying to absorb the full import of what he had just heard. If Claire was right, and he didn't doubt that she was, then the Jupiter-NSA connection would be a major national scandal if it became public. It was the kind of story that would make the front page of the *New York Times*, lead to congressional hearings, and damage or ruin major companies like Jupiter and Pearl. For Will, it was also something he could use to stop the Jupiter merger. Of course, such a move would be grossly unethical and would damage his client's interests, but it gave Will the sense for the first time in days that he had some degree of control over his fate.

Will resolved to start by bringing the due diligence discovery to Richard Grogan in his capacity as co-chair of the corporate department. That was the proper chain of command for him to follow as a partner in the firm, and it might also lead to the scuttling of the Jupiter-Pearl merger. If the disclosure to Grogan did not achieve the desired result, Will could always leak it to the press anonymously, which would surely throw a monkey wrench into the transaction.

"What are you going to do with this?" Will asked, returning the papers to Claire. "You know this is mostly just speculation."

"Yeah, but I just know it's true—and I think you do, too." Claire placed the papers in her purse. "I don't know yet what I'm going to do with it. Probably give it to EPIC. I'm in no state of mind to decide. It's been a tough day."

Will recognized that the Russians must never know about the existence of the list of the Clipper Chip keys. Valter had already asked him to think about whether he could obtain a copy of Jupiter's encryption algorithm. If the *mafiya*, or their friend Aashif, ever got their hands on the encryption keys, they would have the ability to divert electronic funds transfers, commit identity theft, and violate national security on a scale that was difficult to imagine. Finally, Will offered, "How about if I get you a taxi ride home?"

"You know, maybe that's a good idea."

Claire was a little wobbly as they crossed to the door, so Will offered his arm and she took it.

After hailing a cab outside the bar, Will climbed in behind Claire. "I'm just going to see you home. It's on my way, anyway."

The taxi stopped at a new, redbrick apartment building in Jackson Square. Will asked the cabbie to wait and walked Claire to her doorstep.

When they reached the front door, Claire leaned against him as she searched her purse for the cardkey to the lobby.

When she found the key, she slipped it into the front pocket of her jeans and turned her face up to his.

"Thanks for bringing me home," she said. Claire leaned up to give him what he expected to be a chaste kiss on the cheek.

Claire's aim changed, however, and she kissed Will full on the mouth, lips apart. He'd had just enough to drink to drop his workplace inhibitions. They were finally interrupted when the lobby door swung open as a pizza delivery boy with an acne-scarred complexion left the building, pizza box warmer folded under his armpit.

"Was that okay?" Claire asked. "Because there were times when we were working together on the Jupiter deal that I thought maybe you wanted to kiss me. Maybe that was just me."

"No. It wasn't just you." Will knew the firm's general counsel would have hated to hear him say this.

"Would you like to come upstairs?"

"I can't. I'm sorry, Claire."

She pulled back from the embrace. "That's okay. Really. I guess now my day is finally complete."

"There are several reasons why I can't come up, and none of them have anything to do with you. I was your supervisor at the firm. I just can't do this, especially on the day that you were fired . . ."

Claire slid her cardkey through the slot, and the lobby door emitted a metallic click. "Just my luck," she said. "A gentleman."

"Call me if there's anything you need, or if you just want to talk."

"So you don't want to come upstairs, but you're willing to go out of your way to help me. Are you the last nice guy or what?"

"Don't give me too much credit. I never said I didn't *want* to come up."

"See, now *that's* helping." Claire closed the lobby door, and Will watched her until she disappeared into the elevator.

When he turned around, the taxi was gone. He checked his watch—two ten A.M. Tomorrow was going to be a long day, and it was bearing down on him fast.

SIXTEEN

As Will approached the front steps of his condo, his cell phone rang and he flipped it open.

"Hello, asshole." It was Yuri.

"What do you want?"

"Out a little late, aren't you? And is that what you wear out on a date?"

"Where are you?"

"Turn around and take a look. I was wondering how long it was going to take you to notice me. You must have a lot on your mind."

Will turned around to see Yuri walking ten yards back. He looked like an extra from *The Sopranos*, wearing black pants, a leather jacket, and a silvery silk shirt open at the neck to reveal a thick, gold chain.

"Nice, clear signal, isn't it?" Yuri snapped his cell phone closed and approached.

"Can't you just leave me alone?"

"No can do, Will. No can do. You heard what Valter said. I'm supposed to keep a close eye on you. If I have to babysit your ass, at least I will get some work done in the process."

"What do you mean?"

"I mean you're coming with me."

"It's two thirty in the morning. I have to work tomorrow."

"You're not bitching out on me," Yuri said. "Now, we have one rule for tonight. You follow it and we'll be fine. No matter what happens, just keep your shit together and keep your mouth shut."

"Isn't that two rules?"

Yuri gave him an appraising look. "Are you being a wiseass? What, you are not scared of me anymore, Will?" Yuri gave Will a quick, hard punch in the shoulder. "I don't want you getting too relaxed. That's when accidents happen."

Will rubbed his bicep.

"C'mon. I'm parked over here," Yuri said, pointing at a pearl-gray Lexus parked on the street. Will noted that every time he saw Yuri or Nikolai, they were driving a different car. As they climbed into the car, Yuri added, "If you're still a wiseass at the end of the night, I just might be impressed."

As the Lexus effortlessly climbed California Street to the top of Nob Hill, Yuri was in a chatty mood. He popped a CD into the player, and the Cult's "Love Removal Machine" blasted from the speakers. Will told himself, hopefully, that whatever happened tonight could not be any worse than what he had already been through.

"I think we had a good meeting with Valter," Yuri said as

he turned left onto Stockton Street. "If he and Boka make money on this deal, then Nikolai and I will be *mafiya*. Then no more of this petty shit."

"What's happening tonight?"

"Valter is letting Nikolai and me do some of their collections. Nikolai's out covering another route."

"Where are we going right now?"

"We'll be making a couple of stops."

The Lexus pulled into a no-parking zone in front of a large pawnshop on the west end of Market Street, the seedy no-man's-land between Union Square and the Castro. The interior of the pawnshop was as aggressively illuminated as an insect lantern, casting a pool of light on the sidewalk.

Yuri opened the car door. "You stay here. I'll be back in a minute."

In front of the store, a man with stringy, blond shoulder-length hair wearing an Oakland Raiders jacket was standing around with the studied nonchalance of a drug dealer. He interrupted his shoe-gazing every few minutes to cast darting, furtive glances up and down the block. Will tried not to stare at the man who approached. He was wiry and muscular, with greased-back black hair and a sleeveless T-shirt that showed off an arm covered from wrist to shoulder with red and orange tattooed flames; he could have been the bass player in a rockabilly band. The pair glanced at Will sitting in the seat of the nearby car and apparently decided that he was not a cop. Then they shook hands, concealing the palmed exchange of money for product.

Yuri emerged from the pawnshop and returned to the car carrying a fat manila envelope. As he got behind the wheel, he tossed the envelope at Will.

"Put that in the glove compartment."

Will opened up the compartment and saw that there was

a pistol inside. He carefully placed the envelope on top of the gun.

"Why would you bring me along tonight? You're basically making me a witness to what you're doing."

"A witness to what? You saw me pick up an envelope. You think the guy who owns that pawnshop is going to say anything? Do you think *you're* going to say anything? You need to relax, Will. It's the only thing you can do when you're getting fucked up the ass."

Will fell into a glum silence as the Lexus made its way through the traffic of Market Street.

"If I'd known you were going to sit there and pout, I would have let you ride with Nikolai tonight."

Will maintained his silence, hoping that Yuri might get bored and let him go.

But nothing seemed to dampen Yuri's spirits. It occurred to Will that he might be coked up. "You know, I've worked a long time for this, becoming a *patsani* in the *mafiya*. For you, it was probably like when you became a partner in your firm."

"I doubt that."

"How much do you make right now? If things go well in the next few months, I bet I'll be making more money than you."

"That's none of your business."

"Oh, I see," Yuri said. "So you can tell me about the merger of a publicly traded company, but you can't tell me how much money you make."

"You cut me with a razor blade to get me to tell you about Jupiter."

"And I'll do it again if that's what it takes to have a fucking conversation with you." Yuri was beginning to sound genuinely angry. "Okay, I'll start. I'll probably clear a half million a year to start if I get accepted into *mafiya*. That's more than you make, right?"

Yuri was stopped at a light and turned to stare at him, still gripping the steering wheel hard with both hands. His pupils appeared dilated, and his eyes were pinballing. Will looked in those eyes and recognized that Yuri was capable of just about anything. Then he remembered that Yuri was waiting for an answer.

"Yes, that's more than I make."

"See? *And* you pay taxes!" Yuri stepped hard on the gas as the light changed, sending a pedestrian leaping for the median. "I'll bet you probably have to work pretty hard for it, too, don't you?"

"Sure, I put in a lot of hours. I guess the difference is that you're likely to end up in prison. Now that would put a dent in your earning potential, wouldn't it?"

"*Mafiya* don't go to jail. No one fucks with them. You know what the FBI heard John Gotti say on a wiretap? He said, 'The Russians are crazy. We'll kill a guy, but the Russians will kill his whole family.'"

"How do you know so much about the Russian mob if you've never been one of them?"

"Back in Moscow, my father used to tell me stories. He worked as a low-level bureaucrat in the city government. Toward the end of communism, it was hard to tell the difference between his bosses and the *mafiya*, they were so closely connected."

"Did your father have any dealings with the *mafiya*?"

"No, he was too far down the chain, but he saw what was happening. Anyone who had any real power got rich. They'd just take what they wanted and sell it on the black market . . . grain, gasoline reserves, even tanks."

"So that was your dream? Becoming a gangster?"

"Sure, why not? I wanted money, respect. I wanted to be better than my father. Don't tell me this does not sound familiar."

Will wasn't going to argue that point with Yuri. He hadn't entered law school to become a legal aid attorney. He wouldn't have accepted a job at Reynolds Fincher if that had been his intention. Observing his father's frantic efforts to meet sales quotas on copiers and fax machines had left him with a powerful desire to make money. It was a way to carve out a secure place in the world for himself and Anne. Only later had he grown to enjoy the work for its own sake, earning the trust of clients and solving their problems.

Yuri drove down Columbus Avenue to North Beach, the land of Italian restaurants, Beat landmarks, and strip clubs. He parked illegally on a side street above Columbus, blocking someone's driveway. Will remained in his seat until Yuri rapped on the passenger window. "You're coming with me this time."

"Why bring me along?" Will asked.

"Do you know who Enzo the Baker is?"

"*The Godfather*, right?"

"For once, you impress me. You just make like Enzo—follow me and try to look tough. You do not say shit."

Will knew the scene well. Enzo arrives at the hospital with flowers to pay his respects to the bullet-riddled Don Corleone. Sollozzo, a rival mobster, sends his men to the hospital to kill the don, believing that he's unguarded. Michael asks Enzo to stand with him outside the hospital, posing as a tough to convince them that the hospital was still protected. After a car full of Sollozzo's men passes by and the threat is averted, Enzo's hands tremble with fear as he tries to light a cigarette. Michael helps him, lighting the

cigarette with perfectly steady hands. Will loved the way
Coppola lingered on that moment as Michael recognizes
that he is capable of doing things that most people can't
do.

Yuri and Will approached a club at the corner of Columbus and Broadway. A bronze placard proclaimed that in
1968, the club had been the first in the United States with
dancers who went bottomless as well as topless, and thus
"all-nude." The current establishment seemed to be carrying on the same proud tradition because the neon sign overhead read simply, XXX ALL NUDE GIRLS. The club's
marquee urged, LIVE THE FANTASY! TOUCH THE MAGIC!

The doorman, a muscular young man with short blond
hair who looked like a cross between a bodybuilder and
a surfer, looked them over with contempt. "There's a ten-
dollar cover charge, gents," he said in a surprisingly high,
reedy voice.

Gents. What an asshole, Will thought.

"We're here to see Ray," Yuri said.

"Okay. Down that hall. First door on the left."

The walls of the club were painted black, which made
the brightly lit stage the focus of attention. On the stage, a
topless woman with small breasts and a platinum dye job
with black roots shimmied around a chrome pole. Madon-
na's "Secret" played on the sound system. Four or five men
watched her dance, one per table, formless shapes in the
darkness just beyond the stage lights.

They proceeded down a dim corridor, each step producing a smacking sound on the sticky floor. Yuri rapped
sharply on the door and entered.

Behind a desk facing the door was a man who had to
be Ray. He had thinning, light brown hair and was wearing a blue V-neck sweater with no shirt underneath, a few

graying chest hairs sprouting over the V. Ray's face was ill-shaven and deeply lined from sun damage.

"And who the fuck are you?" Ray said, putting down the sports section of the *Chronicle* and standing up.

Ray's desk was occupied by a Forty-Niners mug filled with pens, a photo of his girlfriend or wife, and a desktop computer. It looked similar to Will's own desk at Reynolds Fincher. Will could only guess that Ray used the computer to store mission-critical data such as the number of lap dances performed and the astronomical profit margins on cheap champagne.

"Valter sent me. My name is Yuri."

"Oh, yeah. It's that time again, isn't it? So who's that?" Ray tipped his chin in Will's direction.

"My lawyer."

"Funny." When Yuri did not laugh, Ray eyed them warily, trying to decide if he should be concerned. "Would you two mind stepping into the hallway for a minute? I'll get the money."

"I'll stay here," Yuri said, drawing himself up.

"Oh, what the fuck," Ray said, "but would you at least send that guy out in the hallway?"

Yuri was content to allow Ray this small, face-saving concession. He nodded to Will, who exited.

The corridor was dimly illuminated by the lights from the main room. At the end of the hallway, a door opened and closed in a burst of fluorescent light. A tall stripper with big hair and a curvy figure was briefly silhouetted in the doorway, calling to mind the ideal of female beauty immortalized in chrome on mud flaps. Because her eyes were probably adjusting to the dark, Will was pretty sure that she couldn't see him.

The door slammed shut and the stripper approached, swaying a bit on her stiletto heels.

When she was a few feet away, he heard her sharp intake of breath. She had spotted him. Close up, she appeared younger than he had guessed, perhaps midtwenties. She was a big girl with color-treated red hair, heavy thighs, and large, silicone-enhanced breasts. She was wearing rhinestone pasties and a red thong. Her youth and outsized endowments probably made her a star in that mildewed corner of the entertainment industry.

"'Scuse me," she said in a metallic Midwestern accent, turning sideways to get past Will.

"Sure," Will said, backing up against the wall.

The stripper stepped past him with a flurry of clicking heels, like a skittish horse. Then the rhythm of her steps grew more irregular; the sideways motion was causing her to lose her balance. She tried to plant one heel, then the other, to right herself, but it was too late.

As the girl swayed woozily in front of him, her artificial breasts, with their pastied nipples thrust forward, looked like two eyes frozen in an expression of surprise. With one final, failed stab of her heel, she toppled toward him.

Instinctively (and Will would later question precisely which instincts were at work here), his hands flew up and he caught the stripper. For one long, strange moment, Will stood clutching the woman by the breasts, marveling at the superhuman firmness of the silicone creations. These were indeed world-conquering breasts, indisputable proof of American superiority in the field of plastics technologies.

Will's reverie was interrupted when the stripper regained her balance and brought her knee up into his groin with practiced precision. Will released her and began to slowly fold in on himself like a punctured balloon in the Macy's parade. Will had not experienced this kind of pain since he had collided at crotch level with a tennis net post while playing dodgeball as a second-grader. The pain was dull and nauseating, rolling through him like the pealing of a bell. He slid to the floor with his back to the wall, so that he might lie down for a while and remain very, very still.

The stripper looked down at him indifferently as he rolled on the floor, clutching his genitals, and then yelled, "Bobby!"

The blond bouncer came jogging heavily down the corridor. Will watched him advance, too immersed in his own suffering to apprehend the threat.

When Bobby reached them, already breathing heavily through his mouth, the stripper pointed accusingly at Will and said simply, "He grabbed my tits."

"Okay, buddy," Bobby said, grunting as he pulled Will up roughly. "Time to go." Bobby slammed Will against the brick wall for emphasis. Will felt a sharp pain in his shoulder blade.

Taking a lesson from the stripper, Will brought his knee up into Bobby's groin. A second later, Bobby released his grip on Will's shirt, his attention elsewhere.

"Now you know how I feel," Will said to Bobby as he crumpled to the floor.

The door to Ray's office opened and Yuri stepped into the hallway with another manila envelope in hand. To his amazement, Will was actually relieved to see him.

"Bobby," Ray said. "What the fuck?"

"This guy . . . grabbed Amber's tits." His voice didn't seem to have any breath behind it. "I was . . . just showing him out . . . and the fucker kneed me in the balls."

"Bobby, didn't they say they were here to see me?"

"Well, yeah." Bobby slowly picked himself up on one knee.

"He's with Yuri. And we're doing business with Yuri,

aren't we? So you shouldn't have been putting your hands
on him."

"Sorry, Ray." Bobby managed to stand up and glowered
at Will.

"Don't apologize to me," Ray said, gesturing at Will.
"Say it to him."

Bobby stared balefully at Will and muttered a wholly
insincere, "Sorry."

Yuri stuffed the envelope inside his leather jacket. "See
you next month, Ray."

Ray smiled dimly. "Regular as death and taxes."

"C'mon, Will," Yuri said. "No more titties for you."

When they were back outside on Columbus Avenue,
Yuri turned to Will, struggling to suppress a smile. "So you
like the titties, Will?"

"She fell—"

"No, no, you don't have to be embarrassed."

"I'm not—"

"Listen, Will. I've made my collections for tonight, so
why don't we get a drink? Here," Yuri said, pointing at a
strip club next door, the Klassy Kat. "How's this? Plenty
of titties here."

They entered the strip club, which looked remarkably
like the last one. Another dark room. Another brightly lit
stage. Another boob job. Another dye job. Another pole.
This time, however, the club's sound system was playing
Soft Cell's "Tainted Love." Apparently, the DJ had a sense
of humor.

They claimed a table in the back of the room and ordered drinks, Yuri two Stolis on the rocks and Will an Am-
stel Light.

"So, Will, did you have fun tonight?"

"Not really, no."

An almost-genuine look of hurt crossed Yuri's face. "I thought you said you wanted to see how the criminal element conducts its business." Yuri made air quotes around the phrase *criminal element*.

"You know I never said that."

"Look, I'm sorry you got roughed up back there, but you didn't have to grab that girl's titties . . ."

Will waited for Yuri to tire of his comedy routine.

Yuri pounded down his drinks and began searching for the waitress. Will watched the girl under the lights executing a complicated maneuver. She was supporting herself off the ground with her legs wrapped around the pole, arching her back as she leaned toward the audience. They could hear the amplified squeak of her thighs as they slid slightly down the pole, straining to support her weight.

The stripper was wearing a piece of heavy plastic jewelry around her ankle, which fell halfway down her calf when she was upside down.

"What's that thing she's wearing on her ankle?" Will asked.

"You don't recognize it? That's so the police can track her. She's under house arrest."

"That is so depressing."

"Hey, at least they turn it off during her work hours. She gets to earn a living."

Will studied the stripper's glum expression with new understanding.

"Is Nikolai still doing his collections?" Will was afraid that Nikolai was going to join them later, but he didn't want to ask the question directly.

"How the fuck should I know?" Yuri said, his brow furrowing as he studied the dancer's unsuccessful efforts to gracefully extricate herself from her upside-down position.

He added, conspiratorially, "You know, I don't know why everyone thinks Nikolai is such hot shit."

"What do you mean?"

Two vodkas were set before them by a waitress. Yuri tossed his down immediately.

"Valter treats us as if Nikolai is the man and I am the sidekick. It is not fair. Not just. Sure, Nikolai had his grocery racket in Moscow, but consider this." Yuri was half drunk and in a mood for sharing confidences, which made Will worry that he was going to hear something that he shouldn't.

Yuri thrust an index finger in the air. "First, Nikolai is Chechen. They have their own organized crime, which has nothing to do with *mafiya*. He is not a Russian. I am Russian!"

He raised a second finger. "Two. As you must have noticed, that unassimilated motherfucker doesn't even speak good English. How can you expect to do business in this country if you can't put two sentences together? Without me to act as his fucking UN interpreter, he wouldn't be able to get any of his ideas across."

While using his other hand to signal the waitress for more drinks, he jabbed three fingers at Will. "Third, and I'm sure you have noticed this, as well—Nikolai is no great thinker. I am not saying that the man is simpleminded, but he has not had the benefit of my education. Sure, he is big, and that is good if you are busting balls and collecting the *dan*. But organized crime is a complex business these days. Do you think that Nikolai could have come up with the idea of insider trading? That was my idea. I will not always play second fiddle to Nikolai. Someday, they will see my value. Someday, I will become a *vor*."

"A *vor*?" Will made a mental note that he might be able

to use Yuri's grievances with Nikolai to divide the Russians if the opportunity presented itself.

"*Vor v zakonye*, it means a thief within the code, a godfather."

"Sounds ambitious."

"What is life without ambition, eh? Many steps up the ladder. Right now, I am at the bottom. If I do a good job on collections, then I'll become a *patsani*, a soldier. If I'm a good earner, I become an underboss, a *pakhan*, like Valter. Then, maybe, years from now, if I play my cards right, a *vor*."

Will considered the fact that in all lines of work, including his own, being "a good earner" was usually paramount.

"I've already decided on my *klichki*."

"*Klichki?*"

"Nickname! I've already told you that once. When you become a *vor* you go through a naming ceremony. You get to choose a new name for your new life."

Will sipped his vodka.

"Aren't you going to ask me what my *klichki* will be?"

"Okay. What will it be?"

"The Dagger. See, I've already got the tattoo." Yuri opened his shirt to reveal a tattoo of a long knife on his chest, the blood dripping from its tip rendered in bright red ink.

Because some response seemed to be expected, Will nodded appreciatively.

"Don't tell me you don't have ambitions," Yuri said, his eyes still on the stripper.

"Yeah, sure. What's wrong with that?"

"Nothing," Yuri said, smiling triumphantly as if Will had just proven his point. "There is nothing wrong with that."

His gaze wandered drunkenly for a moment, and then he snapped back into focus, adding, "I'll bet there's somebody at your firm you fucking hate, somebody who's standing in the way of all that ambition of yours."

"Why are we talking about this?"

"I'm just trying to have a conversation with you. Me, I've got somebody standing in my way."

Please don't tell me his name, Will thought.

"His name is Gregor. Ever since Nikolai and I came around, he makes jokes at my expense. He never fucks with Nikolai, only me. I'd like to take that prick out, and maybe someday I will. But there are rules about these things. He would have to fuck up. And I would have to be in a position to do something."

"In a law firm, we also have rules about those things," Will said, thinking of the vote to fire Claire.

Now Yuri was staring gloomily at the stage, pondering his own troubles. Will watched Yuri eyeing the stripper and felt a hard, bright hatred for the Russian. Yuri was as thoughtless and destructive as a virus. Will resolved that he would not allow this stupid goon to destroy the life that he had worked so hard to build. His life was not a consumer item.

"So what happens if you fuck up?" Will said, trying to push Yuri's buttons.

"I can't fuck up," Yuri said. "That's why you should never doubt for a second that I will do whatever is necessary."

Yuri downed another vodka and set the glass down on the round Formica table with a click.

"How do you get to work in the mornings? Yuri asked. "You ride the BART train?"

"Sometimes—it depends—why?"

Yuri seemed about to say something, then decided against it. "No reason. Forget it."

"Wait a second. Why did you ask me that? You had a reason."

Yuri downed another vodka. "Look, I'm going to tell you something, something that could save your life, but you can't let Nikolai know that I told you."

"Sure, I won't say anything to Nikolai."

"We know that there's going to be a terrorist attack on the BART trains. Many people are going to die."

"When is this going to happen?"

"Not right away. But soon."

"How? A bomb?"

"That's all I'm going to tell you. Just drive to work, okay? Take the bus. But stay off the BART trains."

"Are you and Nikolai behind the attack?"

"No, no, of course not! Not directly, anyway. We are businessmen, not fanatics. But we are in a position to know."

"Why are you telling me this?"

"Because we need to keep you alive so you can help us. Nikolai thought it was too risky to tell you this, but I disagree. I think you are smart enough to know not to fuck with us."

That's where you're wrong, Will thought. Yuri's drunken slipup was just the opportunity that Will had been waiting for, a glimpse of the Russians' larger plan. If Yuri thought that he would remain silent while they enabled some sort of terrorist attack, then Yuri had misjudged him. Will would do everything that he could to stop the BART train attack, even if it meant sacrificing his career or his life.

On the stage, it was becoming apparent that the stripper needed to work on her conditioning. Her act, which had begun with crisp, dancelike movements, now looked more like the cooldown of an aerobics routine, her feet shuffling wearily forward and back, her arms vaguely swaying from side to side, the electronic surveillance bracelet bouncing on her ankle.

As they lurched up from the table and headed for the door of the club, Will thought he knew just how she felt.

SEVENTEEN

Tuesday morning. It had been more than a week since Ben Fisher had plummeted to his death on the sidewalk below. Will's stomach turned over as the elevator made a rapid ascent to the thirty-eighth-floor offices of Reynolds Fincher. As soon as he entered the reception area, he detected a subtle disturbance in the daily routine of the law office. Was it the fact that no one said hello to him in the hallway? The way the receptionist skipped her customary smile? Perhaps it was just the queasy hypersensitivity of the hangover.

When he reached his office, Maggie's worried expression confirmed his suspicions.

"What?" Will blurted. "What is it?"

"There are two people here to see you."

"Okay. Who are they?"

"They're from the SEC and the Department of Justice."

Will felt the sudden urge to throw up all over Maggie's desk.

"How long have they been here?"

"About fifteen minutes."

"You should have put them in the reception area, or a conference room."

"They asked to wait in your office. They seemed so official, I just didn't know how to say no to them."

"Okay. I'll just go see what they want."

"They've been interviewing everyone who's been working on the Jupiter deal. It's not just you, so there's no need to worry."

"I'm not worried, Maggie."

Will took some small solace from the fact that Detective Kovach from the SFPD wasn't joining the welcoming party in his office. From that, Will assumed that the SEC and DOJ were not yet aware that he was also the prime suspect in Ben Fisher's death.

He decided he needed coffee to stimulate some activity in his alcohol-sodden brain. He wished that he had stopped at the coffee shop downstairs and bought a creamy latte that might have settled his stomach. Instead, he was forced to rely on the firm's house brew, known to the associates as Black Acid.

When he entered his office, coffee mug in hand, a man and a woman in suits were standing at the window with their backs to him, admiring the view of the Bay Bridge.

"Hello there," Will said.

"Oh, hi. I hope you don't mind us making ourselves at home," the man said, extending his hand. "I'm Dennis Tyler, Securities and Exchange Commission."

Dennis looked more like a young lawyer than a federal agent in his dark gray suit, white button-down shirt, and red power tie. Dennis was medium height and weight, with dark brown hair and regular, plain features, accented only by a neatly groomed mustache and an outsized square jaw. He looked like something that the federal government was capable of producing in mass quantities, like metal desk chairs.

The woman stepped forward and shook his hand. "Hi, Will. Mary Boudreaux, Department of Justice." When Mary said *Hi*, the tiny word elongated to embrace a multitude of vowels. Will guessed that she was from Mississippi. She handed him her business card. Will registered only an elaborate government seal and the word *Enforcement*.

Mary was slender, with shoulder-length brown hair and the slightly doughy complexion of a girl of the Deep South who had been cultivated in air-conditioned rooms. He felt a small shock, like static electricity, when he looked into Mary's eyes and realized that they were processing information about him at a very rapid rate.

"We were just admiring the view," Mary said. "It's a whole lot nicer than what we've got over on Geary Street. How's it compare with your view over at the SEC, Denny?"

"It's better," Dennis said, grudgingly.

"Please, have a seat," Will said.

"Will, we're here to talk to you about the Jupiter–Pearl Systems transaction," Mary said. "We understand that you're heading up the team of attorneys here."

"That's right. Is something wrong?"

Dennis smiled grimly. "I think this is where we say, 'We'll ask the questions.'"

"He thinks he's funny," Mary said. "We'd like to know what you do to protect the confidentiality of a transaction like this one."

"The usual drill for deals involving public companies. We used a code name. We—"

"What was the code name for the deal?" Mary asked.

"Zeus."

"The Greek name for Jupiter. Cute, but not too difficult to figure out. What else?"

"I gave a short talk to the attorneys working on the deal about the importance of confidentiality, the dangers of insider trading. Standard procedure."

"Has everybody been following the rules? Anyone seem a little too interested in how the market is going to react to the announcement?"

"No. Not to my knowledge."

"Not to your knowledge. Nice. I can tell someone's been to law school." Will wondered if Mary smiled with such unrelenting cheerfulness at everyone.

Despite the mild needling, Will was growing more comfortable with the interview. If they had anything incriminating, they wouldn't be asking such mundane questions.

Then Dennis leaned forward in his chair and asked: "You wouldn't happen to know any Russians, would you, Will?"

It took a second for the panic to begin rising. "Russians?"

"Yeah, you know. Citizens of the former Union of Soviet Socialist Republics. They drink vodka. Play hockey."

Did they know about his night with Katya? Worse yet, did they know about his connection to Nikolai and Yuri?

"Why Russians? There are no Russians involved in this deal." The stupid question would buy him at least a few more seconds.

"Remember what I said about the questions?" Dennis looked over at Mary to see if he could get a smile out of her, but her attention was fixed on Will.

"Yeah, right." Will knew that a lie to federal agents could be as bad as the offense itself, but he could see no other way out. "No, I don't think I know any Russians," he said.

Dennis narrowed his eyes. "Are you sure? That was kind of fast. Why don't you take a second to think about it."

They clearly knew something, but how much? He suddenly understood why so many criminal defendants confess—he felt an overpowering impulse to tell the two agents everything. He managed to resist the urge because he realized that they hadn't really said anything that suggested they knew what he'd done.

"Yeah, I'm sure. Of course, I don't know the family history of everyone who's working on this deal."

"Will, you understand that we can't tell you much about what we're doing here, because that could compromise our investigation." Dennis looked over at Mary to confirm that she concurred with this new tack. "But we're going to tell you a little so that you understand what the stakes are."

"I'm certainly curious."

"Uh-huh," Dennis said. "We've detected some unusual trading activity in Jupiter. It's occurring here in the Bay Area, which suggests that someone directly involved in the deal is talking."

"That's very troubling."

"Uh-huh."

"Do you think that the leak is coming from the firm?"

"We'd rather not tell you what we think about that right now." Now Dennis and Mary were both making hard eye contact with Will, neither smiling.

"The thing is," Mary added, "a lot of the people purchasing the stock have Russian names."

Will tried to control his expression. "What do you think that means?"

"We're not sure," Mary said. "But we ran the names and found that several of them have connections to the Russian mob. Nobody who has an actual criminal record in this country, but a few who are known associates of *mafiya* members. Weren't you curious about why a DOJ agent was here along with the SEC?"

"You told me not to ask questions."

"I'm with the Department's Corporate Fraud Task Force," Mary said. "We're running a parallel investigation with the SEC because this appears to be more than just insider trading. Whoever is responsible for the leak may be dealing, directly or indirectly, with members of the Russian *mafiya*. That person is in a great deal of danger."

"Why are you telling me this?"

Mary inched her chair closer to Will's desk. "You're leading the team of attorneys. We thought that you would be in a good position to spot someone who might be involved if you knew what to look for."

Mary removed a series of six wallet-size photos from a leather portfolio and laid them on the desk one by one like playing cards. "Do any of these faces look familiar?"

Will immediately recognized a candid shot of Valter that was probably taken with a telephoto lens, followed by mug shots of four other similarly thuggish-looking Slavic types. The last was a photo of a police sketch artist drawing. There was no mistaking that it was Aashif, Valter's guest that night at Dacha.

"Who are they?" Will asked.

"Five of them are *pakhan*, midlevel members of the city's Russian *mafiya*. Mary pointed at the photo of Aashif. "Homeland Security tells us that this guy is a terrorist who they think has been meeting with local *mafiya*."

"A terrorist? What's this got to do with the merger I'm working on?"

"We don't know. Maybe nothing. But if you recognize any of these faces, or if you see any of them later in any context, we need to know about it immediately."

Will made a show of examining Aashif's photo. "What sort of terrorist is he?"

"His name is Aashif Agha. He's the leader of a radical Muslim cell based in North London. Could be al Qaeda, we don't even know that much. DHS was getting ready to take him down for buying the makings for sarin nerve gas when he went to ground. Now they think he's here in the Bay Area."

"I don't think I've ever seen any of these men," Will said. "But I will certainly let you know if I do."

"Take your time—now is your best chance to speak up."

"I'm sorry. I wish I could be of more help."

"I'm also supposed to tell you that amnesty might be available on a securities charge if you helped us make a case against the Russians," Mary said.

"Why are you supposed to tell me that?"

Protecting his regulatory turf, Dennis interjected, "You understand that was not a formal offer of amnesty, but it would be seriously considered for anyone who came forward with useful information."

Mary placed the fingertips of both hands on the edge of Will's desk, a gesture that was probably intended to be reassuringly intimate. "Would you like to take a few minutes and think about what we've just said?"

As Will returned Mary's attentive gaze, he realized that she and Dennis really did believe he was the one who had leaked the information. Mary was giving him a few minutes to consider the merits of asking for a deal and confessing.

Some clouds parted over the bay, and sun streamed through the windows, blanching the colors of the room. As his blood pressure rose, he could almost feel his heartbeat throbbing irregularly behind his bloodshot eyes. As the bright sunlight filled his office, he felt claustrophobic, a whiteness engulfing his vision, the sense of falling away from his surroundings.

Will was tempted to tell them that he wouldn't say anything more without a lawyer present, but he knew that would be tantamount to designating himself as the focus of two federal investigations.

"There's no need for that," he finally responded, hoping that he hadn't hesitated too long. "I can't think of anyone working on the deal who has any Russian connection. But if I run across anything, I'll call you."

"Will, you seem like a nice guy," Mary said. "I could definitely see someone like you getting in over his head without really meaning to violate any laws. We're going to be straight with you."

"Yes, I'd appreciate that."

"We think you've been lying to us today. We believe you're involved with the insider trading in some way."

"You've got it wrong," Will said, aiming for an indignant tone. "Why would you think that?"

"You can't expect us to tell you everything that we know today," Mary said. "That's not how this process works. But you're going to know soon enough if you don't start cooperating."

"Do you know what a Wells notice is?" Dennis asked.

"No."

"It's a letter that you'll receive from the SEC stating that you're the subject of a securities fraud investigation. You'll have the opportunity to provide a statement refuting the charges in the letter. When you get a Wells notice, it means that the commission has authorized us to file a case against you. It's the first step in a process that, for you, would probably end in a criminal trial."

"And Dennis is just talking about the securities fraud charges," Mary added. "If this is what we think it is, you can add racketeering and criminal conspiracy. Now is the time to get out in front of this. Because once we start going after a defendant like you, a lawyer at a big firm, the press will get interested and then nobody in the department is going to back off until you're in prison. It becomes a point of pride."

"Look, you've got the wrong guy, and I'll tell you why."

"We're listening," Mary said.

"I've only been on the Jupiter deal for a week. I'll bet that the insider trading started long before I knew that I was going to be assigned to the transaction. And this wasn't a project that I sought out in any way. The assignment came from firm management, so why aren't you talking to them?"

"We're talking to everyone," Dennis responded.

"I also heard that Ben had burns on his body. Is that true?"

Mary looked uncomfortable. "We aren't going to comment on that."

"I'll take that as a yes, so someone apparently tortured Ben. Since Ben was the lead attorney on the Jupiter transaction up until a week ago, isn't it fairly obvious that he was the source of the leak?"

"If Ben was involved, and we're not saying he was, we don't think it ended there," Mary said.

"I don't know what else to say, then," Will said. "I guess I better hire a lawyer, huh?"

"That would probably be a good idea," Mary responded, standing up and smoothing her skirt. Dennis stood up like someone who was already tired of being on his feet at nine A.M.

Mary walked over to the window again and gazed out at the sparkling bay and the bridge, still crawling with morning traffic. "I drive over that bridge every morning coming over from the East Bay, but I don't often see it like this."

As the two agents headed out the door, Mary added, "I hope you think about our offer, Will. It's not too late, but it will be soon."

The two agents left Will's office. He sat at his desk for a few minutes staring at his papers, trying to calm himself. Of course they hoped that he would simply confess—it would save the government the trouble of preparing a case. Maybe they didn't have any evidence connecting him to the Russians. But if the agents felt confident enough to pressure him so overtly, then they probably had at least enough to charge him with securities fraud. That meant that his life was about to change soon, and for the worse.

Then Will made the connections. Yuri had told him that there would be a terrorist attack on the BART system. Yuri and Nikolai had just attended a meeting at which the terrorist Aashif Agha was present. Agha was known to be acquiring the makings of sarin nerve gas. The more he thought about it, the more certain he was that Agha was planning a terrorist attack on the BART system that would involve releasing sarin nerve gas on the trains. The *mafiya* was somehow facilitating the attack. They must be planning something like the Tokyo subway system attack in 1995.

He was startled by a knock at his office door. Without waiting for a response, Don Rubinowski entered, looking anxious.

"You seem to have held up okay under the hot lights," Don laughed, though he didn't sound so certain. "Do you think we're going to have a problem here? The agents won't talk to anyone except the people they're interviewing."

"There's been some irregular trading activity in Jupiter, but I don't think they've established any connection to the firm. You know how it goes. It could have come from someone at Jupiter, someone at Pearl. Who knows?"

"Right. Par for the course."

"Yeah."

Don paused. "But if this doesn't just go away, the agents will keep coming back to you because you're heading up the transaction for us. I'm not trying to put words in your mouth, but you should consider pointing them toward Ben. It's looking increasingly likely that he was involved in some fashion."

"I've already said that to the agents."

"Good. If they keep digging, you might also want to suggest that there was another person who was working on the deal who now has an ax to grind with the firm. A person who has been behaving a little erratically lately. A person who was recently fired . . ."

"We have no reason to think Claire had anything to do with this." Will was appalled at the suggestion that the firm might make Claire a scapegoat. It was bad enough that they had fired her.

"No one's asking you to make accusations. The SEC should just know that Claire was working on the deal and that she was fired for performance reasons. That's the sort of thing they'll want to know."

Will was trying hard to restrain himself from saying something to Don that he would surely regret.

"Tough way to start the day, huh?" Don offered. "Why

don't you knock off early this afternoon? You look like you could use some rest." The fact that Don was actually encouraging him to do something that did not involve billing hours gave Will his strongest sense yet that something was wrong.

Will stopped by Richard Grogan's office to inform him of Claire's discovery of the connection between Jupiter and the NSA, hoping that the disclosure would lead to a halt in the merger negotiations. As the co-chair of the corporate department, Richard would be responsible for ensuring that the firm avoided embarrassing press coverage that might follow if whatever Jupiter was up to became public. Will chose not to approach Sam Bowen with the disclosure because he liked Sam and didn't want to make him directly responsible for his CYA disclosure. If the disclosure to Richard did not stop the deal, then Will was prepared to leak the information anonymously to the press, although he preferred not to take that approach because it would be a clear breach of client confidentiality and professional ethics.

Will conveyed the facts to Richard, focusing on the mysterious board minutes. He left out Claire's speculation that Jupiter was partnered with the NSA in a covert spying program, but he did describe what was publicly known about the Clipper Chip program.

When he was done, Richard sighed unhappily, well aware that this was an exercise in risk shifting.

"What do you propose that I do with this bit of information?" Richard asked.

"You might make a discreet inquiry to a member of Jupiter's senior management," Will offered.

"And what would I ask them?"

"Well, you could ask them what sort of dealings Jupiter has with the NSA."

"If Jupiter is doing something that may attract nasty headlines, we need to position the firm so that we won't be viewed as complicit. Clients, even very lucrative clients, come and go, but the firm's reputation can't be tarnished. This could be a sensitive matter, so I'm glad you brought it to me," Richard said, sounding insincere. "Sam and I will discuss this and let you know how to proceed. Any inquiry should probably come from you—that way it will seem more routine." This was Richard's way of putting some of the risk back on Will. If things took an ugly turn, Richard could always spin his own version of what Will had told him in their conversation.

After leaving Richard's office, Will disregarded Don's suggestion and continued to work through the afternoon on the Jupiter transaction. Will reviewed summaries of due diligence findings, looking for additional clues to Jupiter's connection with the NSA or the existence of the Clipper Chip program.

That evening Will returned home, his satchel full of due diligence documents for review that night. In his mailbox, he found a manila envelope with no return address. Inside the envelope was a cell phone, with no note or explanation.

EIGHTEEN

Will awakened from a deadened, sweaty sleep to the ringing of a cell phone. He sat up in bed and took a few groggy seconds to orient himself, his brain commencing its morning reboot. Yes, it was seven A.M. and he should be getting in the shower. Yes, he felt a little better. The pounding headache from yesterday's hangover was gone. And he was fully awake when he remembered that, yes, agents from the SEC and the Department of Justice had interviewed him yesterday, and it had not gone well.

Will lurched across the bed and grabbed the ringing cell phone off the nightstand.

"Turn on the television." It was Nikolai.

"Why are you calling me here?"

"Turn on the fucking TV. Channel fifty-three. Financial News Network."

"You shouldn't be calling me at home. I'm under investigation."

"This is not your phone, remember?"

"So you sent me the cell phone?"

"Of course. It's clean. No one is listening. Now wake the fuck up and turn on TV."

On channel 53, a woman reporter was standing against the teeming backdrop of the New York Stock Exchange trading floor. "One of the big stories this morning is the rapidly spreading rumor that computing giant Pearl Systems is planning the acquisition of the leading maker of encryption software, Palo Alto's Jupiter Software," she said with carefully modulated urgency. "There has been no confirmation from Pearl or Jupiter regarding this rumor, but the market seems to be buying it. And they don't like what they're hearing. Pearl stock has dropped six percent or one dollar sixty-eight cents this morning in heavy trading."

Cut to the anchor, a courtly gray-haired man in a dark suit, who asked, "Christine, why do you think the market doesn't like this deal? This would be a merger of two industry leaders. What's not to like?"

"Well, Mort, an analyst report issued last week by Kincaid & Company criticized Pearl's plans to offer sophisticated encryption products to consumers with their home computers."

"With the growing concerns about identity theft, doesn't the average person want encryption?"

"Perhaps. But the Kincaid analyst questioned whether Jupiter's suite of encryption products for businesses can be offered to consumers in a way that is easy to implement and cost-effective. Consumers may say they're interested in protecting their privacy, but Kincaid believes that they aren't interested enough to pay substantially more for their PC."

"Even many large businesses continue to complain that installing encryption is too costly and difficult."

"That's right. Kincaid believes that Jupiter's strategy is misguided and will allow some of Jupiter's competitors to cut into its market share by offering less expensive computers without encryption features."

"Christine, I can understand why Pearl's stock price has taken a hit. But what about Jupiter, which is down a whopping forty-seven percent? How can a merger with a giant like Pearl not be a good thing for Jupiter shareholders?"

"Investors seem to believe that Jupiter is moving away from its strength and embarking on a speculative strategy that may not work. They seem to agree with the pessimistic outlook offered in the Kincaid report."

"This will be a story to watch this week, Christine."

Christine and Mort moved on to other news from the morning's trading. Will slowly brought the phone receiver closer to his ear.

"You said this deal was sure thing," Nikolai said, somehow sensing that Will was listening again.

"Well, it would have been a sure thing if someone on your end hadn't leaked news of the merger. Besides, it was your decision to invest."

"That is not what Boka thinks."

"What?"

"They were more interested in the opportunity than we thought. They decided to put real money into Jupiter."

"How real?"

"Nine hundred thousand dollars."

"How much have they lost?"

"More than a half million."

"FUCK!"

"Yes, fuck. You appreciate the situation. You are fucked, my friend."

"Look, I did what you asked. I can't control the stock market. There's nothing else I can do for you."

"Calm the fuck down. Stay where you are. Yuri and I will come over."

"Okay, but I have to go to work. When will you be here?"

"Half hour, maybe less. Do not go anywhere."

The phone went dead. Now Will was not only awake, he was in a panic. If, as he had said himself, he was no longer of any use to them, and they had lost more than a half million dollars, then they would surely kill him. Like a housecat laying a bird at its owner's doorstep, Nikolai and Yuri would murder him in a misguided attempt to win their bosses' approval.

Will pulled on a Cal sweatshirt and a pair of jeans and grabbed his wallet and keys from the dresser. He turned on the TV again, still tuned to the Financial News Network, and left it blaring as he stepped into the hallway. Perhaps that might buy him a few extra seconds when Yuri and Nikolai were outside his door.

His breath came in short, ineffectual gasps. He considered whether to take the elevator or the stairs and decided on the stairs, which emerged in the lobby close to the front doors. Will ran down the four flights, taking them two and three at a time. When he reached the door that led to the ground floor, he opened it a crack and surveyed the lobby. It was empty.

He strode through the lobby, shoved open the front door, and took a quick left, forcing himself to walk until he was away from the building.

After a block, and just before he was about to start sprinting, he heard a voice behind him. "This is not respect that you are showing us, Will." It was Yuri. "I've got a gun, so don't even think about running."

Will stopped and turned to see Nikolai and Yuri standing on the sidewalk about five yards behind him. Yuri had a bad case of bed head, his black hair sticking up in tufts. Balding Nikolai was immune to such problems, but his eyes were bloodshot and his clothes rumpled. Yuri's hand was buried in the pocket of his leather jacket, presumably holding a gun. Will guessed that they had also been awakened by an angry call from someone who had been watching the financial news.

"If I go with you, how do I know that you won't just kill me as soon as we're off the street?"

Nikolai spread his hands in a placating gesture. "Nobody's getting killed. We want you to do something for us. If we need you, we can't kill you, right? If it makes you feel better, we can do this in a public place. How about Starbucks?"

"Good idea," Yuri said, scratching his head and trying to tame a devil's horn of unruly hair. "I could use some coffee."

Will's mind raced through a series of impractical escape stratagems. They might have worked, too—if he possessed the physical prowess of Jet Li.

Nikolai added, in an almost kindly tone, "Don't make us hurt you, Will. This time, we would really have to fuck you up."

"There's a Starbucks around the corner. We could talk there," Will said.

"Of course there is Starbucks," Nikolai said. "This is fucking San Francisco. In Moscow. . . ."

"Please, Nikolai, it's too early for that shit," Yuri said. "The cafés in Moscow serve swill. Starbucks is much better."

"You are such a fucking American," Nikolai said.

Yuri looked at Will with a roll of the eyes that seemed to say, *We both know I'm right*, and abandoned the topic.

At Starbucks, they sat down at a small table by the window, as far away from the morning newspaper readers as possible. Yuri took the coffee orders.

The market-tested, earth-toned interior of Starbucks seemed incompatible with the abject terror Will had felt a few minutes ago, although he knew that he was not in any less danger. Nikolai didn't say anything to Will while Yuri ordered the coffees. They both looked out the window at the people walking purposefully to their jobs in the gray morning light.

Across the street from Starbucks was a savings and loan with an oddly shaped, oblong sign. A year ago, a tech company called Blue Gorilla had occupied the building. He could even still see the outline of the company's logo on the savings and loan's signage: a cartoon of a blue gorilla wearing a business suit. He had often studied the expression of smug whimsy on the gorilla's face, wondering what the company actually did.

When Yuri returned, Nikolai said, "I cannot tell you how badly you have fucked up. *Bozhe moi.*"

"I never told you to invest," Will protested.

"Who the fuck cares? We are responsible to our bosses. You are responsible to us."

"There's nothing I can do."

Yuri, who was growing visibly annoyed at Will's assumption that this was a dialogue, interrupted. "You had better hope that's not true. If you don't give us something that we can use, asshole, you are going to die. Badly. And so will that cute little blonde, Claire."

Will was speechless and sick—it was like hearing that a cancer that you thought was isolated had metastasized and spread throughout your body. Finally, he managed, "I'm warning you—leave her out of this."

"Did you hear that, Nikolai? He's warning us!" Yuri said with a chuckle.

"Have you done anything to her?"

"No, not really. We paid Claire a visit at her apartment, just to get acquainted."

"I'm going to ask you again—have you laid a hand on Claire?"

"Do what we say and she will be safe," Nikolai said.

"What do you want from me?"

"We want a copy of the encryption keys for the Clipper Chip," Nikolai said.

Will couldn't have been more stunned if Nikolai had reached across the table with a right jab. How could he know about the Clipper Chip? "I don't know what you're talking about."

"Do you really want to play it like that?" Yuri asked. "We talked to Claire, remember? We know that you're lying."

"Okay, I know about the Clipper Chip. But I don't know how to get at the encryption keys, and that's the truth."

"You are their attorney," Nikolai said. "Figure it out."

"And you better do it fast," Yuri added.

"But while you're working out how to get us encryption keys, we need something else for our bosses," Nikolai said.

"Something we can use," Yuri said. "Information about a public company."

"Maybe something on rich businessman that we could use for . . ." Nikolai searched in vain for the word, then looked to Yuri impatiently.

"Extortion," Yuri offered.

"Yes, extortion," Nikolai said, rolling the word around on his tongue, savoring its illicit flavor. "But it must be valuable."

Yuri licked foam from his stubbled upper lip. "So, Will, are you going to help us or what?"

"Let him think about his answer," Nikolai said. "This is a very important decision for him."

Will took a sip of his coffee and tried to look thoughtful. Even if he had been willing to talk, he couldn't think of anything to offer them. As far as he knew, Reynolds was not currently involved in any other public-company deals. He rarely spoke to the firm's white-collar criminal defense attorneys, who might be privy to damaging personal information about corporate executives.

What seemed like about five minutes passed in silence, as Nikolai and Yuri glared at him like a pet that was too slow to perform a trick.

"Yes, I'll help you. What choice do I have? But I don't know anything that I can tell you right now." The looks that Nikolai and Yuri were training on him told him that he needed to say something more if he wanted to live through the morning, so he added, "But I can get something."

"Are you sure that nothing comes to mind? We could take you out in the alley and put a bullet through your knee, see if that helps," Yuri offered, once more fingering the bulge in his jacket pocket.

"Will that be necessary, Will?" Nikolai asked.

"You have to believe me. I really don't have anything. I've been spending most of my time on the Jupiter deal. I haven't been paying much attention to what else is going on at the firm."

"What do you think, Yuri? Should we give him one more chance?"

"I think we should burn him, but it's your call. I am just so fucking disappointed in this guy."

"I see Yuri's point, Will. I really do. But I have not lost faith in you. Not yet."

"I'm glad to hear that."

"But you should know that if we have to kill you, we're going to kill Claire first. You understand?"

"I understand."

"And I hope you know that we have been gentle with you so far. I know you don't think so, but we have. We are not going to waste our time on that again."

Sensing that the conversation was drawing to a close, Yuri slurped the last of his latte and licked the foam from his lips.

"We're going to let you go, but you are going to meet us here at this time tomorrow," Nikolai said, gnawing on the last fragment of a biscotti. "You will have the encryption keys. If you don't have the keys, you will tell us your plan for getting them, and you will bring something else that we can use. If you're five minutes late, Claire is dead."

Will checked his watch. Eight fifteen. "So we're meeting here at eight fifteen tomorrow."

"Make it eight," Nikolai said as he and Yuri rose to leave, both more alert than when they had arrived, invigorated by either the infusion of caffeine or the delivery of their first threat of the day.

"What do you plan to do with the encryption keys?"

"You don't need to know that," Nikolai said.

Although he knew it was unwise, Will asked, "Do the

encryption keys have something to do with the attack on BART?"

Nikolai's face paled, then reddened, then reddened some more, before he spewed a stream of Russian invective at Yuri. As his anger cooled, Nikolai returned to English. "How could you be so stupid?"

"I asked him. He rides BART!" Yuri stammered. "We don't want him to get himself killed. We can still use him."

"But you didn't have to tell him that! We could have just grabbed him when the time came and kept him off the trains."

"So the encryption keys are going to help in the attack?" Will asked. "What is your friend Aashif going to do? Use them to shut down the power to the trains? Then the riders will be trapped inside with the gas."

Nikolai and Yuri stopped arguing and just stared at him. Will took that as a *yes*.

Finally, Nikolai said, quietly, "I don't think you know how close you are to dying right now." His face had re-turned to its normal pallor. "It was Yuri's mistake to tell you that about the trains. I will be discussing that with Yuri later. But nothing has changed here. You must shut up, and you must do exactly what we say. If you don't, you are going to watch everyone that you care about in your life die, and then you will join them."

"Everyone," Yuri added, apparently not chastened by Nikolai's abuse.

Rising from his seat, Nikolai said, "You are a good son. Yuri tells me the place where your mother lives is very nice."

As the Russians walked out of the coffee shop, Yuri turned back, grinning like he was about to tell a funny joke he had been saving up. "But you should really visit your mother more often, Will. She worries."

NINETEEN

Lullwater Commons was a two-story stucco building in the Richmond District that branched around a central courtyard, resembling an elementary school from the outside. As Will entered the assisted-living facility, the regulars who occupied the couches in the lobby were being herded by the caregivers into the cafeteria for lunch, the clicking of their walkers silenced by tennis balls placed over the front struts.

The lobby was decorated in chintz and flower prints, with a large vase of paper flowers on a table in the center of the room. An ornate, Victorian ceiling fan turned slowly overhead. The lobby was presided over by Barb, a matronly attendant with a gauzy mass of hair that settled around her head like the inhospitable atmosphere of a small, lifeless planet. Barb, who appeared to be only a few years removed from taking up residence at Lullwater herself, surveyed the lobby like a field general. Will had to give credit to the designers of the facility, who had succeeded in creating an environment that was both homey and authoritarian.

Will hurried into the dining room and scanned the tables for his mother. He found Anne sitting alone at a table in the corner of the dining room, a small woman arranging her silverware before her on a paper placemat. Will was relieved to see that she had not been harmed and appeared the same as ever. Her face was still striking, with sharp cheekbones and a long, determined jaw. She might even have been imposing, except that her eyes had lost the intense watchfulness perfected through years in classrooms as a high school history teacher. Now her gaze was soft and unfocused, like she'd lost her glasses.

Anne's light brown hair was combed straight back, but it wasn't enough to cover the large spot on the back of her head where her hair was thinning. Her hair had been a darker brown when he was a child, but the hairstylist at Lullwater used a lighter-colored rinse. She was wearing a flowered sweater and the gray pants with the elastic waistband that he had bought her for Christmas. Once she had dressed him; now he dressed her.

"Oh, sweetie, it's good to see you." She never called him by name anymore, which made it difficult for him to tell if she really remembered who he was.

"Hi, Mom. How're you doin'?" He leaned down to plant a kiss on her pallid forehead. In the bright sunlight, her skin appeared almost translucent, revealing tiny purple veins in her temples and hands.

"Oh, I'm fine, I guess. Sort of a mess."

"Well, I think you look nice. Looks like you had your nails done."

"They only have one color," she said, holding out her

hand and examining the reddish-brown nail polish. "I'm not sure I like it."

"I think it looks good on you."

"I'm cold. Does it seem cold in here to you?"

"Well, maybe a little." He was actually quite warm in the sunlit corner. "Would you like another sweater?"

"No, I guess not. How are you, sweetheart?"

"I'm fine, but I need to know if you've had any visitors lately."

"Visitors? No, I don't think so." Will wasn't confident that she would remember even if Yuri had paid her a visit.

"A man with a Russian accent?"

"Oh, I get so many visitors it's hard to keep track of them all."

Will realized that he wasn't going to learn anything by asking Anne questions, so he decided to just chat. "Mom," he said, "I've got some good news. I made partner in my law firm."

"Oh, that's wonderful, sweetie. Did you know that my father was a lawyer?"

"No, I didn't know that."

"Oh, yes."

Anne's father had been the owner of a hardware store, not a lawyer. He wondered if Anne was now confusing him with her father. A few years ago, Anne would have thrown a party to celebrate the occasion.

"You always used to tell me that I should become a lawyer, and if I worked real hard, that I'd be a partner in a big firm some day."

"I said that?"

"All the time."

"Are you glad you did it?" Her voice had lost the lilt of

small talk, and her eyes were focused on him. Will felt as if the mists had parted for a moment to reveal the old Anne, peering out at him, never one to leave anything unfinished.

"Yeah, Mom. I'm glad I did it."

"Good." Then, with an added note of finality, "Good." And with that, the old Anne seemed to vanish again, if she had ever been there at all. "Now, do you want something to eat? I'm going to have some hot tea."

Anne waved at the dining room attendant, a whippet-thin teenager pushing a cart with lunch plates and plastic pitchers. "Hey there, Anne," he said. "You going to go for some tea today?"

"Yes, please. Hot tea. Not iced tea."

"And how about the entrée? Meat loaf or fish sticks?"

"What kind of fish is it?" she asked, ever the discriminating diner.

"It's just fish, Anne. Can't get more specific than that."

"Then I'll have the meat loaf."

"Good choice. Who you got here with you today?" he asked.

"This is my son, Will. He's a lawyer. Will, this is Daunte."

Will and Daunte nodded at one another and shook hands. "Your mother's a trip, you know that?" Daunte asked.

"Yeah, I do." Before Daunte could push his cart on to the next table, Will asked, "Has Anne gotten any visitors lately? A guy with a Russian accent?"

Daunte gave the question some consideration, then said, "No, I think I would have remembered that. But I'm not here every day. Sorry."

Will said good-bye to his mother, planting more kisses on her forehead, then went back to her room. Every time he visited, he checked her wardrobe to see if she needed anything. Clothes had a way of becoming community property in the facility.

Will was sifting through his mother's dresser drawers when he saw it and froze. On his mother's nightstand was an item that had not been there before—a lacquered Russian nesting doll. He opened it up and removed four colorful figurines of Russian peasant women. They were still wobbling on the nightstand as Will rushed out of the room.

TWENTY

Will returned to his apartment and showered and shaved, nicking his face three times in the process. He turned up the volume on the television so that he could listen for any further news of Jupiter on the Financial News Network. He desperately hoped that investors might discount the rumors and start buying Jupiter, but the stock price remained flat. Mort and Christine moved on to other harrowing collapses and miraculous recoveries in the financial markets. The swift stream of commerce coursed onward, and there was no time to linger over the eddying wreckage of Jupiter Software.

Will tried to call Claire's home number and got her answering machine. He was tempted to go to her apartment and wait there until she showed up to make sure she was okay, but concluded that the best way to keep his mother and Claire safe was to find something that the Russians wanted as quickly as possible. Will had no idea how he would be able to obtain the encryption keys; the high-security and biometric scanners of Jupiter's Sensitive Compartmentalized Information Facility seemed to present an insurmountable barrier. But he did know how to access his law firm's confidential files. Will decided that he was going to give Yuri and Nikolai at least a semblance of the insider information that they were looking for.

Although Will sought to appease Nikolai and Yuri in the short term, he knew that, through his disclosure to Richard, he had also set in motion the process that might expose the Clipper Chip program and end the Jupiter-Pearl merger negotiations. If Jupiter's dealings with the NSA became the focus of national media attention, Will expected that the Russians would give up their efforts to secure the encryption keys and would move on to other, less risky criminal schemes.

He arrived at the offices of Reynolds Fincher at two P.M., prepared to stay at the office all day and all night if that was what it took to find just the right bit of tantalizing but ultimately innocuous pseudo-insider information. As Will approached her secretarial station, Maggie gave him a look that Will had never seen from her before, at once pitying and accusatory. No doubt she was still wondering about yesterday's visit from the SEC and DOJ agents. Will simply gave her a sheepish wave as he passed, not wanting to discuss it.

He booted up his computer and got to work. First, he entered his e-mail inbox and reviewed the most recent messages that he had received from the firm's securities practice group, looking for some mention of a pending public-company transaction.

After wading through about ten e-mail notifications of

practice group meetings and new cases, Will found a copy of the minutes of the practice group's last meeting, one that he had missed because he had been immersed in the Jupiter deal.

The last entry in the minutes was headed *M&A: Work-load and New Matters*. Three corporations were listed in addition to Jupiter: ABT Solutions, Farallon Consulting, and Q-Biologics. These were all publicly traded companies represented by Reynolds Fincher that were apparently in play.

Will accessed the firm's document management system and typed in the names of the three companies, obtaining the client numbers. Next, he searched the system for the most recent documents saved to the ABT Solutions file. A glance at the first document told him that ABT Solutions, a relatively small database management software company, had already been acquired; the deal had closed two weeks ago.

Will next turned his attention to Farallon Consulting. The most recent document on the system was a draft stock purchase agreement dated the day before. Farallon, a technology consulting business, was going to be acquired by personal computer manufacturing giant Koretsu, which was trying to bolster its narrow profit margins on desktop computers with a thriving consulting practice. The fact that Nikolai and Yuri would have heard of Koretsu made this transaction a promising candidate.

The trick would be to find a nugget of publicly available information suggesting that the acquisition was in the works. If a financial newspaper or stock tip website had already guessed at the impending deal, then his disclosure would still be a breach of client confidentiality, but it was less likely to have an actual effect on the stock price of

Koretsu or Farallon. Even so, Will knew that there was no justification for violating attorney-client privilege. He tried telling himself that he was just gathering the information and that he would decide later whether he would actually share it with Nikolai and Yuri.

Will printed the draft stock purchase agreement. He could hear the pages of the document shuffling as they filled the tray of the laser printer outside his office. Next, Will opened his Internet browser and commenced a Google search on Farallon Consulting, looking for news of the transaction.

Will's concentration was interrupted when he saw movement reflected in his monitor screen. He turned to see that Don Rubinowski and Kevin Kaczmarek, the firm's information technology director, were standing behind him, peering over his shoulder at the contents of his screen. Don was holding a sheaf of paper, which Will immediately knew was the stock purchase agreement that he had just printed.

"Will, I'd like you to come with me. Please remove your hands from the keyboard."

"What's up, Don?" Will asked, trying not to sound rattled. "Have we been hit with another virus?"

"We're going to discuss this in private," Don said, in his most ominous managerial tone. "Come with me."

Will followed Don, who was still carrying the agreement, down the hallway to his corner office. He decided it was best not to ask questions until they were behind closed doors because he suspected that the answers would be profoundly embarrassing.

Will took a seat across from Don's desk. His office was ostentatiously simple, adorned with little more than photos of his wife and two children, one of those burbling electric fountains, and a panoramic view of the bay on one side and

Telegraph Hill on the other. There were no papers on the desk, which sent the message that he was now more akin to a CEO than a common lawyer.

"So what's up, Don?" Will said, still attempting nonchalance.

"You're fired, Will."

"Why? What's wrong?" Will did not sound as shocked as he would have liked.

"It's a little too late for that. This firm and its clients trusted you, and you betrayed that trust. But I need you to tell me one thing."

"What's that?"

"I need to know how many transactions you've compromised."

"I don't know what you're talking about, Don." Sick with self-loathing, Will knew just how halfhearted that statement sounded.

"Okay. I thought so. You had a bright future here, but you just pissed all over it. You have a half hour to get out of this office. A security guard will accompany you while you gather your things."

Will had known that he was risking his career with every step he had taken since the night he met Katya at the Whiskey Bar. But when Don Rubinowski spoke the words that ended his more than six years with Reynolds Fincher, and perhaps his entire legal career, it still came as a physical shock. His pulse raced and blood pounded in his ears, drowning out all sound. The only thing he heard was his own voice in his head saying over and over again, *Fucked*.

After what could have been fifteen seconds or five minutes, Will's pulse began to slow and his eyes refocused on what was before him: the implacable, dual-chinned face of Don Rubinowski, watching him with morbid fascination. *Fuck you*, Will thought. The fact that Will happened to be wrong did not make Don any less of an asshole, and he was not about to give him the satisfaction of losing his composure.

"The agents from the SEC and DOJ spoke with me at the end of the day yesterday about their evidence that you leaked insider information on the Jupiter deal," Don said. "Frankly, I couldn't believe it. They suggested that we track your activities this morning, so Kevin set up a pen register on your computer to capture every keystroke you made." Don waved the stock purchase agreement. "It was quite clear what you were doing."

Will considered saying that he was just searching for a form document that he needed, which was a semiplausible story. But Don would have known that was a lie, and saying it might limit his options later. "I think I'd better not say anything until I have a lawyer," he said. Will could muster no enthusiasm for defending himself.

"Then you'd better go. But first, I'll need your office key, access card, parking pass, and BlackBerry."

Will removed the plastic cardkeys from his wallet and placed them on Don's desk. "I'll have to get the Black-Berry from my office."

"You can give it to the guard as you leave." Don paused, then added, "I've got to admit I can't figure out why you did this."

"I don't think I should say anything else until I've spoken with an attorney."

Don simply turned his back on Will and began examining his e-mails. Once, Will had overheard Don grousing about what it was like to be the managing partner of a large law firm. Even in a relatively placid workplace, there was an endless series of employee altercations, personality conflicts, and employment-related lawsuits, actual and threatened, and many of those unpleasant matters were ultimately resolved in Don's office. Even the other partners didn't hear about most of the incidents. Will recognized that he was now just one more potential liability for the firm that had to be managed, lawyered, and eradicated.

When Will left Don's office, a security guard was indeed waiting for him. Will had seen the guard patrolling the Reynolds Fincher building for the past few years, although Will could never quite tell where his official rounds ended and his search for nooks where he could smoke cigarettes began. He thought his name was Jeff, but he wasn't sure. He was a stocky young man in his midtwenties with close-cropped black hair who filled his blue, slightly-too-small guard's uniform like it had been inflated.

"I'm supposed to stick with you until you're out of the building," Jeff said.

"Okay. It's Jeff, right?"

"Yeah. Jeff Wilson."

"How long you been here?"

"Four years."

"Almost as long as me. Sorry we didn't get more of a chance to talk." Will wondered why he had started this conversation, which was making him feel like even more of a jerk.

"Yeah," Jeff said, thankfully choosing not to kick him while he was down.

"I'd just like to stop by my office and pick up a few things and I'll be out of here."

"Okay, but you know I'll have to inspect everything when you leave."

"Sure."

As Will walked with the security guard down the hallway, which was flanked on one side by attorneys' offices and on the other side by secretarial cubicles, he could tell that news of his firing had already spread. The faces of the secretaries displayed variations on the there-but-for-the-grace-of-God-go-I look that Maggie had given him earlier that morning. No one was even making a pretense of working. They didn't want to miss the spectacle of his downfall, a cautionary tale that would be recounted in the firm's lunchroom for years to come.

At the other end of the hallway, but closing fast, was Jay Spencer. Jay was the last person Will wanted to see. He hoped that Jay hadn't heard the news yet, but the smarmy smile on his face told him otherwise.

"I couldn't believe what I just heard," Jay said as they stepped around each other in the hallway. "Say it ain't so."

"I'm a little busy right now, Jay."

"Whatever you say. But I know you can do the time. Stay hard in there, man," Jay added, tapping a closed fist to his chest in a gesture probably cribbed from an Eminem video.

Will was too dispirited to even attempt a comeback. Jeff nodded, urging Will to keep moving.

When they were out of Jay's earshot, Jeff whispered, "I don't know what you did or didn't do, but if being a dick was a crime, they'd lock that guy up and throw away the key." Will smiled a bit at that.

Sam Bowen, who was hovering over his secretary as she worked on a document, looked up as they approached. "Will, buddy, we need to talk. Come on in here." His manner was simultaneously solemn and agitated.

Will looked at Jeff, who shrugged his shoulders. "I'll wait out here for you," he said.

As soon as the door was closed, Sam said, "What the

hell is going on here, buddy? I just heard that you got canned. I couldn't believe it."

Will went to the window to buy himself a few seconds to think. "Sam, you've always looked out for me here at the firm, but there's nothing you can do for me on this one. If I talked to you about it, my lawyer would kill me."

"You retained anybody yet?"

"No. I just found out."

"I know some of the best white-collar defense attorneys in the city. I could make a few calls. . . ."

"Sam, you know you can't help me with this. I shouldn't even be talking to you. You're a partner here, and I don't want to create a conflict for you. If I tell you anything, you're going to be forced to testify against me or lie about this conversation. Everyone knows that we're in here talking."

"Can't I even line up a referral for you?"

"You know I should get my own attorney. I'll find a good one."

"Do you know what they're saying around here? That you may have something to do with the Russian mob! They're even saying that there's some connection to Ben Fisher's death! If it weren't so damn serious, I'd think it was funny."

"Sam, I appreciate that you're trying to help, but I got myself into this and I have to get myself out."

Sam walked to the window and looked down at the traffic on Sacramento Street. "You know, that didn't sound like an innocent man talking there a minute ago," he said. "The part about me having to lie if you told me what was going on."

"Is there such a thing as an innocent lawyer?"

"True enough, but that's no answer."

"I really can't say more than that, Sam."

"I stood up for you and recommended you for partnership just a week ago," Sam said. "You've made me look like a fool."

There was a knock at the door, and Will gratefully opened it. It was Jeff, tapping his watch.

"I've got to go," Will said.

Sam, who was now distractedly fingering a stack of papers on his desk, didn't look up. "You watch yourself, Will," he said.

When Will reached his office, he found that a couple of empty boxes had helpfully been placed on the floor in front of his desk. They wanted him out fast.

Will cleared the collection of toys from his desk. The centerpiece was Atomic Robot Man, a 1950s tin windup with Frankenstein-like bolts jutting from his neck. In ten minutes, he had removed all personal belongings from his desk and walls. He was surprised to see that the items hardly filled a single cardboard box. Inside were his framed law school diploma, a *Black's Law Dictionary*, some laminated offering memoranda tombstones commemorating deal closings, a few CDs, and a Waterman pen. He left the NO SHARKS sticker affixed to his monitor, a caution for the next attorney who occupied the office. Reviewing the meager contents of the box, Will realized just how rigorously he had segregated his personal life from his work.

"I was told to collect the BlackBerry, too," Jeff said.

Will opened his satchel and handed it over.

"You ready to go?" Jeff asked.

"Yeah, that should do it."

"You can take all the time you need to pack up. All I'm going to do is walk around the building for the rest of the day."

"Nah, I'm done."

They rode in the elevator in silence. As he pushed through the revolving door in the lobby, Jeff offered, "Hey, I wouldn't be surprised to see you back here in a few months."

"Maybe, but if I don't have an access card, you'll throw me out on my ass again, right?"

"Fuckin' A." Jeff gave a small nod and left Will standing on the sidewalk.

Will gazed up at the white tower of Embarcadero Four, trying to locate the offices of Reynolds Fincher. Up until that moment, he had been able to tell himself that his work as an attorney was his real life and that everything else that had happened in the past week was a bad dream, a fantasy concocted from too many viewings of the films of Scorsese and Coppola. Will stared up at the building with his box of office furnishings in one arm, CD boom box in the other. It would take a minute or two to turn his back and walk away from his old life to meet his uncertain future. His arms began to ache. He felt like a shipwreck victim clinging to a scrap of wreckage that was slowly going under. As pedestrians flowed around him on the sidewalk, the realization sank in that he was on the outside now. Any protection his relationship with Reynolds Fincher had afforded him was now gone. He and Claire were no longer of any value to the Russians and, in fact, what they knew about their plans posed a threat.

If the Russians had an inside connection at Reynolds Fincher, they probably already knew that he had been fired. Nikolai and Yuri were probably already on their way to kill Will . . . and Claire. He needed to call Claire immediately to warn her.

Will crossed the street and entered a sandwich shop so that he could put down his belongings and try again to call Claire. The phone rang and rang.

Finally, Claire answered. "Hello?"

"It's Will. We need to talk. You're in danger."

"No kidding!" Claire sounded upset. "There's a lot that you didn't tell me, isn't there? I just got back from the emergency room. Nikolai and Yuri came to see me."

"What did they do to you?"

"Don't worry. I'm going to be okay. Just get over here."

"Tell me what's going on!"

Claire banged the phone against something as she shifted it from one hand to the other. "We probably shouldn't be talking about this on the cell."

"Why not?"

"Because I have that thing they're looking for."

Will was growing exasperated. "What thing?"

"The keys. I'll be waiting for you." Claire hung up.

TWENTY-ONE

Will hailed a cab on Sacramento Street, rushing to get to Claire's apartment. He could not imagine how Claire had penetrated Jupiter's elaborate security to obtain a copy of the encryption keys. But if she really had them, then he could only hope that Nikolai and Yuri didn't know that yet. The keys were enormously valuable to the Russians and their bosses, and they would have no qualms about killing to get them. The Clipper Chip keys were also valuable to Will because they served as concrete proof of the hidden relationship between Jupiter and the NSA. With the keys in his possession, Will had some much-needed leverage—leverage that could be used to stop the Jupiter merger or prevent Nikolai and Yuri from killing them.

Will emerged from the taxi into a din of street noise, still carrying the stereo and cardboard box, at the Transbay Terminal on Fremont Street. He needed to make one quick stop to ditch his belongings. The bus station, a gray concrete edifice that straddled Fremont, seemed to have been built from pressed and molded grime. Will knew that his boom box made for an attractive target, so he walked quickly inside, past an array of portable toilets (the restrooms inside were boarded shut). The bus station was a large, barren room of gray tile floors and wooden benches the color of old bones. There were no fixtures of any kind, except for trash cans. The place seemed designed to facilitate regular hose-downs with disinfectant. He purchased a locker and dumped the contents of his cardboard box inside, along with the stereo.

After another short cab ride, Will arrived at the redbrick apartment in Jackson Square where Claire lived. Jackson Square was an upscale neighborhood with good restaurants and bars and small, expensive apartments for workaholics who couldn't bear to be far from their financial district offices.

Claire buzzed him up, peering at him through the peephole before opening the door. Her face was pale and tense and her eyes were bloodshot.

"Are you okay?" Will looked her over for signs of injury. "What were you doing in the emergency room?"

Claire held up her left hand to display a splint on the little finger.

"Is it broken?"

"*Shattered* was the word that the doctor used. Nikolai found the hammer that I keep under the kitchen sink. At least he let me pick the finger."

"Does it hurt?"

"What do you think?"

"I'm so sorry. I didn't mean to get you involved in all

this." Will rolled up his sleeve to reveal his razor wounds. "Look what they did to me."

With a sickened expression, Claire examined the scars, which were still red and swollen. "This isn't supposed to happen to people like us, right?"

Claire's apartment was small, but pleasantly furnished with Oriental rugs and overflowing bookcases that occupied nearly every available inch of wall space. On a desk in the corner of the room was a photo of Claire with the staff of the Electronic Privacy Information Center, her pre–law school job. On the kitchen counter were several pill bottles with the caps off.

"What are those?"

"Oh, I'm just trying to figure out the best cocktail for my particular mix of pain and anxiety." She picked up an oval, pale orange pill from the counter and examined it appreciatively. "I'm thinking Xanax for anxiety. Nothing too heavy to mix with the Vicodin."

"Are you sure about that?"

"Don't worry. I know my meds. But enough about me. Why don't you start by catching me up on what's been happening in your life, Will? Because now it's happening to my life, too."

Will told Claire the entire story, beginning with the morning of Ben's death, through his various encounters with Katya, Yuri, and Nikolai. He even told her of his suspicion that Grogan was involved with the Russians and had gotten her fired because of her discovery of Jupiter's connection to the NSA. Claire listened quietly, shaking her head occasionally.

When he finished, Claire smiled a little self-mocking smile. "I thought that seeing you was about the safest thing

I could do," she said. "But you're not the safe guy at all, are you? Turns out, you're the dangerous guy."

"I'm sorry. I didn't mean to involve you in all this."

"I know," Claire said. "Now don't you want to hear about the encryption keys?"

"Do you really have them?"

"Yes, but let me start at the beginning. Nikolai and Yuri came over here and told me I needed to help them get the encryption keys to the Clipper devices. They said that they'd kill both of us if I didn't cooperate. Yuri held my hand down on the kitchen counter, and Nikolai broke my finger. Yuri said it was to make sure that they had my attention. They said they'd be back soon to check on my progress."

"So how did you manage to get past all that security at Jupiter?" Will asked.

Claire washed down the Xanax with a swallow from a bottle of water. "It wasn't hard, actually. Do you remember Riley Boldin? The programmer at Jupiter that I introduced you to?"

"The one with the crush on you."

"Uh, right. Well, I went to Jupiter's offices and visited Riley. They let me go back to the due diligence room because they don't know yet that I've been fired. They still have my security pass on file. Technically, I'm still employed by Reynolds until the end of the month. I stopped by Riley's office and chatted him up about what he was working on. He was very happy to talk."

"I'll bet he was."

"I asked Riley about all of the high-tech security at Jupiter guarding the encryption keys, and he told me that one of the projects he was working on involved 'testing key strength' or something like that. He said that it was such a pain for him to constantly go through the biometric scanners and other security devices of the SCIF facility that he had managed to obtain a complete set of the encryption keys that he kept at his workstation. He said even his supervisor didn't know that he had it. He held up this little memory stick. He called it 'the keys to the kingdom.'"

"But how did you know that the stick contained the keys to the Clipper Chip, and not just Jupiter's standard encryption keys?"

"I told him that as part of the due diligence, I'd noticed that there seemed to be connections between Jupiter and the NSA, but I couldn't figure out what was going on.

"He said that he knew all about that stuff, but it was top secret. If that sort of information was going to be disclosed to Reynolds Fincher as part of due diligence, the okay would have to come from senior management.

"I pointed at the memory stick and said, 'I bet all of the secrets are on that little memory stick.' He just laughed and said, 'Like I told you—keys to the kingdom.'"

Will recalled his indiscretion with Katya regarding the Jupiter acquisition and wondered how many times throughout history the most precious secrets had been disclosed because a guy wanted to impress a girl. "So how did you manage to get it?" he asked.

"I asked him to get me a cup of coffee, and while he was gone I put the memory stick in my pocket. I was gone before he got back."

"But he's going to know that you took it," Will said.

"Yes, but I don't think he'll tell because he'd probably lose his job if he did. He wasn't supposed to have his own copy of the keys." Claire walked over to her answering machine and played a message.

Riley Boldin's voice on the tape crackled fuzzily, but

his desperation came through loud and clear. "Claire, this is Riley. I know that you took something from my office today. That was incredibly uncool. You have no idea how serious this is. Please call me right away or we could both be in a lot of trouble."

Claire removed a silver memory stick from her pocket. "What do you think I should do now?" she asked.

"You should make a copy and then give the memory stick back to him. I don't think he'll report it to his bosses. He'll figure that there was no harm done, and if he tells, he could still lose his job."

"You know, I wanted to help you by getting this," Claire said, holding up the memory stick. "But we can never let them have it now. Not with what you know about their plan for the BART trains."

"I know. We'll make sure that they never get it. In fact, I think we need to report the plan to release nerve gas on the BART trains. We could do it anonymously."

"Right," Claire said. "They could decide to go forward with the attack even without the encryption keys."

Will picked up the memory stick, turning it over in his hand. Something that held the keys to the country's most sensitive information should be heavier than this, he thought. "We also need to get this out of here right now. Nikolai and Yuri could come back anytime."

Before they left Claire's apartment, Will examined the pills spread out on the kitchen counter. He picked up a Xanax. "So these are good for anxiety?"

"They take the edge off."

"You mind if I . . ."

"Help yourself," Claire said. "I'm sure you could use it."

Outside on the sidewalk, they could feel the evening chill seeping into the afternoon as they searched for a taxi to take them to the bus station, where Will intended to stash the memory stick in the locker that he had purchased. When Will looked back up the street, he saw Nikolai and Yuri walking toward them, about fifty yards away. Yuri extended his arms in a mock greeting.

Will grabbed Claire's arm and pulled her in the opposite direction. "Run," he said.

They took off across Walton Square. When he looked back, he saw that Nikolai and Yuri were pursuing, their arms flailing awkwardly like men unused to exercise. On the other side of the square, Will and Claire ran down the sidewalk of Davis Court. Will was wearing hard-soled shoes, and he felt each stride on the concrete sidewalk in his knees.

Yuri was out ahead of the lumbering Nikolai, and he was gaining ground on them. Will saw no place for them to hide; the Russians were too close.

Claire and Will ran through a landscaped park next to the Maritime Plaza building. Looking up at the white towers ahead of them, Will realized that he had, probably through force of habit, headed for the familiar territory of Embarcadero Center. When they reached Clay Street, they were brought to a halt by a stream of cars. Will looked back and saw that the Russians were now only thirty yards behind them, so he dashed out into the thick of the traffic. They made it to the other side in a fanfare of car horns and squealing brakes.

Nikolai and Yuri crossed Clay without incident and continued to close the distance. Claire's breathing was growing labored, and so was his. They would not be able to outrun them.

They dashed through the lower level of Embarcadero Two. As they turned onto Sacramento Street, nearly overturning a sidewalk hot dog cart, Will began to formulate a plan.

"We're going up into Embarcadero Four," Will gasped. "The firm's offices."

"They'll trap us in there."

Will's knees were sore, and his calf muscles burned. His hair was pasted to his forehead, and beads of sweat rolled down his face and stung his eyes. As he ran down the familiar corridor of Sacramento Street in front of the Embarcadero Center towers, he had the surreal sensation that he was a runner nearing the finish line of a race. But the crowd was not cheering him on. Instead, he saw only unfriendly, suspicious faces turned to observe the spectacle as they flailed their way through the sidewalk throng. Men and women in business suits came to a complete stop on the sidewalk to stare at them.

Will turned into Embarcadero Four, and they scrambled up the escalator past the shops to the second-floor lobby of the office building. Before stepping through the revolving door and passing the security guard, they slowed to a walk and quickly smoothed down their wild hair, mopping the sweat from their faces.

Pushing through the revolving door, they saw Nikolai and Yuri climbing the escalator behind them, their faces bright red.

Will stuck his hand into the closing door of an elevator, which opened to reveal one passenger, Betty Sanderson, a litigation paralegal at Reynolds Fincher. Will and Claire climbed inside, both unable to do anything but gasp.

Betty was a small, capable woman in her midforties who seemed to be willing herself to become even smaller as she pressed herself into the corner of the elevator and stared intently at the CNN headlines on the elevator's video screen.

Betty's eyes darted ever more rapidly from the video screen to Will. Their eyes met as he looked up from his hunched posture, hands on his knees. Will gave her a nod of recognition that he hoped was reassuring. Betty quickly looked away, no doubt envisioning tomorrow's headlines about the fired attorneys who returned to their law firm's offices and the shooting rampage that ensued.

"We can't go—to—firm's offices. . . ." Claire gasped. "They won't let you in."

"I know—that's not—where we're going," Will said, punching the button for the sixth floor. The reception area of Reynolds Fincher was on the thirty-eighth floor.

The elevator doors opened on the central hallway of the sixth floor, which was shared by an accounting firm and an ad agency. Will got out and took Claire by the arm to pull her after him.

"Have a nice day, Betty. Say hi to everyone for me," Will said. As the elevator doors slowly closed, Will saw Betty's facial muscles twitch, as she tried to decide whether it was more dangerous to acknowledge Will or ignore him. As the doors shut, she gave a curt, spastic nod in his direction.

"What do we do now?" Claire asked.

"There are two of them. They probably figure that we're going to try to hide in Reynolds' offices. One of them will take the elevator up to the firm on the thirty-eighth floor. One will stay in the lobby to see if we come out."

"Yes, that sounds like a very good plan for *them*. But what do *we* do?"

"We take the elevator back down."

"No. Like you said, we can't go back to the lobby."

"We won't be going to the lobby. We're going to take the freight elevator down to the ground floor. The office lobby is on the second floor."

Will went to the far end of the bank of elevators and pressed the separate set of buttons for the freight elevator. They waited for the elevator and anxiously eyed the bank of elevator doors, hoping they would not open to reveal the Russians.

Finally, the freight elevator arrived, its interior covered with green mover's padding. Will pressed *G*.

"There's just one possible problem," Will said. "Let's hope no one at the office lobby level has punched the button for the freight elevator. If the doors open in the lobby, they'll see us."

The floors ticked down on the elevator's digital display. *5 . . . 4 . . . 3 . . . 2 . . . L*. Will and Claire exhaled simultaneously as the elevator continued downward to *G*.

The doors opened on the ground floor, filling the elevator with afternoon sunlight and a view of the Crabtree & Evelyn store, which was plastered with posters for a sale on scented soaps and bath powders. Will peered out of the elevator to see if the Russians were waiting for them, but he saw only a familiar mix of shoppers and office workers.

Will and Claire stepped out of the elevator and onto the sidewalk of Sacramento Street. As they crossed the street, Will glanced back to confirm that they were not being followed.

On the second floor of the Embarcadero Four tower, behind the lobby reception desk, was a floor-to-ceiling glass window. After scanning the ground floor of the building, Will's eyes drifted upward to the second-floor window— and there he saw Nikolai and Yuri standing in front of the glass, watching them walk away.

As they headed for the entrance to a BART station, Will touched Claire's arm and pointed at the Russians.

Without hesitation, Claire made a gesture that he was sure would register with them even at that distance. Feeling a swell of affection, Will put his arm around her as they climbed on an escalator that would take them down to the trains.

TWENTY-TWO

Will and Claire sat in silence as the BART train rattled across town toward the Civic Center, leaving Nikolai and Yuri far behind. The train car was crowded, and several people were standing in the aisle, businessmen lurching and bumping along side-by-side with the homeless.

"Where are we going?" Claire asked.

"Neither of us can go home, so we'd be better find a place to stay tonight. Someplace they'd never think to look for us."

"And you have an idea?"

"I have an idea."

Will knew of a dumpy motel far out on Geary Street near Golden Gate Park that would serve as a good hiding place for the night. He was afraid that if they stayed at one of the better hotels, the Russians might get lucky cold-calling front desks. Although they could have paid cash and signed in under a fake name, he thought that paying a two- or three-hundred-dollar hotel tab with twenties might attract suspicion. At a good hotel, there was also a chance that he might run into one of his former law firm colleagues or clients. Once they had found a safe place to stay for the night, they would have time to ponder their next move.

The driver of the train tapped the brakes and sent the standing passengers grabbing for the handrails. Will could hear the faint thump of bass, possibly Jay-Z, coming from the headphones of a boy in a black hoodie standing next to them.

The lights in the train flickered for a moment, then went out. It was not an uncommon occurrence, and it usually didn't last long. Nevertheless, Claire gripped his hand tightly in the darkness.

In that moment, Will was overcome by sickeningly vivid images of what would happen if Aashif Agha carried out his plan, and he knew that Claire must be thinking the same thing. It would start just like this, with the lights going out, and then the train would come to a stop.

After he had learned from the federal agents of Agha's attempts to purchase sarin gas, Will had read some online articles about the Japanese subway attack. He figured that Agha's plan might be executed in much the same fashion.

First, Agha's associates would probably bring liquid sarin solution onto the train in water bottles or other containers. In each train, one of the terrorists would puncture the bottle containing the sarin and leave it under his seat, just before getting off at a stop. As the train doors gasped shut, the sarin would already be leaking out of the punctured bottle, spreading across the floor of the train and emitting a toxic gas that was five hundred times as deadly as cyanide.

The sound of the darkened train thundering through the tunnels now seemed to grow unbearably loud. If the terrorists were able to use the encryption keys to somehow shut down the BART system, the fatalities would be multiplied many times over. There would be panic as the passengers shoved against each other to reach the doors. With the power out, it would be almost impossible for the clamoring, screaming throng to pry the doors open and reach the fresh air in the tunnels. The passengers would start choking and bleeding from the eyes and nose. Then they would begin collapsing. Even if power was restored in a matter of minutes, it would already be too late.

The car's lights sputtered and came back on as the train pulled into the Powell Street station.

"I have to get out of here," Claire said, still clutching his hand, her breathing quick and shallow.

They hurried up the steps of the escalator to get to the open air. Once among the crowd of shoppers on Powell Street in Union Square, Will and Claire walked aimlessly for a while, both trying to shake off their shared nightmare.

"Did you ever think that one day someone would call you a terrorist?" Claire asked, leaning in close so no one else could hear.

"We're not terrorists."

"But that's what they'll say, if this goes public."

Will paused for a moment as they threaded their way through a wave of shoppers emerging from Macy's. "We haven't really done anything yet," he said.

"I don't know about you, but I've stolen the encryption keys from Jupiter, which are basically a national security secret. And anything that even resembles aiding terrorists is enough to get you thrown in prison for a very long time."

"I promise to visit you in San Quentin. You should know that the inmates call it Q."

Claire narrowed her eyes at him. "Oh, go ahead and laugh, Mr. Aider-and-Abetter."

After a bit of silence, Will said, "I have been thinking about what could happen if the encryption keys were in the hands of a terrorist like Aashif Agha. The attack on the trains is just the part of their plans that we know about."

"I've been thinking the same thing."

"Paragon is the most widely used encryption product. Anyone who had a back door to decrypt Paragon transmissions would probably be able to access banking records and commit identity theft on a scale that no one's ever seen before. People would lose their life savings. Lives would be ruined."

"I don't think we have any way of knowing how much damage could be done," Claire said. "What if they got the access codes for New York City's power grid? Or the identities of U.S. spies? Or anti-terrorism plans? We really have no concept of what we're messing with here."

"I sort of wish you hadn't been so clever in getting the keys from your friend Riley," Will said. "I never meant to get you involved like this."

"They said they were going to kill you if they didn't get the keys. I wasn't about to let that happen."

They took a taxi from Union Square to the Richmond District and the far reaches of Geary Street, finally arriving at the Parkview Inn, a faded motel circa 1965. The motel stood by itself among some apartment buildings of similar vintage across the street from Golden Gate Park. The Parkview had a neon sign out front that looked as if it hadn't been lit since the 1970s that read COLOR TV— VACANCY. The neon lights that would have allowed for the option of "No" Vacancy had been inartfully removed from the sign. The afternoon was rapidly darkening as a storm blew in. There was only one car in the parking lot, and Will guessed that it belonged to the manager.

"Didn't I read about this place in *Conde Nast Traveler*?" Claire deadpanned, walking past the curtained windows of the other rooms, which showed no signs of life.

"I wanted a place where there was no chance we'd be found."

"Then I'd say mission accomplished."

After registering, they opened the door and were greeted by a room that was small, dingy, and spartan, but serviceable. The walls were adorned with paintings of sailboats that were intended to be realist in style, but were so crudely executed that they looked more like abstracts. When Will switched on the television set with the imitation wood-grain finish, it gave the evening newscasters a sickly green tint.

The room had two windows, one in front facing the street and another on the rear wall. He walked to the back of the room and drew the rear window's curtain back gingerly with one finger, as if examining a crime scene.

"How's the view?" Claire asked skeptically. "They call this place the Parkview, right?"

"I think they better start calling it Parking Lot View."

"Do you think we're safe here?" Claire asked.

"Yeah, sure. For now. I don't see how they could find us here, and I didn't see anyone following us."

"What should we do now?"

"I think we have to report what we know about the BART attack. It's one thing to keep quiet about an insider trading scheme. It's something else to withhold information about a terrorist attack."

"I agree," Claire said. "But how do we do it?"

"I'll take care of it," Will said. "I'm going to make a call that no one will be able to trace, but I'll need to go out for a while."

Will walked down Geary until he found a convenience store, where he paid cash for a cell phone with prepaid minutes. Will entered the parking lot of a gas station that was closed for renovations. He scanned the parking lot and the sidewalks in all directions until he was certain that there was no one within fifty yards of him to overhear, then dialed the number of the vice unit of the San Francisco Police Department. Will bypassed the department's hotline number because he was sure that those calls were recorded. He didn't want to give anyone the opportunity to use voice recognition software to identify him. Will had considered dialing Homeland Security or the FBI but figured that he should not underestimate the ability of those agencies to trace a call.

Will spoke quickly and tried to deepen his voice as he recited his statement, which warned of a terrorist attack on the BART trains using sarin gas sometime in the near future. He even mentioned Aashif Agha and Boka by name and noted the involvement of the city's Russian *mafiya*.

He hung up the phone just as the police officer on the other end of the line was beginning to stammer out a question. Will knew that the message was detailed enough to be taken seriously, particularly when the police figured out that Aashif Agha was a real terrorist who was known by Homeland Security to be in the Bay Area. The BART trains would probably be swarming with police in time for the next morning's commute.

Will tossed the phone into the maw of a garbage truck as it passed by on its rounds. If the police managed to track the location of the phone using its GPS receiver, it would probably be on the other side of the city by the time they found it.

As Will walked back down Geary to the motel, a few heavy raindrops began to splatter on the sidewalk. A storm was sweeping in, turning the afternoon to night in a matter of minutes, as if a curtain had been drawn.

TWENTY-THREE

Will awoke to the sound of a dull thump and a muffled curse. As his eyes adjusted to the dim light, he saw Claire pulling on her jeans in the dark. She had stubbed her toe against a chair and was hopping on one foot.

"Hey, where are you going?" Will said softly, drunk with sleep.

"I'm going to get a soda from the machine. Do you want anything?"

Will pondered for a moment. "Nah."

"Okay, back in a minute."

Claire opened the door, and a gust of cold, damp air entered the room, rousing him. He sat up in bed and realized that he was cotton-mouthed and that he did want a soda. He climbed out of bed and pulled on his jeans, shirt, and running shoes.

Outside, the storm had arrived. The rain sounded like the

hiss of a blank tape turned up to thundering volume. Turning to check that the door was locked, he paused, brought up short by the sense that he had just seen something.

The streetlamp outside the motel illuminated the shifting patterns of the rain against the night's black backdrop. Will thought that he had just detected a movement behind him in the darkness that wasn't from the rain or wind.

Will turned back around to face the street. Just outside the arc of the streetlamp, he saw two figures walking toward the motel. Behind them was a shadow that bore the distinctive Detroit stylings of the Lincoln Town Car.

When they saw that he had spotted them, Nikolai and Yuri began running toward him. Like a bear, Nikolai was incongruously fast for his size.

Will looked down the motel's walkway, searching for Claire. He saw a sign labeled VENDING that pointed around the corner. He knew that if he went after her, they would cut him off.

Will clawed at his pocket for the room key and unlocked the door. He slammed the door shut and fumbled attaching the chain. Will's heart rate accelerated, and his mouth dropped open as he strove to take in enough oxygen to operate his personal disaster response system.

His eyes darted around the room, settling on the rear window, the only escape route. Will grabbed Claire's purse from the dresser and dug in it for the memory stick, but all he found were car keys, cosmetics, and Kleenex. The Russians were now trying to kick in the front door, producing sounds like the muffled boom of depth charges. He dumped the contents of the purse on the dresser and at last found the memory stick.

Will didn't turn to look as he struggled with the sash, which had probably not been opened in years. He tore fingernails trying to get a better grip. Then he heard the sound of shattering glass as Nikolai and Yuri turned their attention to the front window, a more yielding point of entry.

Finally, with an unhappy groan, the rear window opened. Will punched out the wire mesh screen and climbed out, tripping and falling forward to land heavily hands-first on the parking lot asphalt. He scrambled across Geary Street and into the dense woods of the park. Branches whipped at his face and arms.

Will stopped running when he heard the sound of the Russians talking at the edge of the park. He didn't want to draw them with the sound of crackling underbrush.

"Will! Don't make us come in there after you!" Nikolai shouted. "We have Claire."

Next came Claire's voice. "Just run, Will! They—" It sounded like she was cut short by a blow.

At that moment, he considered standing up and walking out of the woods to stop them from hitting Claire, but he knew that would do no good. Unarmed, he would be no match for them. And once they had the memory stick, Nikolai and Yuri would have every reason to kill them both. The memory stick was probably the only thing keeping Claire alive. Will quietly crept deeper into the woods.

"What kind of man are you? You are going to let us do this to your girlfriend? Claire, why would you want to be with such a pussy?"

For a moment, there was silence.

Then Will's cell phone, which was in his pants pocket, began ringing—loudly. Will pulled the phone from his pocket and shut it off, cursing his stupidity. The Russians had his cell number and had called him so that the ringing would give away his hiding place.

"I heard it! He's over there!" Yuri said. Then, to Will,

he taunted, "You should have answered it, asshole! I had something very important to say to you!"

There was the sound of snapping branches as Yuri and Nikolai came after him. Will fled in the opposite direction but soon reached sparse brush at the edge of the woods. Ahead of him lay the grassy expanse of the park, where he would be easily spotted. He changed direction, moving through the woods parallel to the park and away from the motel. The noise of Nikolai and Yuri blundering through the underbrush was growing more distant. He only hoped that they could not hear him as clearly as he could hear them.

Will hunkered down on a muddy slope in a stand of trees and waited for his heart to stop hammering. His face stung where it had been whipped by branches. After a while, he no longer heard anything but the sound of the rain, the rustling of the wind in the trees, and the more distant sound of the swish of car tires on the wet pavement of Geary. Yuri and Nikolai must have been moving in the opposite direction because he could no longer hear their voices.

He pulled his phone from his pocket and dialed Yuri's cell phone number. He thought he heard Yuri's phone ringing distantly somewhere in the woods to his left, but he might have been mistaken.

"Da."

Will whispered into the phone in case they were closer than he thought. "I have a proposal for you."

"I'm listening."

"I'll give you the memory stick on one condition—you let Claire go. And you don't hurt her. You don't lay a hand on her."

"No problem. So let's get out of these wet fucking woods and get this over with."

"I'm not an idiot. We're not making the exchange out here. We'll do it in a public place, with lots of people around. I'll call you tomorrow morning to arrange the meeting."

"If we don't find you tonight."

"Yes."

"Because if we find you, then I do not think we would be able to honor the deal."

"And I won't honor the deal if I find out you've done anything to harm Claire." Will shut off the phone.

As his pulse slowed, he began debating the question of how Nikolai and Yuri had managed to track them down at, of all places, the Parkview Inn. Only a few logical possibilities presented themselves. He doubted that the Russians had somehow followed them ever since they got on the BART train. If they had, they wouldn't have waited so long to move on them.

Will was still carrying the cell phone that the Russians had given him, and he wondered if it might contain a tracking device. He threw the phone into the bushes far away from him. Perhaps they had been tracked using the GPS in Will's own cell phone, but that seemed awfully sophisticated for Nikolai and Yuri. Nonetheless, Will removed the battery from his cell phone.

There was also the possibility that Claire had tipped the Russians to their location. Claire had been conveniently out of the room when Nikolai and Yuri had come to kill him. He found it difficult to distrust Claire, but it was the simplest explanation, and thus the most plausible.

She had certainly sounded sincere when she urged him to run. And a real blow seemed to have cut her short. Most persuasive of all was her smashed finger. But then again, he hadn't actually seen what was underneath that splint. Will was left with some strong suspicions about Claire, but not nearly enough to abandon her to two Russian thugs.

He decided to stay in his hiding place for a while longer. If he tried to leave the park now, he would be much easier to spot crossing a street or an open field. In an hour or so, Nikolai and Yuri would probably tire of searching for him in the rain.

Will checked his watch—it was one thirty A.M. He listened to the falling rain until he heard patterns in the sound, and then nothing at all. He concentrated on the ticking of waterlogged branches, trying to tell if it was the sound of someone creeping closer through the woods. After a while, his thoughts drifted to subjects beyond the immediate danger. He wondered if the BART attack would proceed without the encryption keys, and whether the police would be able to stop it if it did. He hoped that Nikolai and Yuri weren't hurting Claire. He pondered the fact that he would not be reporting to the offices of Reynolds Fincher. He wondered how he would hold up in prison. He shuffled and reshuffled these concerns as he waited in the darkness, shivering and wet.

In a way, this terrifying night seemed oddly familiar to Will; he had a recurring nightmare that involved flight from pursuers. It began with him sitting in a movie theater watching a George Romeroesque zombie picture. The theater was one in which he had seen many movies as a young boy—the Cameo in Brookfield, Missouri. It was the only theater in his father's hometown, a Depression-era shoebox about ten seats across with creaky wooden floorboards. The childhood reminiscence ended and the nightmare began when the zombies shuffled off the movie screen and proceeded to hunt him through the small town, from the strangely pristine alleys of Main Street to the gazebo in the town square. Despite the fantastical nature of the scenario (and the thinly veiled allegory regarding fears of conformity and parental control), it prompted a very real terror. Will jerked upright in bed after waking from one of these episodes, gasping for breath like he had been submerged in dark water, rather than a dream.

He was in the middle of a real-life reenactment of that familiar scenario as he sat on the muddy ground in his hiding place. But the terror was not as wild and untrammeled as in the nightmare. He found himself absorbed primarily in pragmatic thoughts of his physical discomfort and routes of escape. Observing his steady hands, smeared with mud, Will thought of Enzo the Baker.

Will checked his watch again—three thirty A.M. Nikolai and Yuri had probably given up their hunt for him by now. Will dislodged himself from the muck and began making his way through the park, skirting the edges of the woods so that he wouldn't stand out.

Will eventually found a cabbie who was willing to pick him up despite his dirty and disheveled appearance. When he arrived at the Holiday Inn on Van Ness, he noticed that the street was festooned with rainbow banners in anticipation of the Gay Pride Parade. By the time Will checked in, he already had the beginnings of a plan for making the exchange.

TWENTY-FOUR

The next morning, Will didn't dare return to his condo to get clean clothes, so he purchased a new and too-youthful outfit at the Gap: a vivid green-and-blue-striped shirt and a pair of jeans that seemed a little too tight no matter which size he tried. Will no longer looked like something that had crawled from the swamp. In fact, he looked ready for his senior year of high school.

Will returned to his room, showered, and called the Russians.

Will already knew the first question that he wanted to ask. "How did you find us last night?"

"That is none of your fucking business."

"You want the memory stick, right?"

No response.

"Then you'd better tell me because that's the only way

you're going to stop me from going straight into the FBI witness protection program."

"Ah, I see. You are having doubts about Claire. You think she may have betrayed you? Relationships must be based on trust, my friend."

Will remained silent, waiting for an answer.

Finally, Yuri spoke. "You shouldn't have used your credit card when you bought the room, fuckhead."

"No offense, but I'm surprised that you two have the connections to run a trace on a credit card."

"Not us. The people we work for. *Mafiya* has people inside at the credit card companies. Identity theft is big business for them." Will shuddered as he realized that it was sheer dumb luck that he had paid for his current room with cash he had gotten from an ATM on Van Ness. If he had used his credit card again, then the Russians would probably already have him. "Any more questions?"

"Yes. Is Claire all right?"

"Sure. That was our deal, right?"

"Put her on the phone."

A few seconds passed, and then he heard Claire's voice. "Will? Is that you?" She sounded tremulous and distant, but he couldn't tell how much of that was attributable to the weak connection.

"It's me, Claire. Are you okay?"

She seemed not to have heard his question. "Don't try to—they're going to kill you." There was a scrabbling sound on the line as the phone was taken from her hand.

"There. You see? She's okay. Now can we get on with this? What—"

"If you hurt her, I'm going to make sure that Homeland Security and every anti-terrorism agency in the country knows about that memory stick. If you think the government doesn't like organized crime, wait till you see how they treat terrorists."

"Where are you? We'll bring her to you."

"I'll meet you at the corner of Market and Battery. In the middle of the Gay Pride Parade."

Will heard muffled conversation in Russian as Nikolai discussed the proposal with Yuri. "Okay. We'll meet at noon."

According to the bedside alarm clock, it was already eleven thirty. "I can't make it there that fast. I'm too far away."

"Just be there." The connection went dead.

Will dressed frantically and quickly hailed a cab. As the taxi stalled in traffic, he realized that reaching Market and Battery in a half hour was going to be even more difficult because many streets were blocked for the parade. Festive crowds were migrating toward the parade route on Market Street, adorned in feather boas, leather, and sparkle makeup.

Will finally abandoned the taxi at eleven fifty-five A.M., still three blocks north of Market. He pushed his way through the parade crowd, which ranged from curious straights in jeans and polo shirts to drag queens who had thrown their scant sartorial caution to the wind. As Will approached Market Street, he saw that the parade was underway and was being led by a convertible bearing the parade's grand marshal, the seemingly hungover Sir Ian McKellen, who grimaced in the bright sunshine and waved feebly to the crowd.

He recalled hearing that Reynolds Fincher was organizing a float for the parade, but he had been told that no attorneys would be participating, only gay staff members, of which there were many. In most other cities, an old-guard law firm would probably not have participated so prominently in the parade, but given the political and economic clout of the gay community in San Francisco, Reynolds had decided that it was good business to sponsor a float. Paradoxically, many of the firm's gay and lesbian partners and associates did not seem to feel that it was good business for them to participate personally in the parade, or to be openly gay, for that matter.

Will scanned the throng for a glimpse of Nikolai, Yuri, or Claire, to no avail. The next float to pass had a Wild West theme, with sagebrush and cacti, bearing the slogan LEATHER PRIDE. The float, sponsored by the Leather Community, featured men wearing chaps, cowboy hats, and little else. A few of the leather men brandished bullwhips.

Ordinarily, Will would have enjoyed this uniquely San Franciscan spectacle, as the Gay Pacific Islander and Gay Saudi Arabian delegations filed past, followed by the Dykes on Bikes, several of whom were topless, with buzz cuts and nipple rings. On this day, it barely registered as he tried to locate the Russians.

In order to gain a better view of both sides of the street, Will pushed forward to the iron barricade. He wished that he had specified which side of Market they were to meet on. As he examined the faces, his view was blocked by a shirtless young man bearing a placard that read GAY VEGANS TASTE BETTER. The young man caught Will's grim expression and returned a beaming smile. "Happy Pride!" he said.

"Happy Pride," Will muttered.

Then Will saw Yuri on the opposite side of the street. Yuri had already spotted him and was baring his tight-lipped, angry smile, waiting for Will to notice him. When their eyes met, Yuri gave him a finger-waggling, homosexual-mocking wave that drew disapproving glares from several people standing nearby. Yuri motioned for him to cross the street.

Will did not see Claire or Nikolai but assumed they must be nearby. He slowly wedged himself through a gap in the barricade and waited as the Bank of America float chugged past.

A cop on horseback about twenty yards away saw Will standing on the wrong side of the barricade and admonished him with a pointed finger.

"Look, a horsey cop," said a young man standing behind Will.

"This is San Francisco," his partner corrected him. "The term is *mounted policeman.*"

As he crossed Market Street, Will saw a float bearing down upon him with a dozen men in six-foot-tall wigs, one of which contained a replica of the Transamerica Building. They were belting out a musical number—it was the cast of *Beach Blanket Babylon*.

He was startled when he glimpsed a cop approaching through the crowd. When he turned, however, he saw that it was only a leather man wearing a leather version of a policeman's peaked cap. Refocusing his attention on the south side of Market, he found that he had lost track of Yuri.

Then Will spotted him, standing about ten yards away with Nikolai and Claire under a black fiberglass sculpture. The crowd was less dense there, so he could see them clearly. Claire looked grim and tired, but she did not seem to have been harmed.

Nikolai and Yuri waited for him to approach. Will did not walk over to them immediately, taking a moment to assess the situation. Nikolai noted Will's hesitancy and grabbed Claire by the arm, squeezing it hard enough to make her wince. Will took a step toward them, then another, his eyes darting from Yuri to Nikolai and back again.

Yuri was watching Will while Nikolai scanned the crowd. When Will was still ten yards away, Nikolai froze. He had spotted something or someone. He made a sharp remark to Yuri. After hearing their exchange, Claire started to shout something at Will.

An instant later, Yuri's hand was reaching inside his leather jacket. Will stopped abruptly, as if he had come to the end of a tether.

Yuri drew a pistol from his jacket. In a moment of excruciating clarity, Will saw the glint of afternoon sun on the barrel of the gun, the concentration on Yuri's face as he aimed.

An instant later, Will was shoving his way through the parade crowd, throwing elbows like Shaquille O'Neal. He heard no gunshots. Will managed to make it to Market Street and, drawing several shouts of resistance, clambered over the barricade into the street. He heard the cries multiplying behind him and knew that Nikolai and Yuri were plunging through the throng after him.

As he staggered onto Market Street, he found himself surrounded by a group of men dressed like nuns who had been outfitted at Frederick's of Hollywood. It was the Sisters of Perpetual Indulgence, a troupe of drag queen performance artists. The Sisters took his intrusion in stride—one blessed him, and another attempted to spank him on the ass with a ruler. Standing in the middle of Market Street, with Nikolai and Yuri at the barricades and once more able to take aim at him, he felt more exposed than the burly Sister standing next to him wearing fishnets over a thong.

The Sisters did not have a float that Will could hide behind, so he tried to stay close to the performers while moving against the tide of the parade. When he looked back to spot Yuri and Nikolai, he saw them climbing over the barrier. Will wondered if they were actually brazen enough to shoot him in the midst of a televised parade.

Looking for cover, he was relieved to see a float rumbling toward him. It was a large, rolling lump of papiermâché covered with plastic flowers and bearing the slogan MORE THAN A LAW FIRM and, in smaller letters, CELEBRATE DIVERSITY! REYNOLDS, FINCHER & McCOMB HONORS SAN FRANCISCO'S LESBIAN, GAY, BISEXUAL, AND TRANSGENDER COMMUNITIES. The float was manned by about a dozen people who were standing at a low railing along the side throwing Mardi Gras beads to the crowd.

Will scanned the railing for familiar faces. There was Jeannie Cruz, a secretary. Martin Reznik, a librarian.

A string of beads hit him in the chest. When he looked up, he saw that they had been thrown by Craig Logan, a paralegal he had worked with on the Jupiter deal.

"Didn't expect to see you back so soon! Happy Pride!"

Will walked backward to face Craig and keep up with the float. "Can I join you up there?"

"This isn't your coming-out party, is it, Will?" Craig reached down and extended a hand. Will climbed the steps built into the side of the float and joined Craig at the railing.

Craig put his arm around Will's shoulder and looked out at the crowd. "How about a big smile for Don Rubinowski? I'm sure he's watching this at home. He'll be so pleased to see that you've returned to the fold."

"Craig, I need your help. Is there a place around here where I could hide?"

"Once that closet door is open, Will, there's no more hiding."

"I'm serious, Craig. I need to get out of sight. Right now."

"Well, there's a cabin in the back where the driver sits. . . ."

Will inched past a line of bead throwers on the narrow walkway. He reached the rear of the float and opened a hatch to reveal a Teamster sitting behind a steering wheel in a cramped cabin, peering through a narrow window in the float's façade.

Before ducking inside the cabin, Will glanced around for Nikolai and Yuri. It was then that he saw Nikolai beside the float, staring straight at him.

Will leaped over the opposite railing, hitting the pavement with an impact that launched him forward onto his hands and knees. He rose to his feet quickly and, without looking back, sprinted down Market Street in the direction of the parade.

A series of loud pops, each one accompanied by a flat, metallic echo like the sound of an aluminum bat hitting a ball. Gunshots.

There were screams and he heard the parade crowd pressing on itself in panic, the sound of people desperate to run but unable to move.

Will continued to run. He didn't feel as if he had been wounded, but he fully expected his legs to fail him at any moment. Perhaps his life was already leaking out of him, and only adrenaline, that reality suppressant, kept him from recognizing the fact.

He staggered to a halt as he approached a woman who was standing in the center of Market Street, pointing a gun at his chest with legs braced and both hands on the weapon in a perfect Weaver stance. She looked like anyone else in the crowd in her jeans, running shoes, and short-sleeve blouse. She was in her early forties and had a hard face, made harder by dark aviator sunglasses.

"Department of Justice," she said. "Get down on the ground and put your hands behind your back."

Will examined the front of his shirt for traces of blood. "Have I been shot?"

"Not yet," she answered. "And if you don't want to be, you better get down."

Will placed his palms down on the hot, gasoline-smelling pavement. He was pulled up to his knees, and the agent twisted his hands behind his back. The handcuffs pinched his wrists as they clicked shut. Market Street was no longer rumbling with the vibrations of parade vehicles. The procession had come to a halt, and those who hadn't run for cover at the sound of the gunshots were staring at the scene—the crowds of onlookers on both sides of Market, the Sisters of Perpetual Indulgence, the Reynolds Fincher staff on the float, and, presumably, the television audience at home.

The DOJ agent hauled him to his feet and walked him over to a knot of people a few yards away. Although he drew his share of curious stares, the crowd's attention seemed to be focused on what lay before them.

Six men and women in sunglasses were arrayed in a circle around two figures on the pavement. They seemed to have formed the circle intentionally to block the view of the crowds and cameras.

The two figures sprawled on the asphalt were Nikolai and Yuri. Nikolai was lying facedown and motionless, arms splayed. Yuri was lying faceup in the street, his hand clenching in a fist and unclenching, as if by that action he were somehow managing to keep his heart pumping. The agents broadened their circle slightly as they inched away from the shockingly large pool of blood that drew everyone's eyes to the Russians like a big red spotlight.

Will searched the crowd for Claire's face, but she was nowhere to be seen.

A young agent wearing a bright blue polo shirt and cargo shorts was shouting into a cell phone.

"Where's the ambulance?" the agent barked. "The parade has stopped and we're on fucking television!" He paused to listen to the voice on the other end of the line, then shouted, "If it was only half a block away, why isn't it here yet?" Another pause. "That's what the cops are there for! Get them to clear the goddamn intersection!"

Will waited with the agents for an ambulance to arrive. Numb from shock, his eyes wandered over the scene, from the dead and dying figures of Yuri and Nikolai on the pavement, to the anxious attitudes of the agents, to the morbidly curious faces of the parade crowd.

"Shouldn't somebody be helping them?" Will asked the woman agent.

"One of 'em's already dead. The other one's probably gonna be gone soon. There's not much we can really do till the ambulance gets here, anyway."

The noise of the parade had died away, leaving a strange quiet that was punctuated by the troubled murmuring of the crowd and, finally, the wail of an ambulance siren. The floats and the parade marchers shifted to the opposite side of Market Street to make way for the ambulance, which crept fitfully toward them as obstacles were removed from its path.

When the ambulance finally arrived, its rear doors slammed open. Three EMTs bearing gurneys emerged in a practiced drill. Nikolai and Yuri were borne into the ambulance. Nikolai was brusquely hoisted aboard like so much cargo. Yuri was lifted with more care, an indication that he was still alive. Yuri's fist was no longer clenching, but his eyelids were half open and he seemed to be breathing.

"Come on," the woman agent said. "You're going with them in the ambulance."

"Why?"

"The one that's still alive might have something to say to you."

Will and the agent climbed into the back of the crowded ambulance, with Nikolai and Yuri on the gurneys and a paramedic. The other two paramedics rode in the front.

"If it were my decision, you wouldn't be back here," the paramedic said. He was a small, muscular man with bushy, black eyebrows. He didn't seem particularly alarmed by the life-and-death event before him.

"It's not your decision," the agent said.

When Will looked over at Yuri, he saw that the Russian's glassy, heavy-lidded eyes were fixed on him. Will couldn't be sure if he was really seeing him, though. Perhaps his attention was already directed inward. The interior of the ambulance was brilliantly lit. Watching the harsh lights flicker and fade in Yuri's eyes, Will felt as if he were standing outside a house that was being prepared for a vacation, the windows going dark one by one.

A gurgling rose in Yuri's throat, followed by a garbled Russian phrase.

Will looked at the agent and the paramedic to see if they had heard.

"He says, 'Fuck you,'" said the agent. "Loose translation."

"You speak Russian?"

"That's why I'm here." *She's hoping Yuri will say something that will incriminate me,* Will realized. That's why he was allowed to ride in the ambulance.

Will returned his gaze to Yuri, who was still staring at him intently over the head of the now-busy paramedic, with a look that he read as hatred. He had been taught to feel compassion for all living things, but at that moment he was simply glad that Yuri's career of inflicting pain was drawing to a close.

Will noticed that the ambulance had stopped. No one seemed to be in a hurry as they climbed out into the sunny spring afternoon.

"He's gone," the paramedic said, removing the IV from Yuri's wrist.

The paramedic, the agent, and Will stretched for a moment in the driveway in front of the emergency room, glad to be out of the ambulance's cramped quarters.

The agent turned to Will and pulled an identification badge from her wallet. "I guess it's time to introduce myself. I'm DOJ Special Agent Joan Fisk. The San Francisco PD is going to let us take you down to our offices for questioning now." She glanced at him. "It's better for you than spending the night in jail."

"Is it better? Because I think I'd take the night in jail."

Agent Fisk ignored him. "I guess you already know this drill, but I'm required to tell you that you have the right to an attorney."

"Actually, I don't know the drill. I do corporate work. I'm not a criminal attorney," Will said, absently.

"Oh, yeah?" Agent Fisk responded, returning the badge to her wallet. "Well, as far as we're concerned, you're a criminal attorney now."

TWENTY-FIVE

Will was taken to the DOJ's offices on Geary Street and ushered past an expanse of cubicles into a conference room. Agent Fisk offered him coffee, which he accepted.

He was still carrying the memory stick that contained the encryption keys, and he worried that soon he would be asked to empty his pockets. Once the agents figured out what the encryption keys were, the proceedings were likely to take on an entirely different tone.

After returning with a cardboard cup of something luke-warm, Agent Fisk left the room without a word. This, he thought, must be the point in the process where the suspect is left alone with his thoughts to ponder his fate. If the tactic was intended to make him anxious, it was working.

Will's first-year criminal procedure class was a hazy memory. Everything he knew about the process of arrest and interrogation he had learned from television. He had already decided that as soon as his interrogators arrived, he was going to "lawyer up," as they said on the cop shows. The question was, who would his lawyer be?

Although he had spent most of his adult life working in law firms, Will knew very few criminal lawyers. Major law firms generally did not handle criminal cases, except for some white-collar criminal defense work. The top firms viewed criminal law as low-rent, dirty, and, worst of all, not particularly lucrative. Even though many of his peers had formed their first notions of the legal profession watching Michael Kuzak try criminal cases on *L.A. Law*, that was not the reality of the practice of law for most graduates of good law schools. In order to pay off the sizable student loans required by a top-twenty law school, graduates needed to earn top salaries—which were paid by the major law firms. And those firms did not do criminal work.

As he sipped the coffee and scanned the ceiling, trying to spot cameras and microphones, he searched his memory in vain for the name of a criminal lawyer that he could trust.

The conference room door opened and Dennis Tyler and Mary Boudreaux, the two agents who had interviewed him at his office, entered.

"Hi, Will," Mary said, frowning sympathetically.

"Will," Dennis said, curtly. Will thought that they must be almost as tired of this good-cop, bad-cop routine as he was.

Dennis and Mary sat down opposite Will at the conference table. "It's pretty clear that you weren't being straight with us at our last meeting," Mary said. "But we're not going to hold that against you for now. Clearly, you were under some pressure."

"What do you want to know?" Will asked.

"Someone phoned the San Francisco PD with an anonymous tip about a terrorist attack on the BART system. It involved the Russian *mafiya*." Mary paused. "And Aashif Agha." Another pause. "And sarin nerve gas. We know it was you that placed that call, Will."

"I don't know what you're talking about." Will felt that if he told the truth, he and Claire would be convicted as participants in a terrorist plot. The theft of the encryption keys alone was probably enough to ensure that they would spend the rest of their lives in prison. If Will reached the point of disclosing everything, he would do it only after consulting with a criminal defense attorney, and he wasn't about to say anything that would incriminate Claire.

"Do you really expect us to believe this crap?" Dennis said. "Who else is going to make that call? We already know about your links to the *mafiya*. After today's little incident, surely even you can't deny that. In our last meeting, we told you about Agha and his efforts to purchase sarin. Obviously, you put that information together and left the message warning about the BART attack."

"We know that you were trying to do the right thing," Mary said. "And that will be taken into account if you tell us the whole story. Why don't you start with how you got involved with the Russians?"

"I don't think I can respond to questions like that without a lawyer present."

This was enough to redirect the line of questioning. Dennis pointed behind his back through the plate glass window of the conference room. "Do you see those people working out there in those cubicles?"

"Yes." Will was unsure where Dennis was heading; it sounded like a question when he said it.

"Do you think you're better than them?"

"No, Dennis, I don't."

"Good. Because very soon you'll be wishing to God that you could do the things that they can do. Little things like taking a walk outside. Eating a hamburger. Sleeping in a real bed."

"I get your point."

"No, I doubt that you really do. If you don't cooperate with us right now, and I mean *right now*, you're going to lose the ability to do all of those things for a very long time."

Will did not respond, briefly mesmerized by Dennis's performance, which was that of a journeyman actor who was finally being allowed to take center stage. As with most B-actors, however, Dennis's performance lacked subtlety and modulation. He tended to overplay.

"Do you appreciate what that means, Will?"

"No, I guess I don't."

"It means that your life as you know it is now over. I'm guessing that you're a guy who's spent a lot of time trying to separate himself from everybody else, trying to get ahead. You probably made good grades, went to a good college. Top law school. Got hired by a good law firm. Made partner. I respect that. We both do."

Mary gave a slight nod of support for Dennis's statement. Will gave her credit for not smirking or even allowing a twinkle of humor to show in her eyes. She might not be getting many lines in this scene, but Will recognized a gifted performer when he saw one.

"Thanks, Dennis."

"Just shut up and listen, wiseass. If you go to prison, you probably think it's going to be one of those artsy-craftsy minimum-security places, where they put people like Milken and Boesky. Well, I've got news for you . . . they

don't exist. You'll be going into the general prison popula-
tion, and that's not a very inviting place for someone like
you. When you finally get out, everything you've worked
for will be gone. You'll never be able to practice law again.
All your skills, all your education, it won't mean shit. An
ex-con who knows how to work a drill press will be more
employable than you. You want to be forty-five years old
and starting over from square one?"

"Just tell us the story," Mary said. "Beginning to end.
How you got involved with the Russians, the insider trading, the planned BART attack, Claire—"

"Where is Claire?"

"She's being questioned down the hall."

"And she is talking," Dennis added. Will did not believe
him.

"There is one thing I'm curious about," Will said. "How
did you happen to be there at the Gay Pride Parade?"

"You know what? I'll tell you that much. Call it a show
of goodwill," Mary said. "The joint investigation of the Jupiter deal caused us to step up surveillance of some of the
local *mafiya*. We saw Nikolai and Yuri meeting with some
known Red Fellas . . . in a Starbucks, no less. We didn't
know who Nikolai and Yuri were, but we caught a break
when they led us right to you. Do you have any idea how
lucky you are to be alive right now?"

Will did not respond. He was not feeling particularly
lucky.

"Unfortunately, Yuri made one of the agents in the
crowd, and that's when the shooting started," Dennis said.
"He probably figured that you had set him up."

"There's a narrow window here where we can make
the next ten or fifteen years of your life a whole lot bet-

ter," Dennis continued. "That window's closing fast. If you come clean now, it can still make a difference."

"You should listen to him, Will," Mary said. "You know, we don't even have to be in here right now. We don't need a statement from you to make our case."

"Then why are you here if you don't need my statement? You know, I am familiar with these interrogation techniques. I watch *Law & Order*."

"If you just tell us what happened," Dennis said, "there will be less paperwork and less court time. Saves everybody money. We'll be able to move on to other things. It's the kind of thing that gets favorable consideration in sentencing."

"Am I being taped?" Will asked.

"Yes," Mary said.

"Who else is listening to our conversation right now?"

"No one." Will didn't believe that, either.

"I want my lawyer." Will said the magic words like an incantation and waited for a reaction, a puff of white smoke, something.

Dennis stopped talking, placed his hands on the table, and looked over at Mary with a look of profound disappointment. "You sure this is the way you want to go?"

"I want . . . my lawyer."

"Okay. Have it your way," Dennis said, pushing himself up out of his chair. "The longer you go away for, the better it looks in our files. Isn't that right, Mary?"

"He's right. This is going to be good for our résumés, bad for yours." Mary's voice had lost much of its southern drawl, and she looked at him with a keen glare that didn't seem like an act.

"You should also know that if you don't talk to us, we can't offer you protective custody," Mary said.

"Why do you think I need that?"

"Because two members of the Russian mob have just been killed. Their bosses just might consider you responsible for their deaths. We've been trying to build a case against the Red Fellas in this city for years. You have no idea what they are capable of."

"I think I have some idea."

"Nikolai and Yuri were so low on the totem pole that we'd never even heard of them before you showed up. If their bosses come after you . . . well, you better just hope they don't find you."

"Can I have the protective custody while I think about whether to talk?"

"No," Mary said. "You can't be arrested until you've been charged. And we can't put you in protective custody unless you've agreed to cooperate."

"I thought you were going to charge me with securities violations."

"Don't worry, we'll have you behind bars soon enough," Dennis said. "But we can't hold you for insider trading yet. That's not how it works. There's a procedure here that we have to follow."

"Can we get you a soda?" Mary asked.

"No, thank you. Can I leave now?"

"There's some paperwork we need to finish up," Mary said. "Just sit here for a while and we'll be back."

"I want to leave now. If you're telling me I can't do that, then I want to call my lawyer."

"Suit yourself," Mary said. "You can use that phone on the desk outside the conference room."

Will walked purposefully over to the phone, even though he still wasn't sure who he was going to dial. Finally, his mental Rolodex produced the result he had been searching for since he had arrived, a name that he hadn't thought of in at least seven years: his former law school classmate Jon Coulter. He dialed information on his cell phone and got an address for the Law Offices of Jon Coulter on Mission Street, not exactly the hallmark of a successful law practice.

When Will told the receptionist that he was being questioned at the offices of the Department of Justice, he was immediately put through to Coulter.

"Will Connelly!" Jon exclaimed in his flat Chicago accent. "It's been, what, seven years?"

"Are you still doing criminal law?" Will asked, cutting short any reminiscences.

"Yeah, what's up? What are you doing at the DOJ's offices?"

"I'm not in a place where I can speak freely right now, but agents from the DOJ and the SEC are here trying to ask me questions. I think they might charge me. I told them I wanted a lawyer. You're the only real criminal lawyer that I know."

"What do you think they might charge you with?"

"Well, they're talking about insider trading . . . and involvement with organized crime . . . the Russian mob . . . and a planned terrorist attack. Oh yeah, and I'm also suspected of murdering one of my former colleagues at Reynolds Fincher."

There was a lengthy silence on the other end of the line, and Will began to wonder if the connection had failed. "I'll be over there in a half hour or less," Jon said at last. "Don't say anything else until I get there."

"Okay."

"Don't even make small talk with the agents. I mean it—say nothing."

"Okay. I get it."

As he waited in the empty conference room for Jon to arrive, he recalled the day they met nine years ago when they were both first-years at Boalt Hall. Will first took notice of Jon in his contract law class. Each session, Professor Arthur Silver selected one student for Socratic dialogue, a form of intellectual blood sport in which the instructor quizzed one student throughout the entire hour on the minutiae of a single case.

Will still remembered the day that Professor Silver called on Jon. Everyone in the class took a particular interest in the contest that day because the student more than held his own. For someone who had obviously not spent a great deal of time reviewing the case, Jon acquitted himself surprisingly well, relying on a cursory reading of the case, quick-witted intelligence, and chutzpah.

Professor Silver was a small, balding man who had an impish sense of humor that he used to ingratiate himself to the class as a whole while simultaneously terrorizing and humiliating individual students with his belittling jokes. When Silver resorted to lamely mocking Jon's mispronunciation of *demurrer* ("Oh, so the defendant was shy and modest?"), the class recognized that, to the extent possible in the rigged game that was the first-year law school classroom, Jon had achieved a victory. It was a bloodied-but-still-standing, Rocky-Balboa sort of victory, but a victory nonetheless.

After class, Will congratulated Jon on his showing, and they had struck up a friendship and alliance for the remainder of their first year. Jon was only twenty-five then, but the blueprint for the middle-aged man was already apparent: slightly pudgy and his black hair was already thinning at the temples. A Chicago native, he was loyal to the ways of his homeland—chain smoker, drinker of Old Style beer, hopeless Cubs fan.

As a study partner, Jon displayed all of the virtues and the failings that were hinted at in Professor Silver's classroom that day. He had a quick mind and was able to master the course materials well enough to get a B or a C with relatively little effort. But his studies never achieved the histrionic meticulousness of those who were motivated by the fear of classroom humiliation. As a result, Jon never rose to the level of an A student.

Will always felt a little guilty that he had let his friendship with Jon slip away after the first year. The *Law Review* took up much of his time after class, and he began to hang out with the journal's staff and editors, whose sense of themselves as budding masters of the universe was unhealthy but contagious. Will continued to see Jon over the course of the remaining two years of law school, but their conversations grew shorter and more rote, ultimately reduced to a few comments on the latest travails of the beleaguered Cubbies.

After graduation, Will perused a list in the law school alumni magazine of the jobs that his classmates had taken. Jon had joined a criminal defense firm in Oakland that Will had never heard of. Now he had apparently opened his own practice. Will decided to reserve judgment as to whether that constituted a step up or a step down.

As promised, Jon arrived in less than a half hour, pushing through the conference room doors with Dennis close behind. Jon looked very much like he had eight years ago, only more so. The waistline had spread a little more and, obeying some principle of male physics, the hairline had receded in inverse proportion.

Jon shook hands with Will and whispered, "What the

fuck, Will?" Without waiting for a response, he then turned to face Dennis. "I'm going to need a few minutes alone with my client, but not in this room."

"Even if we had the recording equipment turned on, which we don't, it wouldn't be admissible," Dennis responded.

"Just the same. I'd like to use that unoccupied office over there."

Dennis grimaced. "Go ahead."

Once they were behind closed doors in the empty office, Will launched into an abbreviated version of his story. As Will spoke, Jon turned from time to time to watch Mary, Dennis, and the other agents as they filed to and from a room adjacent to the conference room.

When Will got to the part about the BART attack and his anonymous call to the police, Jon got up out of his chair and started pacing.

When Will had reached the end of his narrative, Jon said, "Holy fucking shit, man! You've managed to be my first organized-crime case, *and* my first terrorism case— all rolled into one—with a murder charge thrown in for good measure. I didn't think that anyone could manage that trifecta, much less one of my old law school classmates. This is some serious shit, Will. But at least you haven't been charged yet. Frankly, I'm not sure what they're waiting for."

"What do you propose that we do?"

"We're going to see if we can walk you out of here without someone deciding to place you in custody. Then we're going to regroup at my offices, where I can hear the whole story in more detail. But first I want to see what's going on in there," Jon said, pointing at the room into which Mary had just disappeared. "Wait for me in the conference room."

Jon entered the room adjoining the conference room. About thirty seconds later, Will heard raised voices inside. Then the door flew open, and Jon, Mary, and Dennis strode into the adjacent conference room, none of them looking happy. Will was startled to see that following them was Detective Kovach of the SFPD. Kovach was accompanied by someone Will had never seen before—a man in a dark suit, with graying blond hair and squinty eyes. Kovach and the squinting man had apparently been observing the proceedings in the conference room on a video monitor.

The entire group joined Will around the conference room table, with no one taking a seat.

Jon was the first to speak. "So exactly what kind of multi-jurisdictional clusterfuck is this, anyway?"

"Watch your tone," Dennis said.

"First, let me get the players straight," Jon said. "I understand what the DOJ, the SEC, and the SFPD are doing here, but who are you?" he asked the squinting man.

"David Pace. Department of Homeland Security."

"And what brings you to the clusterfuck?"

"I wish you would stop saying that," Pace said, looking pained. "There's a woman present."

"Oh, don't mind me," Mary said, clearly tickled by Jon's dramatic flair.

"I'm sure Mr. Connelly could probably explain my presence as well. His friends in the Russian *mafiya* are apparently doing business with a terrorist named Aashif Agha, whom we're trying to locate. An anonymous call was placed to the police about a possible attack on the BART system by Agha. We believe that call was placed by Mr. Connelly."

"Is my client being charged with something?"

"I'm just here in an observational role for the time being. We're trying to learn as much as we can about the dealings between Agha and the Russian *mafiya*."

"You sure you want to take this case on, counselor?" Dennis asked. "Where there's smoke there's usually fire, and we've got more smoke here than when the Oakland Hills burned."

"That's a good way of putting it, Agent Tyler," Jon said. "All I've heard so far is a lot of smoke and circumstantial evidence. Does anyone have an actual case against my client? If not, will someone please explain to me why we're still here? Apparently someone said something to Will about some paperwork. . . ."

"That was me," Mary said.

"And what sort of paperwork is that?"

"Just interview notes, which are now completed."

Jon swiveled to make eye contact with everyone gathered around the table. "Then I think we're done here."

There was silence around the table. Will noticed that Mary, Dennis, and Kovach were all casting glances at the man from Homeland Security, probably because his was the agency with the broadest discretion to detain Will, if he chose to use it.

The DHS agent simply shrugged. If Pace had known that Will had sat across a table from Aashif Agha, then Will would probably already be in a federal detention facility, and he most likely would never have even been granted access to a lawyer.

"You're free to go," Mary said, opening the door to the conference room.

Jon reached into his pocket for a handful of business cards and slid them around the table like he was dealing a hand of poker. "I probably don't have to say this, but I expect that there will be no further direct communications with my client."

Mary examined Jon's card, then said to Will, "You'd better hope that this guy is very, very good."

TWENTY-SIX

Jon drove Will back to his office on Mission Street, which was in a narrow two-story brick building wedged between a bodega and a pawnshop. Stenciled on the second floor window in elegant script were the words LAW OFFICES OF JONATHAN COULTER. In a cruder block-letter style, apparently added after market realities sank in, were the words ABOGADO—YO HABLO ESPAÑOL.

Mission Street, the main street of the city's Latino community, was never quiet. It clattered to the rhythms of five-and-dime commerce, with *taquerías* and bodegas coexisting alongside vintage clothing stores and bars catering to hipster youth. Most of the stores seemed ready to spring into a defensive nighttime posture, their doors and windows bracketed by steel-accordion fences and medieval iron bars.

They climbed the stairs of the building, past the offices

of a Spanish-language record label on the first floor. When Will opened the door, he thought that he had mistakenly entered a doctor's waiting room. Each of the three people seated around a coffee table wore bandages or casts. They all looked up at him with the simmering, subdued eyes of those in pain.

A receptionist with an attractively angular Spanish face was on the phone behind a desk. "You are what?" she asked, in a high, thin voice.

She narrowed her eyes as she listened, as if that would help her understand the person on the other end of the line. "You have been *what*?"

Another pause.

"Incarcerated!" she exclaimed. "You are in jail! What is the charge?"

She nodded into the phone. "Uh-huh. Well, that's not good." More nodding, as she saw that Jon and Will had arrived. "I'll put you through to Mr. Coulter."

"I have to take this," Jon said. "I'll join you in my office in a minute. By the way, this is Ingrid. Without her, this place couldn't exist. Hell, I couldn't exist."

Ingrid dropped her managerial frown and smiled.

Jon led Will back to his office, then went into an office next door to speak with his newly incarcerated client. "I'll be back in a minute," he said. "Deep cleansing breaths. Try to relax."

Two large windows let in the gray afternoon light and looked out on some surprisingly ornate cornicework on the adjacent building. On his desk, which was littered with files, was a photo of Jon and Ingrid grinning on a beach, his arm around her waist. Next to the framed picture sat a baseball signed by Ernie Banks, enshrined on a Lucite pedestal.

Ten minutes later, Jon returned and tossed a notepad on his desk.

"So you're a criminal lawyer," Will said. "Just like Perry Mason."

"Yep, *yo soy un abogado criminal.*"

"Sounds dramatic."

"Sounds that way, doesn't it? Actually, it has its moments. I do a little criminal defense, a little PI work. It was kinda dicey a couple of years ago, but now I'm pretty confident I can keep the doors of this place open."

"I saw the sign out front. I didn't know you spoke Spanish."

"Ingrid's the interpreter; she really helps me out with that. But I'm picking it up pretty fast. You open a law office in the Mission, you better *habla* that *español*. There's a guy down the street who advertises himself as *el mejor abogado*, but I've decided not to engage in an advertising war. Live and let live, I say."

Jon leaned forward and placed his elbows on the desk. "Will, I need to understand how you ended up in this shitstorm. I need to hear it all, and from the beginning."

"First, I need to know if Claire's okay."

"She's fine. They've taken her statement, and she was released before you were. Right now they seem to be viewing her as an innocent third party who got entangled in this mess because she was your friend."

"That is actually a pretty accurate statement."

"Okay," Jon said. "Now that we've gotten that out of the way, let's hear it."

Will told the story from beginning to end without holding anything back, from the morning that Ben Fisher died to his first encounter with Katya at the Whiskey Bar to his disclosure of insider information and his meeting with

Aashif Agha. He even admitted the theft of the encryption keys, although he minimized Claire's role to protect her. Will wasn't sure what loosened his tongue more, the presence of attorney-client privilege or the fact that his old friend Jon was sitting across the desk from him, his sympathetic nods interrupted only by muttered exclamations like "Jesus!" and "Holy shit!"

Finally, when he had reached the end of his story, Will asked, "Can you help me?"

"Well, this is not my usual turf. I'm sure you could find someone who's better qualified. I could get you a referral. . . ."

"I know this is not what you usually do. But I want someone I can trust, someone who won't view this as just another case. So what I'm asking is, *can* you do it? Because if you can, then I'd like your help."

Jon considered the question for a moment. "Well, yeah, I could do it. I've handled securities fraud defense cases in the past, and I've defended a couple of murder charges. I might need some help, though, in thinking about how best to protect you from an anti-terrorism prosecution if anyone finds out that you've taken those encryption keys. But even if we're just talking about securities fraud, I want to make sure that you understand the stakes. You may be best served by bringing in a heavy hitter."

"And what are the stakes?"

"Well, the evidence against you for Ben Fisher's murder is pretty circumstantial right now. But if Ben's cell phone turns up with that video on it, then it's a whole different ball game. Right now, I'm more worried about the securities fraud case. They're probably much closer to charging you there. That's why the SEC was leading the interviews today, and the PD and Homeland Security were in the background. You could be looking at as much as five to ten years in a federal prison on an insider trading conviction."

"Why such a heavy sentence?"

"Two reasons. One, you were with a big law firm, and it will make headlines and send a message if they put you away. The SEC doesn't have a big enough budget to pursue a lot of prosecutions, so they like cases that they think will have an *in terrorum* effect. Besides, every time an affluent white guy with a law degree goes to jail, another SEC agent gets his wings."

"Thanks for finding the humor in my nightmare." Will was surprised at how quickly they fell back into their old mocking banter. Maybe they just knew no other way of talking to each other. "Okay. So what's the other reason?"

"This is a joint prosecution with the DOJ. If they think you can help them make a case against a member of the Russian mob, they'll apply every bit of pressure that they can. So you'll have two federal agencies competing to see who can fuck you over the most."

"But I don't really know anything about the Russian *mafiya*. I only dealt with Nikolai and Yuri, and they're both dead."

"What about that memory stick you mentioned? Where is that?"

Will had forgotten that he was carrying it. He reached into his pants pocket and placed the silver plastic memory stick on Jon's desk.

"So that's it?"

"That's it. The back door to everyone's most confidential information."

That silenced Jon, but only for a moment. "Those agents are such screwups. They could have easily detained you in a holding cell, at least for a while. And if they had processed you, they would have taken your possessions and found the memory stick."

"I guess I was lucky."

"Maybe. Does the Russian *mafiya* know that you have this?"

"I don't know. Nikolai and Yuri knew that we had stolen it, but they're both dead. I guess it's possible that they didn't tell anyone else. Maybe they wanted to be heroes and bring it to their bosses by themselves—to make up for the loss on the Jupiter investment."

Jon rubbed his temple. "Do you know much about the Russian mob here in San Francisco?"

"Only what Yuri and Nikolai told me, and it was always hard to tell how much of that was just posturing."

"Well, I don't represent wiseguys. I don't even represent dealers, only possession cases. But when you do criminal law, you hear a few stories. The head of the *mafiya* here is supposed to be a guy called Boka."

"That's who Nikolai and Yuri said they were working for."

"Have you met him?"

"No."

"Good. Do you think that he knows who you are?" Jon sounded anxious.

"Yes, he must. If the Jupiter investment really cost him a half million, then I'm sure he knows all about me. And I'm sure he knows about the plan to get the encryption keys. You're going to scare me now, aren't you?"

"It's likely that you could help yourself on the securities charges if you cooperate in making a case against Boka and his crew. Have they offered you protective custody yet?"

"They offered it, if I start talking. But I wasn't ready to do that yet."

"Some of the regulars down at the courthouse tell a story about a witness who was going to testify against Boka's organization in a RICO case."

"What happened?"

Jon looked away. "For all I know, it's just a bullshit story. The courthouse is full of them."

"Just tell me!"

"They say that when they found the body he was missing his head, his hands . . . and his balls. It's supposed to be their trademark."

Will slumped in his chair. "Talk about your *in terrorum* remedies. I'm a dead man, aren't I?"

"Well, you're definitely in danger until you're in custody. And if you decide to talk to the feds, you'll probably have to go into witness protection, which they should be willing to offer. You need to understand where this could go before you say a word."

"Just tell me what you think I should do."

"Well, the one thing you had going for you was that you probably weren't dealing with real members of the Russian mob, just a couple of wannabes. But if they know you have the encryption keys, or they even suspect it, then that raises the stakes."

"So what do you recommend?"

"I think we need to open up a dialogue with the DOJ and SEC. Try to feel them out on what kind of case they have. In the meantime, you should lay low, stay out of public places, and we'll see if there's a deal to be made with the feds. I can hold the encryption keys for you if you like."

"No, I need to be responsible for that. If you held them, that would put you at risk."

Jon picked up the memory stick and examined it. "Do you even know for sure that this is what you think it is?"

"Well, no, not really. A programmer at Jupiter told us that the keys are stored on it."

"Can you think of any reason why we shouldn't take a look to confirm?" Jon asked. Will shook his head.

Jon removed the cap on the memory stick and inserted it into a port on his desktop computer. He opened the file with a click, and a large table appeared on the screen full of long strings of numbers. Each number changed every ten seconds or so, making the document seem as if it were undulating like a living thing. Jon and Will stared at the flickering numbers. What had Riley called it? The keys to the kingdom.

"So what if the government does learn that I've taken the encryption keys?" Will asked.

"I've never handled a terrorism case, but my understanding is that if the government has solid evidence, they'll bring it to criminal court. If the case is not so good, they might try you before a military tribunal."

"What would happen then?"

"I don't know," Jon said. "How long can you hold your breath underwater?"

TWENTY-SEVEN

Taking Jon's advice, Will went into hiding. He knew better than to return to his condo in the marina. Instead, he purchased another disposable cell phone at a convenience store and headed for the Hyatt Regency at Embarcadero Center. Checking in at the registration desk, Will hoped that he was as small and anonymous as he felt standing under the enormous vaulted atrium of the John Portman–designed convention hotel. This time, he paid cash for the room. Will slept fitfully that night as his thoughts kept returning to his plans for the coming day.

Will waited for the sun to come up, then used the disposable phone to call Jon's office at seven thirty A.M. Fortunately, Jon was an early riser, and he reached him. "What's up? Are you okay?" Jon asked.

"Well, no, I'm not, but that's not why I'm calling. I wanted to know if you've managed to reach the feds yet."

"I did. I spoke to that DOJ agent, Mary Boudreaux, at the end of the day yesterday. I got a funny vibe from her."

"Funny how?"

Jon hesitated. "Are you calling me on a clean line?"

"Yeah, it's safe."

"Well, mine isn't. Let me give you a number." Jon gave Will the number of a pay phone outside his office.

When the conversation resumed, Jon said, "I think maybe they're not satisfied with their case against you."

"What did Agent Boudreaux say?"

"The same line as before. That you should come in and cooperate because you're in danger. That sentencing would be lighter if you talked. I think they're trying to bluff you into taking a deal."

"I thought they'd given up on all that and were just going to bring charges."

"Yeah, I thought so, too. I tried to press her on when you would be charged and I got the impression that it won't be anytime soon."

Will stood up from his couch. "How did she put it . . . exactly?"

"She said, 'We're assembling our case. Tell your client not to go anywhere for a while.'"

"For a while."

"Yeah. For a while."

"Do you think maybe this is not as bad as we thought?"

"I wouldn't go that far. It wouldn't take much to establish a link between you and the Russians . . . a handwritten note, a phone record, a security video. Maybe they already have enough to charge you, but want to wait until they're confident that they can convict. This case will get press coverage, so they don't want to start something they can't finish. On a positive note, though, look at what we do know. Nikolai and Yuri are both dead. You didn't actually purchase or trade in Jupiter or Pearl stock. There's circumstantial evidence that you tipped Nikolai and Yuri, but, as far we know, there isn't a paper trail."

"There's the fact that I was caught looking for insider information on the firm's computers."

"At most, that was grounds for terminating your employment. It doesn't really help the feds make their case. Besides, you said yourself that you could have just been looking for a form."

"And how about the case Detective Kovach is trying to make against me for Ben Fisher's murder?"

"I don't think it's as strong as they would like," Jon said. "It wouldn't be hard to establish reasonable doubt. For starters, they don't have motive. They can place you with Ben immediately before his death. The fact that you deny that you met with Ben looks bad, even if it's true, but that doesn't prove that you killed him."

"There is that video on Ben's cell phone."

"Yes, if they had that, they would prosecute. Let's just hope it never turns up."

"What about Claire?"

"They have nothing on her. She hasn't even been seriously threatened with charges. As far as they can tell, she's just your girlfriend and was kidnapped by the Russians to put more pressure on you. As long as no one figures out that she took those encryption keys, she'll be okay."

"She may be okay with the SEC and DOJ, but what about the Russians?"

There was silence on the line. "I could talk to her, tell her that she should find a place to hide out for a while."

"And my mother. They know where my mother lives. What am I supposed to do?"

"I think you should leave town. Don't leave the state, though, and keep me posted on where you're staying in case they decide to charge you."

"You think I'm in danger?"

"I sure wouldn't hang around waiting to find out."

"What about you? If I'm in hiding, they're going to figure that you would know where to find me."

"Don't worry about me," Jon said testily. "I know how to stay out of trouble."

After his call with Jon, Will stood under a hot shower as the thoughts that had been ricocheting around in his head the night before began to order themselves. He was not going to simply hide out, waiting for federal agents to make their case against him or for Boka's men to come for him, or his mother, or Claire. And he had no interest in committing himself to the half-life of a witness protection program. Even if he went to prison, he was sure that the Russians could get to him if they wanted to. If he was going to extricate himself, he would need more information about Boka and what he wanted from him. He needed to know if his suspicions were right and it really was Richard Grogan who had betrayed him at the firm. And he also needed to find out who had Ben's cell phone and the incriminating video. The only place where he could go for that kind of information was Katya.

———

Will figured that Katya's workplace would be a neutral and relatively safe place where he could ask her a few pointed questions. The offices of Equilon Securities were located in an inauspicious building at Folsom and Second Street, an address that was fine if you were looking for a tattoo, not a growth fund. Most securities firms were located in the

financial district a few blocks north, closer to the Pacific
Stock Exchange, but commerce abhors a vacuum, and so
many unlikely businesses were drawn to "SoMa," the south
of Market area, by favorable rental rates.

The directory in the cramped lobby showed Equilon Securities in Suite 302. Will took the elevator to the third floor
and stood before the door to 302. There was no sign in the
hallway and no sound of voices or ringing phones coming
from within. Will recalled how busy the place had sounded
when he had called Katya before their meeting at Justin
Herman Plaza.

Will tried the door, which was unlocked. Inside was
a large office suite that was almost entirely empty, except for some desks and a few disconnected phones. Will
knew he was in the right place, though, because a glass
placard bearing the Equilon Securities logo lay on the
floor, propped against what had once been the reception
desk.

Equilon Securities was a sham business—probably one
of a long line of phony operations that the *mafiya* had used
to defraud the gullible. The security guard downstairs told
Will that Equilon must have moved during the night because he had shown up for work two days ago to find the
offices deserted.

Next, Will went to Katya's house on Pacific Street,
where he had spent the night with her, only to be greeted
in the morning by Nikolai and Yuri. He sat in his car down
the block from her building, waiting for her to appear. The
morning fog burned off and the sun came out. The interior
of the car warmed up and he rolled down the windows.

After an hour and a half, Katya emerged from the building, wearing jeans and a peasant blouse. Katya got into her
Toyota Camry, which was parked out front, and drove away.

Will followed her at a discreet distance as she made her way to Geary and the Russian restaurant Dacha. After parking on the street, Katya disappeared into the restaurant.

Will figured that the restaurant was probably under federal surveillance, particularly after his anonymous call linking Boka to the terrorist plot, so he parked his car far down the block. He knew that he shouldn't be seen anywhere near the place, but he wasn't willing to just wait for the next bad thing to happen. He watched the surly waitress arrive for her shift.

Screw it, Will thought, *I'm going in.* He needed to know who at the firm had set him up, and Katya was the only person that he could ask. He knew that it was dangerous to walk into Boka's headquarters, but there was some security in knowing that the feds were watching. Boka and his men would certainly be aware of that, too.

When Will entered the restaurant, his eyes took a moment to adjust to the gloom. Then he saw Katya sitting at a corner table, already observing him. As usual, he couldn't quite tell if she was smiling. In the past, the trait had lent her an appealing aura of mystery. Now it just annoyed him.

Will approached Katya's table. "I thought you'd be a little more surprised to see me."

"I am surprised that you would come here," she said. "Not a very good idea."

"Why is that?"

"This is Boka's place. You should be running *away* from Boka."

The waitress materialized at their table, waiting for their order with her customary pained expression.

"Vodkas," Katya said. "He'll have a double." After the waitress departed, she added, "I don't expect you to believe me, but it is kind of nice to see you again."

"But you didn't think you would, did you? You thought Nikolai and Yuri would have killed me by now."

Katya shrugged noncommittally, then stood up from the table and motioned for Will to stand. "I am willing to have this conversation with you, but first . . ."

Katya patted him down for a wire, and when she was satisfied, they sat down again at the table. "Okay, ask your questions. Maybe I can even answer a few of them."

"First, how can I trust anything you say?"

"There's no need to be insulting," she said. "You know you can't trust me. I think we established that. But you don't have anyone else to ask, do you?"

"What is your role here, anyway? Were you sleeping with Yuri?"

"Yuri and I had known each other for a long time. We were together sometimes, on and off. We understood each other."

"So what exactly is your connection with Boka?"

"He looks after me."

"But what is it that you actually *do*?"

"What they ask. Sometimes it's as simple as working as a receptionist in one of their fake businesses. Sometimes they need me to be nice to someone like you."

"You know there's another word for that."

She smiled, as if she couldn't begrudge Will his opinion of her. "Someday, Boka is going to finance my restaurant, and then I'll be on my own."

"If you think that someone like Boka will ever give you anything, then you're not as smart as I thought."

"Who are you to say? You don't know Boka, do you?"

"No, but am I wrong about him?"

Katya didn't answer, turning to the waitress, who had brought the vodkas. The waitress lingered for a moment, probably trying to decide if they posed a threat to the glasses or crockery. Katya said something to her in Russian, and she returned to the kitchen, appeased.

"You and your friends knew about the Jupiter deal, and you knew right away that I had been assigned to take over from Ben. That tells me that you are working with someone else at the firm. I need to know who that is."

"We do have a mutual acquaintance. I was going to say a friend, but I guess that is not the right word."

"Who is it?"

"I can't say. I probably shouldn't have said that much."

"I thought it was strange that you knew about the company."

Katya smiled. "I could have known that. And, like I said, I do read the *Chronicle*. Okay, maybe I exaggerated about the *Wall Street Journal*."

"How did you know I would be at that club?"

"We followed you from your office. Simple."

"You knew they were going to torture me, maybe kill me."

"I knew that Yuri had a lot riding on the deal. He was just doing what he thought was necessary. As he used to say, 'It's not personal, just business.'"

"Yeah, that sounds like Yuri, all right." Even from the grave, Yuri continued to pay homage to Coppola.

Will continued, "This isn't just business. Did you know that they threatened my mother—my mother who's in a nursing home?"

"I am sorry about that, Will—really. But that's not my part of the job. You can try to make me feel guilty if you want to, but that's not a very good use of our time, is it?"

"I need to know who has Ben Fisher's cell phone."

"I really don't know, Will. And I couldn't tell you if I did."

Will tossed back his vodka and stood up. "Is there anything else that you can tell me about the person who gave you my name?"

"It's someone you wouldn't expect."

"That doesn't exactly help, does it?"

"If I say anything more, I'll have to answer to Boka. You're really not so dumb. You'll figure it out."

Searching for a cigarette, Katya rifled through her purse just as she had when she first caught his attention in the Whiskey Bar.

With a small look of triumph, Katya produced a cigarette from her purse, then looked up to meet his gaze. He stared back at her with contempt.

Seemingly reading his thoughts, she stood up and stepped in close, as she had that first night in her apartment on Pacific Street. Then she leaned upward on her toes and kissed him, but the kiss was nothing like their first. Their teeth struck as she pressed her lips hard against his in a kiss that would have been the perfect complement to angry sex. Will found himself returning the kiss in the spirit in which it was given. Finally, she broke away, biting his lip and giving him a shove in the chest.

Will touched his finger to his lip. When he drew it away, it was smeared with blood.

Like a fighter breaking from a clinch, Katya stepped back from him. Her face was flushed as she stood watching him, waiting for him to leave, adjusting her skirt. There was absolutely nothing left to say.

As if on cue, a door at the rear of the restaurant opened. It was the same door that Valter had left through the night that Nikolai and Yuri had brought him there. Two men emerged, wearing matching Puma tracksuits in chocolate brown and moss green, respectively. One was tall, with short blond hair and a puffy, vaguely misshapen face; he looked like a once-handsome middleweight who hadn't stopped boxing quite soon enough. He wore the jacket of his tracksuit zipped all the way up like a turtleneck. His companion was stocky, dark, and hirsute, like a cross between a shot-putter and a trained bear cub, with a dense thatch of matted fur exposed above the zipper of his open jacket. A gold medallion nested in the thicket of chest hair.

"Come with us," the tall man said, taking his arm. "Boka would like to see you."

"I'm not going in there," Will said, pulling away. "There are people who know that I came—"

"Now is not the time to plead for your life," he said. "That comes later."

TWENTY-EIGHT

The Russian track team forcefully escorted him through the doorway at the rear of the dining room. He was led down a short corridor thick with cigarette smoke into an office. Inside, the tall man patted him down, doing a much more thorough job than Katya had. When he was satisfied, he motioned for Will to take a seat in a chair in front of a large desk.

Behind the desk sat a small, well-groomed man in a three-button, gray Armani suit. The man had a hard, un-lined face; he looked like he had been designed in a wind tunnel. The man's eyes were fixed on some papers before him on the desk.

Will almost smiled. Ignoring the newly arrived guest was a classic method of asserting dominance. Will had first encountered the technique when he was a first-year associate arriving in a partner's office with his first completed assignment.

While being studiously disregarded by the man behind the desk, Will examined his surroundings. The office was surprisingly well appointed, considering it was located in the back room of a dive restaurant. The walls were decorated with framed Kandinsky lithographs. On a corner of the mahogany desk sat a large amber paperweight with a spindly primordial insect imprisoned inside.

After a few protracted moments, the man looked up and trained his deep-set, pale gray eyes on Will.

"Will Connelly." He had a heavy Russian accent and a voice that glided from one note to another like an oboe.

"Yes."

"My name's Boris. My friends call me Boka. Do you know who I am?"

"The boss?" Will ventured.

This drew an approximation of a smile. "Yes. Exactly so." The smile hung frozen on his face like a theatrical scrim, concealing as much as it displayed.

"You've got balls showing up here like this," Boka said. "But it is not good for either of us. It reflects poor judgment. Makes me wonder who the fuck I am dealing with."

"I got tired of waiting for something to happen."

"He wants something to happen," Boka said to the tracksuits, amused. Then, to Will, "You pull shit like this, something is going to happen, but I don't think you are going to like it very much." One of them snorted appreciatively.

"But you are clearly an impatient man," Boka said, "so I will get to the point. You have cost me a lot of fucking money. The only reason you're not dead right now is because it was not your idea."

"I never told them to put money in Jupiter stock."

"Yes," Boka said. "I believe that's what I just said." He paused, then resumed in a calmer, didactic tone. "Do you know how many imbeciles I deal with in the course of a day?"

Will decided that the question was rhetorical.

"Fear makes people stupid. And when someone is sitting where you are sitting right now, they are usually afraid. I try to reassure them, calm them down, but it is no use. So all day long I find myself dealing with idiots, people who are so focused on their own fears, their own needs, that they have lost the ability to listen." He gently tapped his forehead once with the flat of his palm. "Their eyes never stop moving. They are unable to concentrate, unable to help themselves. It can be quite frustrating. I'm sure you encounter this in your profession."

"Yes."

"Okay. I am going to try to forget about the many foolish things that you have done and assume that you are a person of intelligence. I will speak to you directly, with respect. And I will expect the same in return."

Will nodded.

"Okay. You have spoken to the federal agents. What have you told them about us?"

"Nothing. I've said nothing to them about any of you." Will decided that this answer, in addition to being true, was probably the least dangerous.

"But surely you must have said something to them about Nikolai or Yuri?"

"No."

"What about Valter . . . and Katya?"

"No."

"So you have not explained to them how you got involved in that ugly scene at the parade? It is only natural to want to explain yourself."

"I just listened to what they had to say, then I asked for my lawyer."

"You cannot make *this* stop by asking for a lawyer, though, can you?"

Boka picked up a stick of rock sugar from a saucer and swirled it in a cup of tea that sat on his desk. He sipped the tea and, unsatisfied, stuck the rock sugar in his mouth like a lollipop. In the silence of the room, Will could hear the crystals click against his teeth.

"You know that we could be taking a more . . . *rigorous* . . . approach." Boka uttered the word with the clinical but freighted intonation of a doctor describing a radical therapy.

"Yes."

"Methods that would make that blade that Nikolai and Yuri used on you seem gentle by comparison."

"Yes, I appreciate that."

Boka gave a small, dry laugh that sounded more like a clearing of the throat. "Now when you say *that*, I believe it." He waved his hand. "Please, keep talking. Tell me more about your conversation with the agents."

"If I told them what I know about Nikolai and Yuri and the rest, then they would know that I was guilty of securities fraud. It was in my own best interest to keep quiet and let my lawyer handle things. If I incriminate myself, I'll never practice law again."

"Is it that important to you? Practicing law?"

"It's what I do."

"I see. But how do we know that your lawyer is not simply getting you the best deal in exchange for what you know about us? Maybe they are telling you that you can still salvage your career if you testify."

"Because we don't think they have a case against me that will stand up."

Boka started to nod. "And why is that?"

"With Nikolai and Yuri dead, there is nothing to directly link me to the trading in Jupiter stock. It's not enough for a criminal prosecution."

"No smoking gun, as you say."

"Right. So there's no need for me to make a deal."

"I hope you aren't tempted to give them information just because you think we are bad men who belong in jail."

"I really don't know anything about you."

"I hope you know enough to be scared. You should also know that we have this." Boka reached into his desk drawer and held up a cell phone. "This is Ben Fisher's phone, with the video implicating you in his murder. I think Detective Kovach would find this very interesting. And then, of course, there's your mother—and the girl, Claire."

"Clearly, you've got me. So what do you want from me?"

"I want two things. The first is your silence. But I don't want you to just say it. I must know that it is true. You know, in many ways, it would be simpler just to kill you. But the Department of Justice is already watching us, and they know that we may be connected to this matter. If we killed a potential witness, they would be swarming around here like gnats for the next year. That kind of attention adds to the cost of doing business. For now, they are focused on Yuri and Nikolai, who were outsiders, for all their ambitions. And that's how it will stay."

"You can trust me to remain silent." Will's eyes wandered to a plaque on the wall behind Boka's desk. Inlaid in lacquered oak and brass was a photo of a girls' soccer team. The players looked to be about eleven years old. Standing in the center of the picture and beaming with pride was

Boka. He was wearing a soccer jersey and a chrome-plated whistle hung from his neck.

Boka noticed Will looking at the picture. He picked up the amber paperweight and rolled it from one hand to the other. "We are not afraid of Justice or the FBI. They've been trying to make a case against us for years. But if they can't put you in jail, then they think they have to at least harass you to justify their miserable fucking existences. You see, if we kill you, then I'm going to have to explain to my daughter Natalya why there are men sitting in the stands at her soccer match taking pictures of me, making their rude and unfunny jokes. And I would rather not have to do that. Besides, my girls are going to be defending their league championship this season. They need to focus."

"If you let me walk out of here, I swear you will never hear from me again."

"I appreciate the sentiment, but if I have you shot and buried in a construction site, I won't hear from you again, either."

"What do you want me to say? I won't talk. I don't really know anything, anyway."

Boka studied him for a bit. "Then I'm going to ask you another question," he said.

"Yes?"

"I want to know if you have the encryption keys for what they call the Clipper Chip. You know what I'm talking about, don't you?"

"Yes, but I don't have them."

"You should answer me truthfully, Will."

"Yuri and Nikolai wanted me to get them, but I didn't know how. Jupiter uses every high-tech security measure imaginable to protect those encryption keys."

"I was wondering why Nikolai and Yuri would chase you like that at the parade."

"I really don't know—I thought they just wanted to kill me. They didn't have a chance to say anything to me before they died."

Once more, Boka studied him. Will was certain that his face revealed just how addled by fear he was.

"I'm glad that you came here," Boka said. "It gives me a chance to see if you seem clever enough to know what is best for you. Some decisions must be based on personal observation."

Finally, Will asked the question that he knew could be his last: "So, what have you decided?"

"I think I will let you live—let you carry on with your fucked-up life. Aren't you going to say *thank you*?"

"Thanks."

"You know, Will, we don't like civilian casualties. We've already had one in this matter. Besides, you did not seek us out. We came to you. If you were some fool who had borrowed money from us, or came to us with his fucked-up business, that would be another story. Then I would have to kill you—as a matter of principle. Also, you are lucky that Nikolai and Yuri were freelancers. If you had been responsible for the deaths of men who really worked for me then, again, I would have had to kill you."

"I'm grateful. But can I ask you a question?"

"Okay."

"I believe that you were working with someone at the law firm. Someone other than Ben Fisher. I would like to know who that is. In exchange for my silence."

"I am letting you live in exchange for your silence. Isn't that enough?" Boka paused. "Did Katya say something to you?"

"No, it just seems logical."

"You are pressing your luck, Will Connelly."

"You think I've been lucky?"

"You are the luckiest son of a bitch alive on the planet," Boka said, casting a meaningful look at the two men in tracksuits.

Will recognized with a queasy shock that Boka's look was meant to convey irony. He was making a joke that he thought Will was too stupid and distracted to appreciate. Will was anything but lucky, because Boka did intend to have him killed after all. He just wasn't going to do it in the restaurant, which was his base of operations. The FBI and DOJ probably had the place under surveillance. Boka was simply taking advantage of the opportunity that Will had provided to question him about his conversations with the federal agents and try to determine whether Will had the encryption keys. Because Will had apparently convinced Boka that he'd been unable to obtain the keys, Boka saw no further reason to let him live.

Boka waved his hand with an air of exasperation. "We're done here. Go. Go now."

Will rose from the chair slowly and walked somewhat unsteadily to the door, still uncertain whether he would feel the impact of a bullet before he could turn the knob. He felt an overpowering sense of relief as he opened the door and entered the hallway leading back to the restaurant.

Katya was gone. A cadre of elderly Russians played cards at a corner table. Will hurried out of the smoky restaurant, and his head immediately felt clearer in the fresh air. He walked quickly down Geary for several blocks, looking behind him repeatedly for a glimpse of a tracksuit or a slow-moving sedan.

He cast a suspicious glance into a Russian grocery, mo-

mentarily struck by the paranoid notion that the man behind the butcher's counter with the bloodstained apron was
watching him. Staring at the butcher through the plate glass
window covered with Cyrillic lettering, the scene looked
like a frame from an incomprehensibly subtitled foreign
film.

As he put more blocks between himself and the restaurant, he grew more confident that he was not being followed.
He walked on past the alternating Russian and Korean establishments until he stopped before an onion-domed Russian Orthodox church, which was incongruously adjacent
to a Shell station.

Passing through this patchwork neighborhood, he did
not get the sense of a transplanted culture with its roots
sunk deep, as he did in New York's Little Italy or San
Francisco's own Chinatown. Instead, the various Russian,
Korean, and Thai merchants looked like they were fight-
ing a losing battle to preserve their tenuous beachheads on
Geary Street against the encroachments of 7-Elevens, Taco
Bells, and Jiffy Lubes.

He entered a Russian deli and wandered the aisles, examining the foreign labels with their cartoonish depictions
of black bears and Cossacks in fur hats. The Russian émi-
grés who were the store's customers took their time at the
counter to speak in Russian with the proprietor behind the
register, which seemed to be as much a part of the transaction as the purchases of smoked salmon and pickled
herring. Will watched the dark-haired, high-cheekboned
people file in and out of the store. He found it difficult to
imagine that someone he knew formed the link between
himself, this insular community, and the thieves' world that
existed beneath it.

Will compiled a mental list of the Reynolds attorneys

who had played roles in the deal. There was Dave Gleason, the securities specialist. Judy Carlson, the fifth-year associate who had drafted several sections of the merger agreement. Richard Grogan and Sam Bowen, the heads of the corporate department, who had ensured that the deal was appropriately staffed with associates and provided veteran advice on managing board communications. And, of course, Claire had led the due diligence team. Although he still had no proof, he felt certain that Richard Grogan was the attorney who was working with the Russians. It explained why Richard had been so determined to have Claire fired right after she uncovered the connection between Jupiter and the NSA.

Will needed to find a way to positively link Richard to Boka's organization. If he was going to get out of the crosshairs of the DOJ, the SEC, the SFPD, and Homeland Security, he had to give them someone better to focus on. He would give them Richard Grogan. Will decided it was time to visit Claire, who knew almost as much about the Jupiter-Pearl merger and the workings of the firm as he did. Perhaps Claire could help him make the connection that was eluding him.

He was still standing in the aisle of the Russian grocery, and the proprietor was now eyeing him suspiciously from behind the register. Will replaced a can of imported salmon on the shelf and hurried outside, a bell jangling as the door smacked shut.

TWENTY-NINE

Will pressed the buzzer in the doorway of Claire's Jackson Square apartment building and shoved his hands into his jacket pockets. The temperature was already beginning to drop as the afternoon sun hung low, bouncing an orange glare off the windshields of the parked cars on the street.

Claire's voice crackled through the intercom. "Who's there?"

"It's Will."

The buzzer sounded. By the time he reached the second-floor landing, Claire was standing in her doorway, wearing a gray sweatshirt and sweatpants. Her blond hair was disheveled. Pulsing dance music was coming from the stereo, and on the television a suburban ninja army of a dozen men and women in aerobics outfits were throwing punches at the air in unison.

"My Tae Bo DVD," she gasped. "Let me turn this off."

The music stopped, and the figures on the screen froze mid punch.

Will grabbed her by the shoulders and gave her a kiss. "I've missed you. I wanted to come sooner, but I wasn't sure if it was a good idea with the kind of scrutiny we're under."

"I'm glad you did."

"How did your interviews with the SEC and DOJ go?"

"I really couldn't tell. That's why I was working out—to relieve the stress of not knowing."

"What did you tell them?"

"The truth, or at least parts of it. I said that we were seeing each other, that you took me out to that hotel by the park, and that I was kidnapped by the Russians. I left out the part about me stealing the encryption keys from Jupiter. And I said you didn't really tell me what was going on."

"You lied to federal agents. We need to make sure they never figure that out."

"I know. But the alternative was calling a lawyer. If I had done that, they would have viewed me as a suspect."

Will told Claire about his meeting with Boka and his theory that Richard Grogan had set him up.

"Well, I always thought Richard was evil," Claire said, completing an orbit of her small apartment. "But I thought he was just law-firm-partner evil, not FBI's-Most-Wanted evil."

"Did you ever notice anything, or hear anything, about Richard that would suggest that he could be involved in something like this? Maybe some bit of gossip among the associates?"

"I've got nothing," Claire said. "Maybe you should think of this like a legal research project, like you were searching for a case on Lexis. What you need is another term to narrow your search."

Will walked to the window and looked down at Jackson Square. After a moment, he turned and pointed to Claire's computer. "Do you mind if I use this?"

Claire nodded. "Have a seat."

Will connected to the Internet and went to the Reynolds Fincher website. Claire watched the monitor over his shoulder for a while, then went into the kitchen and started putting dishes in the dishwasher. "I find it calming," she explained.

He was not optimistic that he would find any clues on the website, but now that he was an outsider to the firm, his resources were limited. Will began by looking at the biography of Richard Grogan.

Will found nothing but the usual recitation of degrees and honors. He was not surprised to see that Grogan's biography was far too long to fit on a single webpage, a sure sign of an unchecked ego.

He tried another tack, Googling his own name along with the word *Russia*, hoping that the Internet might, in Ouija board–like fashion, reveal the nexus between himself and the *mafiya*. Although the search results failed to turn up anything, he was surprised to find that the browser still produced links to his bio on the Reynolds Fincher website. The browser obviously used archived pages for its searches because all references to him had been immediately expunged from the website after his firing. Maybe, in this alternate Internet universe, there was still a version of himself showing up for work each day at Embarcadero Center.

Will returned to the law firm's website and explored it like someone peering in the windows of a house where he once lived. On the home page, he noticed that the website had a search feature. He typed in the search term *Russia*.

Seconds later, he was presented with five search results.

First, there was a link to the brochure for the firm's international law practice, touting representation of a U.S.-based oil company that did business in Russia. Next were the bios of three attorneys who claimed to speak Russian. Last, and most surprisingly, was a link to the bio of Sam Bowen.

A shot of Sam appeared on the screen, alongside a list of his credentials. Duke Law School. Articles editor, *Duke Law Review*. Experience in mergers and acquisitions. Will froze when he saw one of the last items: "Author, 'Doing Business in Russia: Opportunities and Perils in the Post-Soviet Economy,' *International Lawyer*, February 2000."

As Will studied the grinning photo, he reflected on his dealings with Sam over the years for signs of something sinister behind the hail-fellow-well-met demeanor. Did he see corruption in the professionally lit face in the photo? He definitely recognized in Sam someone who might pursue a lucrative opportunity, whether in the post-Soviet economy or elsewhere, and, through an overabundance of confidence in his own abilities, fail to recognize the perils. However, an article in an obscure legal journal was hardly proof of Sam's involvement with the *mafiya*.

Will called out to Claire, "You worked on some deals with Sam Bowen, right?"

"That's right. You don't think it's Sam, do you?"

"I don't know yet. He does international transactions. Do you know if he's ever done one in Russia?"

"No, I don't think so." Claire paused with a dish in her hand, then placed it on the counter. "Wait a minute . . . he did start one, but it never went anywhere. I was going to be on the deal team."

"What kind of transaction?"

"A joint venture that was going to bring U.S.-style supermarkets to Russia."

"Supermarkets?"

"Yeah, a regional chain in the Midwest, Branson's, was going to share some of their distribution and supply-chain management know-how with a group of Russian entrepreneurs who understood how things get done over there."

"So what happened?"

"I don't know. My guess is that Branson finally figured out how screwed up the Russian economy is. One day Sam was calling us from Moscow, giving us a travelogue about seeing the Kremlin and Red Square, stuff like that. Then all of a sudden, he was back in the office. When anybody asked, he just snapped at them, which was unusual for him."

"Sam is nothing if not a nice guy."

Katya had lied to him about many things, but he didn't doubt that she had been speaking the truth when she told him the story of Nikolai "the Grocer" and his brief success in the thuggish world of Moscow commerce. He did not know how Nikolai and Sam had crossed paths, but he was certain that the failed U.S.-Russian joint venture was the connection. It was Sam who had brought Nikolai and Yuri into his life. Sam, with whom he'd worked daily since he was a first-year associate. Sam, his mentor.

Will turned off the computer and stood up.

"So does this mean you think Sam is the one, not Richard?"

"I think so, yeah."

Will moved toward the door. Claire came around the kitchen counter to block his path.

"Where do you think you're going?" she asked, mopping a strand of blond hair off her cheek.

"I just need some time to sort this out. Figure out what to do next."

"I'm going with you."

"I'm fine, really."

"I know you probably want to go and threaten Sam Bowen or something silly like that. Well, I'm not going to let your raging testosterone get you into trouble." She blocked the door, her chin up and a smile tugging at the corner of her mouth.

"Raging testosterone, huh?"

"Totally raging," she affirmed.

He laughed, for the first time in quite a while. It was nice to have someone on his side.

Claire quickly washed up in the bathroom and changed into a pair of jeans and a yellow T-shirt. As she was picking up her purse from her desk by the window, she paused, looking out at the street.

"That's funny," she said.

"What?" Will asked.

"There are these two guys outside wearing Puma track-suits. And they really don't look like they're members of a track team."

Will dashed across the room to the window.

"What did I say? It's not *that* weird."

"Where were they?"

Claire pointed to the sidewalk across the street. "Right there. They were there just a second ago."

"We need to get out of here," Will said.

THIRTY

"I think better when I drive," Will declared, hopefully, as he maneuvered his BMW through the traffic on Kearney. Studying the rearview mirror through a succession of abrupt turns, he was finally convinced that he wasn't being followed by the Russians. In the space of a few blocks, they had gone from the Italian enclave of North Beach to the outskirts of Chinatown. San Francisco was a lot like Disneyland—a series of colorful, tourist-ready attractions jammed together for easy access. All the city needed was a monorail.

"So, how's it going then? Any ideas?" Claire asked.

"Well, I could confront Sam, but if I did, he'd probably just deny everything. And then I'd have given away my one advantage—the fact that they don't know I know."

They stopped briefly at the Hyatt Regency so that Will could go to his room and pick up the memory stick with the encryption keys. He'd been keeping it in the hotel room's safe, which was far too obvious a hiding place if he was ever found.

When Will returned, they drove south to Mission Street. They were approaching the Transbay Terminal, where he had purchased the locker on the day he was fired to store his office furnishings.

He parked in a driveway in front of the bus station. "Let's stop for a second. I'm going to hide the memory stick in a locker that I got here."

Will left Claire in the car while he made his way inside, past two homeless men who were erecting a cardboard fortress around their sleeping area on the sidewalk. Inside, the dim electric lights and falling darkness made the air of the vaulted station lobby seem dense and oppressive. The terminal had the modernist architectural flourishes of a WPA project, but in its current state it was difficult to imagine the place as anyone's idea of progress.

He struggled with the padlock on the locker door, finally opening it with a clang. He began to worry about attracting attention. There was movement in the shadows that draped the corners of the lobby. Will had crumpled the cardboard box to fit it into the locker, and now he struggled to press it back into shape to hold his belongings.

Back at the car, he handed the box to Claire, who placed it on her lap. As they drove away, she began sifting through his things.

"What's this?" Claire asked.

"Six years of my life. It's what left from my office at Reynolds."

Claire hefted the battered copy of *Black's Law Dictionary*. "You ever actually use this thing?"

"Not really."

"Me neither."

"Everyone thinks it's a good idea to get one before they go to law school, and it's just too big and impressive-looking to ever throw away."

While they were waiting for a stoplight to change, Claire removed a tiny silver key from the box. "What's this?"

"Key to my gym locker."

They drove past the office towers of Spear Street and headed south on the Embarcadero toward AT&T Park. At the next stoplight, Will examined the keys hanging from the ignition.

"What is it?" Claire asked. "Did you lose something?"

"No. I didn't." He turned off the car and held up a tiny silver key that was identical to the one that Claire had found in the box. "*This* is the key to my gym locker."

"It looks just like this one, though. Is it a duplicate?"

"No."

"Then who do you think it belongs to?"

The light had turned green, and the car behind them honked.

"You asked me about the last thing that Ben Fisher said to me. Remember what I said?" Several drivers behind them were now leaning on their horns.

"Oh my God," Claire said. "He asked you if you'd seen the key to his gym locker."

The day before he died, Ben had asked Will about his lost gym locker key for a reason. The key had never been lost. Ben had placed it in Will's office so that he would find it later—if something happened to him. Will started the car and drove away fast, making a U-turn on the Embarcadero and heading back to Embarcadero Center and the gym that he and Ben had belonged to.

––––––––

The Athletic Club was favored by professionals who worked in the adjoining office towers of Embarcadero Center. It was eight P.M., so the place thrummed like a factory to the sound of machinery turning—in this case, treadmills and elliptical trainers.

Will entered the men's locker room and went to Ben's locker, four down from his own. Claire followed him in, sneaking past the attendant at the front desk. They were alone in the locker room.

"He's probably still paid up on his membership, so I'll bet they haven't cleared out his locker yet," Will said.

He inserted the tiny key into the padlock, and it opened with a click.

Inside were a pair of moldy-smelling running shoes, nylon running shorts, deodorant, and other assorted toiletries. And a white, letter-sized envelope.

Will slowly removed the envelope and examined it. There were no markings on the outside, and it was unsealed. He removed a sheet torn from a yellow legal pad, which was covered with jagged, steeply slanted handwriting that he recognized as Ben's.

The note read:

If you're reading this, then I'm probably dead. I know how melodramatic that sounds, but there's no other way to say it. I'm an attorney at the law firm of Reynolds, Fincher & McComb. If I am dead, it is because of the actions of Sam Bowen, a partner at the firm. Over the past year, Sam has disclosed confidential information about several wealthy clients to members of a Russian organized-crime family in San Francisco, which is led by a man called Boka. Innocent people have been the victims of extortion and terrorized. Now Boka has asked

Sam to disclose insider information about the upcoming merger of two publicly traded companies, Jupiter Software and Pearl Systems. Until very recently, I didn't know that Sam was involved. Two Russians who work for Boka named Yuri and Nikolai used threats and intimidation to get me to disclose information about the Jupiter transaction. It all started when I met a girl named Katya Belyshev at a movie. At least I think that's her real name. I eventually learned that she also works for Boka. Sam had told Boka and his people to approach me so that when federal agents found out about the insider trading, everyone, including me, would think that I was the source of the insider information, not Sam. Tonight I tried to talk Sam into joining me in going to the Justice Department to tell the whole story and help them make a case against the Russians. He said he was going to, and that we would go together to the offices of the Justice Department tomorrow afternoon at 3. I'm writing this letter because I'm starting to suspect he was lying.

The letter went on to provide additional details about the information that Sam had disclosed to Nikolai and Yuri, the various client relationships that had been compromised.

"We knew Ben had been murdered by the Russians, but now we know for certain that Sam played a role," Will said, turning the letter over in his hands. "And we have the evidence to prove it."

"So were you approached by this Katya person, too?" Claire asked.

"Yes."

Claire looked at him for a moment, apparently deciding not to ask her next question, at least for the time being.

They took the letter with them and drove aimlessly about the city. If he went directly to the Justice Department or the FBI with Ben's letter, it might be enough to successfully prosecute Sam and Boka. But then again, it might not. Because the defense wouldn't have the opportunity to cross-examine Ben, the letter would probably have little probative value in court. And even if the letter proved effective as evidence, it would still fall to him to be the government's primary witness in a case against the *mafiya*. If there was any truth to Jon's story about what had happened to the last witness against Boka's organization, it meant that there was a distinct possibility that he could lose his head, hands, and balls, none of which he was prepared to part with. Even in a best-case scenario, he would probably have to give up his legal career and spend the rest of his life hiding in a witness protection program.

By the time they had driven out to Ocean Beach, Will had formulated a plan. By the time they had returned to the financial district, he had managed to convince Claire that he wasn't crazy.

Will wanted to consult with Jon and hear his defense lawyer's take on the value of the letter in a prosecution. But Will did not want to implicate Jon by telling him what he planned to do next, and he also didn't want to lie to him, so that conversation would have to wait.

They stopped at a copy shop on Geary to have Ben's letter scanned and an electronic copy saved to a diskette. If the long-haired young man behind the counter read the letter, Will was ready with a story that it was a prop in a low-budget mystery thriller being filmed in San Francisco. But the copy shop clerk, his eyes glazed with boredom, didn't glance at the letter as he scanned it, sliding the diskette and the original back across the counter to Will without comment.

After leaving the copy shop, they drove to Embarcadero Four and the offices of Reynolds Fincher. They circled the tower, counting the lighted office windows on the thirty-eighth floor. Only two windows were lit, but it was impossible to tell whether attorneys were still at work up there.

Will pulled his cell phone from his pocket and dialed the number for Sam Bowen's office, which he knew from memory. The phone rang five times, and then Sam's voice mail picked up, laying on the honeyed north Florida accent a bit too thick for Will's taste, like one of those airline pilots determined to impress you with how right his stuff was. "Hi, you've reached voice mail for Sam Bowen at Reynolds, Fincher & McComb. Leave me a message and I'll call you right back."

After hanging up, Will muttered to himself, "Hello, Sam, you two-faced bastard."

THIRTY-ONE

The guard in the front lobby nodded in recognition as Claire pushed through the revolving door and approached the security desk. Will's heart sank when he saw that it was Jeff Wilson, the massive guard who had escorted Will out of the building just a few days ago. He obviously had no idea that Claire had also been fired.

Will wore a Giants cap pulled low over his forehead and tried to look everywhere but at the guard. *If he gets a good look at me,* Will thought, *this little mission is over before it has begun.*

Claire could have commanded Jeff's attention without even trying, but she took no chances, bustling up to the security desk. "It's so nice and quiet here at night, isn't it?" she said sweetly.

"Yeah, I guess it is," Jeff conceded, surprised to be engaged in conversation.

"I'm moving some things out of my office." Unnecessarily, she held up the empty cardboard box. "I'll just be a few minutes."

Will hung back, pretending to be fascinated by the electronic touch-pad directory of the building's tenants.

Claire nodded over her shoulder. "My boyfriend's going to help me carry the stuff out. Does he need to sign in?"

"Nah," Jeff said, with a magnanimous wave. "He's your guest."

Claire swiped her electronic card key over the pad on the security desk, and the guard activated one of the elevators so that they could go up to the thirty-eighth floor. Claire was receiving two months' pay while she looked for another job, which technically entitled her to access to the offices. But both parties understood that she wasn't actually supposed to show up, and especially not after hours.

There would be no record that Will had entered the building. And it was true that Claire had never cleared out her desk. If anyone questioned her, she would just say that she had been too embarrassed by her firing to show up during regular business hours to remove her things, a story that had the advantage of being true.

The elevator doors opened on the dimly lit reception area. The brightest source of light was an open office door at the far end of the hall.

"I'll come by your office and get you when I'm finished," Will whispered before heading for Sam's office. Claire went in the opposite direction to her office, carrying the empty cardboard box. If they were discovered, she would be able to produce a box full of her office items to support their story.

Will recognized that the lit office at the end of the hall belonged to Richard Grogan. Richard was the type who might actually be working at this hour. Richard's office was two doors beyond Sam's, so he would be able to enter Sam's office without passing the open door.

If Richard or other attorneys were working on the floor, they weren't making any noise. He crept down the carpeted hallway, past several works from the firm's bland collection of modern art. At night, the tower creaked softly like a ship at sea. He quickened his pace, anxious to get out of the hallway, where he could be easily spotted.

After confirming that Sam's office was empty, he ducked inside and shut the door, slowly releasing the doorknob so that the lock wouldn't click. It took his eyes a moment to adjust to the darkness. The office was lit only by moonlight streaming through the narrow, vertical windows that ran from floor to ceiling along one wall. He turned on a brass lamp and sat down behind Sam's desk.

As he waited for Sam's computer to boot, he examined the framed photo of Christine, Sam's wife. She had a strong chin, streaked blond hair, and a bemused expression. Everyone who worked with Sam knew that he used his allegedly domineering wife as an excuse for every event that he wanted to skip.

Will froze as the computer's speakers chimed with the musical tones that heralded a Microsoft product. He doubted that anyone could hear that sound through a wall or a closed door. Just the same, he listened, motionless, for footsteps in the hall.

He entered Sam's password, *Azalea*. He knew the password because Sam had once given it to him when they were working on a deal together. Sam had needed Will to access his e-mail to retrieve draft documents sent by opposing counsel while he was on the road. Sam had felt the need to explain, noting that his wife had enlisted him into gardening. The azalea was Christine's favorite flower.

An instruction box appeared on the screen: *Password is incorrect. Please enter password again.* He retyped the password and got the same result.

Will felt like slamming the desk with his fist, but he couldn't afford to make the noise.

He tried to think it through. The system required that attorneys change their password every three months. What did Will do when he was asked to make the change? He usually just added a number to his current password.

Will tried again, typing in the password *Azalea1*.

Wrong.

Next, he entered *Azalea2*.

Wrong again.

Nearly ready to give up, he tried *Azalea3*. A few seconds later, he was staring at the contents of Sam's e-mail inbox.

Will removed the diskette from his jacket and slipped it into the computer's disk drive. He opened the imaged copy of Ben's letter and saved it as an attachment to a blank e-mail.

Consulting the business card that she had given him, he typed the following e-mail to mary.boudreaux@doj.gov:

Dear Ms. Boudreaux,

I understand that you've been investigating the connection between the Russian *mafiya* and insider trading in Jupiter Software stock. When you read the attached letter, which was written by my former colleague Ben Fisher, I think you'll agree that we have a lot to talk about. Please meet me at the bottom of the escalators in Four Embarcadero Center at 10 P.M. Thursday night.

Sam Bowen

Will paused for a long moment, his finger on the mouse, before sending the e-mail. Even if he had not actually pushed Ben off the roof of Embarcadero Center, Sam had killed him just the same. He deserved what he got.

Will entered Sam's outbox of sent items and deleted the record of the e-mail to ensure that Sam didn't see it, then turned off the computer.

It was then that Will heard footsteps coming down the hallway, followed by a voice. Sam's voice. He frantically searched for a hiding place, but the desk was the only option. Turning off the desk lamp, he got down on all fours and crouched beneath Sam's desk.

The lights came on.

"So all that's left is to revise the indemnification provisions and prepare the exhibits, right?" Sam said, sounding tired and irritable.

"That's it. Then I'll e-mail the revised draft out, and the ball's back in their court until tomorrow." It was Jay Spencer.

"They can't say we're holding up the deal this time," Sam said.

"Well, they can," Jay said, "but they'd be wrong."

Will heard Jay leave and Sam's footsteps as he walked around the office. There was a sound of shuffling paper. Sam was probably picking up some files from the working table in the corner of the office.

By placing his face nearly flush with the floor, Will had a sliver of a view from beneath the desk. He saw an expanse of green carpet and Sam's tasseled loafers.

The shoes began moving across the floor. Will hoped that he was leaving, but he passed the office door. He was approaching the side of the desk.

Will drew a deep breath and began formulating the lame

story he would tell as he climbed out from under the desk. Sam's response would likely be outrage, tempered with paternal disappointment. Always most comfortable in the role of good guy, Sam would make a show of not reporting him to building security. He would probably let him walk out on his own. But as soon as he was gone, Sam would call Boka and have him killed, just as he'd had Ben Fisher killed.

But Sam's shoes were now facing the door.

"Claire?" Sam sounded surprised.

"Hi, Sam." Will exhaled with relief at the sound of Claire's voice.

"I don't mean to sound rude, but what are you doing here?"

"Just cleaning out my desk. I preferred to do it when no one was around. I'm sure you can understand."

There was a long pause. "Yeah, sure. Hell, I remember what it's like. I was laid off myself when I was a young attorney."

"You're working late," Claire offered. She was stalling, trying to figure out a way to get Sam out of the office.

"Yeah, we've got a closing. Grogan and Spencer are here, too. I'm too old for this shit."

"What's the problem? Are you short of associates?"

Sam gave a tentative chuckle. "Glad to see you haven't lost your sense of humor. These things always sort themselves out. You'll see. Well, I'm afraid I've got to—"

"I just wanted to say that I really enjoyed working with you." Claire wasn't going to be able to stall Sam much longer. He wanted to get back to work.

"Same here, Claire. Same here. Are you going to be able to get all of your things out tonight?"

"Yes. There's not that much stuff left."

"Good. I hope you'll take this in the spirit in which it's offered, but you probably shouldn't come back up here after hours while you're in your severance period. Don't want anybody getting the wrong idea."

"No problem," Claire said, with a slight edge. "I'm done here."

"Well . . ." Sam said, trying again to break off the conversation.

"Hey, Claire!" It was Jay Spencer.

Sam stepped away from the desk and walked over to the doorway.

"Claire's just packing up the last of her things," Sam said. "I don't think she expected to find so many of us working tonight."

"I sure didn't," Claire said. "Hello, Jay. Richard."

Richard Grogan answered. "Claire. I hope all is well with you."

"Thanks, Richard. I'm fine," Claire said coolly. "And you?"

"Fine as well."

Will pictured Claire standing there, refusing to allow them an easy exit from the conversation, while Sam, Richard, and Jay grew impatient.

Finally, Jay broke the silence. "Sam, Richard and I were wondering if you could come take a look at the new indemnity language. If it looks okay to you, then I think it's ready to go. Excuse us, Claire, but we're kind of under the gun here."

"I understand," Claire said, sounding relieved.

From his vantage point under the desk, Will watched Sam's loafers exit the office as he followed Richard and Jay down the hall.

Will emerged from beneath the desk. Peering from the

doorway, he saw that the hallway was now empty. He hurried to meet Claire in her office so they could make their escape. Roaming the office's hushed corridors after hours had always made him feel vaguely conspiratorial, but never more so than that night.

THIRTY-TWO

A bank of fog rolled across the city like a rising tide, lapping at the office towers of the financial district, pooling in the hollows around Russian Hill, flowing languidly through the warrenlike streets of Chinatown. Seen from Nob Hill down the corridor of California Street, the Bay Bridge was a connect-the-dots abstraction of support pillars and spires, with nothing in between. Will felt almost as if he were intruding on something intimate as he steered his car down an empty Geary Street at three thirty A.M. on a Thursday, watching the fog and the city nestle against one another in the night like an old married couple.

He drove past Dacha Restaurant three times until he was satisfied no one was there. Then he circled twice more, trying to spot any law enforcement surveillance. He decided that if the FBI, the DOJ, or the San Francisco cops were staking out the restaurant, he probably wouldn't be able to spot them, anyway. He was willing to take that risk.

Will pulled into the alleyway behind the restaurant. There was the rusted iron door that Yuri and Nikolai had shoved him through on the night that they introduced him to Valter.

He parked beside a Dumpster and reread the message that he had printed on his home computer:

Boka—

I can't do this anymore. Meet me at the entrance to Justin Herman Plaza, next to Four Embarcadero Center on Thursday at 10 P.M. I want out. But I have something for you—a going-away present.

                                        Sam

He placed the sheet of paper inside an envelope bearing the Reynolds Fincher logo and sealed it. Will slipped the envelope beneath the restaurant's back door.

THIRTY-THREE

On Thursday afternoon at five P.M., Will drove into the parking garage beneath Four Embarcadero Center. He started on the first parking level and worked his way down, until he found Sam's blue Mercedes SLK parked on the third level in a corner far from the elevators. He parked his BMW in a nearby spot.

Sam should appear sometime in the next couple of hours. Even if a transaction was on the brink of closing, he was likely to leave the final preparations, and the attendant all-nighter, to his associates.

Will searched for video surveillance cameras and spotted several, but they did not appear to be trained on the corner of the garage where Sam's car was parked. He knew that he would attract the attention of patrolling security guards if he loitered near Sam's car, so he took the elevator up to the street-level shops. Sam would have to pass this

way to take the elevator down to the garage. Will bought
a cup of coffee, took a seat on a concrete bench twenty
yards from the elevators, and waited. The shadows grew
long, the night fell, and a cold wind whipped through the
walkways of the shopping center. The shops closed, and
the pedestrians dwindled to a few office workers hurrying
home, late for dinner.

He ran his fingers over the stippled plastic grip of the
pistol that was cradled in the pocket of his leather jacket.
Like a new dental filling, he just couldn't get used to the
feel of it. Claire kept the gun for security and had allowed
him to take it only after an argument.

Will's attention drifted for a moment as he watched a security guard pass. When he looked again, he almost failed
to notice Sam, who was already standing before the bank
of elevators. Will checked his watch: It was eight fifteen
P.M.

Sam was carrying a briefcase and wearing a brown
suede jacket and white khakis. He looked anxiously over
his shoulder once or twice as he waited for the elevator to
arrive.

Will approached while Sam was facing the closed elevator doors, his back turned. He reached him just as the doors
slid open with a pneumatic gasp. Sam stepped inside, and
Will followed.

Sam jumped when he turned around and saw Will.
"Will! You scared the shit out of me! What are you doing
here?"

"I'm here to see you."

"Well, it's good to see you, buddy. I was just thinkin'
about you today. How's that job search going?"

"I haven't really gotten around to it yet. I've been kinda
busy."

"Don't wait too long," Sam said, slipping effortlessly into a tone of avuncular concern. "You don't want too big a gap in your résumé."

The doors shut, and the elevator slowly descended.

"Sam, I'm under investigation by the SEC, the DOJ, and the SFPD, so it's not the best time for me to be going out on interviews."

"Really? That's tough. I didn't know the investigation was still going forward."

"Sam, cut the bullshit, okay?"

Sam smiled disarmingly. "William, if I cut the bullshit, there wouldn't be anything left."

"I know that you set me up."

Sam looked incredulous. "What did you say?"

"You told Nikolai and Yuri about my involvement in the Jupiter deal. You gave them insider information on the transaction, and then you set them on me so I would think that I was their source. I was bound to be one of the first suspects, anyway, since I was running the deal."

Sam laughed uncomfortably. "I know this has been a rough time for you, but you can't just go around pointing fingers. You gotta take it like a man."

"I know that I probably wasn't your first choice," Will continued. "You tried to use Ben Fisher, but he wanted the two of you to turn yourselves in to the Justice Department. Yuri and Nikolai were probably the ones who shoved him off the roof. Or maybe you did it yourself. Were you in the office that morning?"

"You need to get some counseling, Will. I don't think you realize how pathetic this sounds." Despite his bluster, Sam was shaken. He was probably trying to figure out how Will could have known that Ben wanted them to turn themselves in to Justice.

"Look, I know about your trip to Moscow for the super-market joint venture deal. I know about Nikolai's connection to the deal. The only thing I don't understand is why you did it."

Sam was anxiously watching the floor numbers, which were turning, ever so slowly. "What are you doing here, Will? You wearing a tape recorder? Is that what this is about?"

Will opened up his jacket and patted the front of his shirt, showing Sam that there was no recording device. The gun was now tucked into his jeans against the small of his back. He didn't want to brandish it in the elevator for fear that security cameras or someone entering the elevator would see it.

"You should go home, Will. Don't make things any worse for yourself than they already are."

"That's just it. For me, how much worse can it get? But you, things could still get a lot worse for you."

"If you start saying crazy shit to the feds, they'll see it for exactly what it is—a poor son of a bitch trying to cut himself a deal by slinging some mud."

The elevator doors opened. Sam stepped out and turned to face Will.

"I'm going to get in my car now. So stop following me."

"I have a gun. And you're going to go for a drive with me. In my car."

"What are you going to do, shoot me? That would be the stupidest thing you've done yet."

"I just want to talk. I think you owe me that much. Now that I know."

"You don't know shit. And I don't owe you shit." When

Sam was belligerent, he sounded much more like someone who had grown up in north Florida.

"I don't want to shoot you, Sam, but I will if I have to."

"You couldn't kill someone, and you know it."

"Maybe, but I would have no problem putting a bullet someplace where it's really going to hurt."

"All right," Sam said. "You want to talk, we'll talk. You're the man with the gun."

"Get in," Will said, pointing to his car. "On the driver's side."

When they were both in the car, Will handed the keys to his BMW to Sam.

"Drive us out of the garage," he said.

Once they were on the street, Will directed Sam to head south across Market. Will removed the gun from his jacket and trained it on Sam, holding it low so that it wouldn't be seen by other drivers.

A few minutes later, they were under the Bay Bridge in a desolate area occupied by parking lots that were nothing more than vacant, unpaved expanses of dirt demarcated by chain-link fences. If you were an office worker in the financial district who could not afford thirty-dollars-a-day parking downtown, this was where you ended up. It was a way to fight the high cost of working in the city, as long as you didn't have to go down there after dark.

Will told Sam to stop next to one of the Bay Bridge's massive supports. Even at night it seemed to cast a shadow, blocking out the faint glow of streetlights and deepening the darkness. He cut off the engine and the headlights.

"Am I supposed to be scared? Is that why you brought me to this place?"

"That's up to you," Will said. "I just wanted a place to

talk where no one would see us. I need to know the rest of the story."

Sam turned in his seat to face Will. "Okay," he said. "I'm going to be straight with you. Up to a point, anyway. I just want you to know that it wasn't personal. Those people are animals. You know what they're like."

"Thanks to you, I do, yeah. How did you get involved with them?"

"Nikolai and a couple of his thug friends showed up at my hotel room in Moscow when I was there to negotiate the Branson deal. They said that my client's supermarket joint venture was going to put their small, local grocery stores out of business."

"So they threatened you?"

"Sure, there was that, but it was all pretty businesslike, by and large. We reached an accommodation."

"What kind of accommodation?"

"I got them in as investors on another transaction that I was working on over there."

"You brought them in as investors? Are you insane?"

Sam shrugged. "It seemed like a good idea at the time. And it got them off my back. Nikolai was running a very profitable business. Even in that cut-rate currency, he was very liquid. And I thought the company was a sure thing."

"What kind of company was it?

"Medical supplies." He grimaced. "You have no idea how fucked up the health care delivery system is in the republics."

"So the deal blew up, and you owed them something."

"Right. That was when I started feeding them information on a few firm clients. The stakes rose from there. They wanted a bigger score, and I thought the Jupiter merger might be it, particularly when I learned about the company's connections to the NSA."

"So you knew about the Clipper Chip program from the start?"

"Of course. That's why I chose that company—the insider trading was always secondary to that. But before I could give the Russians information on Jupiter, I had to give them you to cover my tracks."

"I've always been your go-to guy, haven't I?"

"If it's any consolation, it's true that you weren't my first choice. I always liked you, Will. That was why I chose that dweeb Ben Fisher to take the fall—no pun intended. Unfortunately, he was such a straight arrow that he wouldn't play ball. Like you said, he was going to the feds, and he wanted me to go with him. He forced our hand. He was such a loner that we didn't have anyone we could use to threaten him with. With you, we had your mother and Claire. By the way, how did you know that about Ben?"

"Lucky guess," Will said. Will gestured with his gun for Sam to keep talking. "And then you framed me for Ben's murder."

"You have to admit the access card thing was a nice touch. It focused the suspicion squarely on you and away from me, but it wasn't enough to convict you with. That way, we could continue to use you."

"Were you the one who put Ben's security key in my pocket?"

"Of course it was me. Yuri and Nikolai couldn't get access to the building that early in the morning without attracting attention."

"So that means you were also the one who pushed Ben off the roof."

Sam's face darkened. "I wasn't about to go to prison. Can you see me spending the rest of my life in a federal prison?"

"Actually, I can."

"Well, I can't. It just came down to a choice between him or me, and I chose me."

"So why did you pick me to replace Ben?"

"You were leading the negotiations, so you were the logical choice."

"And when the SEC and DOJ began suspecting me, I acted convincingly guilty because I actually thought I was the source of the leak. . . ."

"Pretty clever, huh? I had to have a decoy when it came to insider trading. The SEC tracks that stuff too closely. And I sure didn't want anyone at Homeland Security to know my name."

"So when Nikolai and Yuri cut me with the box cutter, they weren't really looking for information, they were—"

"Just two boys having fun."

"I thought that Nikolai and Yuri were just petty criminals. Are you saying that they were really in with Boka the whole time?"

"No. That part was pretty much true. Nikolai was using me as his entrée into the *mafiya*. Yuri was just along for the ride. They were both trying to prove themselves to Boka and his organization."

"Aren't you worried that they're going to blame you for the money they lost on Jupiter?"

"That's not a problem because they never actually invested very much money in Jupiter. We made up that story about losing a half mill just to turn up the pressure on you. We needed you to be highly motivated to get us what we really wanted—the encryption keys to the Clipper Chip."

"If the Russians just wanted money, how did this turn into a terrorism scheme?"

"The *mafiya* could have used the encryption keys to commit identity theft or any number of crimes, but that would have drawn the attention of Homeland Security and the NSA. That was more heat than even they were willing to deal with. But they had no problem with selling the keys to a group of interested parties from the U.K."

"You mean Aashif Agha."

Sam looked surprised. "How do you know that name?"

"He was at Dacha one night when Nikolai and Yuri brought me there." Will drew a breath. "All right, I'm going to ask you again. Why did you do this?"

"It's pretty obvious, isn't it, Will? It was the money. Boka pays me well for what he gets. And the encryption keys are going to go for a very big price. I'm going to retire early with what I make on this one. There were actually several terrorist organizations bidding. For them, the encryption keys were perfect. They offered the opportunity to do an enormous amount of damage to U.S. industries like financial services, health care, airlines, and defense. But not only that, it would be a huge embarrassment to the federal government because the keys weren't even supposed to exist. Who knows? A scandal like that might even be enough to bring down a president."

"People are going to die. They're going to shut down the BART trains and release sarin nerve gas. But you knew that, didn't you?"

A look of surprise crossed Sam's face before he could disguise it. He clearly wanted to ask Will how he'd learned of the planned attack on the BART trains, but he knew he wouldn't get an answer.

"What have you given the Russians so far?" Will asked.

"Not that much, really. A tip on a real estate development deal. Some personal information on a few clients that they could use for extortion."

"You're a partner. You make a good living. Why were you so desperate for money?"

"You really thought making partner was going to solve all your problems, didn't you?" Sam asked contemptuously. "After a while, 'making a good living' is just not fucking good enough. You know how many deals I've worked on that ended up making other people rich? There's a big difference between having a nice car and a nice house and being *liquid*. I got preferred shares on some of the tech deals I worked on, and I thought that was going to put me over the hump, but that's all for shit now."

Sam observed a brief moment of silence for his lost tech stock portfolio.

"Didn't you ever think about the consequences of what you were doing? The attack on the trains is just the part of the plan that I know about. What if a thousand people died? Or a hundred thousand?"

"We're living in an information age, Will," Sam said matter-of-factly. "Information is just a commodity, like any other. I had some and I sold it. I can't be responsible for what the next guy does with it."

Will checked his watch again: It was nine forty P.M.

"You have to be someplace?" Sam asked.

"Just start the car," Will said. He had heard enough.

Driving back to the financial district, Sam seemed to grow more relaxed. "Will, buddy," he said, "I knew you weren't going to shoot me."

"Why's that?"

"Because everyone has a threshold they won't cross, a thing they won't do, even if it's necessary to their success. Successful people just have that threshold set a bit higher than everyone else. Take you, for example. You've been willing to do the things that are necessary to make it at a competitive place like Reynolds, but you've reached your limit. This is as far as you go."

"What self-help book have you been reading? *The Seven Habits of Highly Effective Sociopaths*?"

Sam laughed with a snort. "That's funny. I'm going to use that."

"Don't get too comfortable over there," Will said, growing annoyed. "I'm still pointing a gun at you."

"You may be holding a gun, but that doesn't mean you're in control of the situation."

"Explain that one to me."

"Nothing you can do changes the fact that I've got Boka behind me. If you do anything except sit still for your prison sentence, you're not going to live very long."

"Now is not a good a time to be threatening me, Sam."

"That's not a threat, it's just the reality of your situation."

Will instructed Sam to drive north on the Embarcadero and stop in front of the Ferry Building. "Are we done here?" Sam asked, as the car came to a halt.

"Yeah. You can get out now."

"One more thing," Sam said, an assertive note in his voice. "I want you to give me the encryption keys."

"I don't have them."

"I know you better than they do. You're a capable guy, and Claire's very sharp. I figure you two probably had enough connections over at Jupiter to find a way, particularly since you're desperate." Sam stared at Will for a long moment. "Whether you have them or not, I'm going to tell Boka that I think you do. So if you have them, you might as well hand them over. Boka is a very persuasive guy when he wants to be."

After a long pause, Will reached in his pocket and removed the memory stick, which was in a plastic baggie.

Sam grinned. "God, I love being right."

Sam climbed out of the car and came around to the open passenger's-side window to face Will. "You take care of yourself, buddy." Sam squinted meaningfully at Will, the same look that Bill Clinton used to signify deep empathy. For Will, it was the ultimate expression of Sam's arrogance. After everything that he had done, from murdering Ben to setting Will up to face a prison sentence, Sam still thought that he held some sway over him. Like a parent who always sees their child as a needy six-year-old, Sam would always see Will as the first-year associate who had once been so anxious to impress him.

"Good-bye, Sam," Will said.

Sam turned and strode across the Embarcadero toward Justin Herman Plaza, crossing the broad median lined with palm trees. Will watched as Sam walked away. Will had no doubt that Sam planned to contact Boka to have him killed as soon as he was out of his sight. Sam had clearly been alarmed by the degree of knowledge that Will had displayed about Ben Fisher, Aashif Agha, and the planned attack on public transit.

There was a chill in the air, and the fog hadn't rolled in yet. He had a clear view of the empty expanse of the plaza, which was lit by a nearly full moon. This was the place where not so long ago he had met Katya after his first encounter with Yuri and Nikolai. On the right was Vaillancourt Fountain, the enormous sculpture that resembled corroded ventilation ducts. On the left were the concrete ramps scarred by skateboard wheels.

Looming over the far end of the plaza was the white tower of Embarcadero Four. Underneath the tower was the garage where Sam's car was parked. When Will dropped Sam off, he knew that he would walk in that direction to retrieve his car.

When Sam reached the center of the plaza, two figures wearing Puma tracksuits, one chocolate brown and one moss green, emerged to meet him. Will checked the time by the Ferry Building clock tower. Everyone was right on time for the ten P.M. meeting that Will had arranged.

When he saw the two Russians, Sam stopped and looked back in Will's direction. Even at that distance, Will thought he could feel Sam's eyes lock on him. Or maybe he was just searching for an escape route.

Sam must have known that if he tried to run, he would never make it, so he continued walking toward the Russians, more slowly now.

Sam and the *sportsmeny* stood talking for a minute or so. Sam's hands stabbed in the air. It was his last negotiation, and one in which he had no leverage.

One of the men in tracksuits produced a laptop from a shoulder bag. He placed the laptop on the ground and, crouching on one knee, plugged in the memory stick to examine its contents.

When the tracksuit completed his review, he began shouting at Sam. Moments later, Sam was on the ground. They must have used a silencer because Will did not hear a shot. At first, he thought that Sam might have been shoved or tripped, but he didn't rise and he didn't move.

After that, things happened quickly. The federal agents that Will had invited to meet Sam at the escalators of Em-

barcadero Center must have been watching the exchange
from the concourse of the office building.

Shouts carried faintly across the plaza. In response, the
Russians turned to face the building, raising their guns. Before they could aim, there was the sound of at least fifteen
shots, crowding on one another like the explosions at the
finale of a fireworks display. When the shots stopped echoing across the square and in Will's head, he saw that the
two Russians were slumped on the concrete of the plaza
next to Sam. One of the Russians tried to sit up, the palms
of his hands pressed against the concrete, as if it required
all of his strength to oppose gravity.

When the federal agents examined the memory stick,
they would see that it was blank. If they checked for finger-
prints on the memory stick, they would only find those of
Sam and the Russians. Will had been careful.

As four agents emerged from the office building and
approached the bodies, Will reached for his keys to start
the car. But before he could turn the key in the ignition,
the passenger side door of the car opened and Aashif Agha
climbed inside, pointing a pistol at Will's chest.

THIRTY-FOUR

"Where is your gun?" Aashif asked.

"I don't have one."

"Where is your gun? I saw you pointing it at Sam." Aashif was dressed nondescriptly in a gray North Face fleece jacket, khakis, and a white button-down shirt.

Will pointed to the glove compartment. After Sam had walked away, he had placed the gun there, so there was no way he could reach it with Aashif sitting in the passenger seat.

Aashif removed the gun and ejected the clip. He tossed the bullets out the window and then replaced the gun in the glove compartment.

"What do you want from me?" Will asked.

"You know what I want," Aashif responded. "Drive away slowly."

He started the car and drove down the Embarcadero,

unnoticed by the federal agents who were still gathered around the bodies of Sam and the Russians a few hundred yards away in Justin Herman Plaza.

After driving for only a few blocks, Aashif said, "Pull over. Here."

Will parked beside Pier 15, a hangarlike concrete building that bore the sign DELTA BAY TUGS. The corrugated iron door to the building was raised halfway.

"Get out," Aashif said. "We're going in there."

As they approached the doorway, the Port of San Francisco flag atop the roof snapped in the cold wind. Aashif peered inside, confirming that the place was empty. The cavernous, warehouselike space had a series of small windows near the roof that let in dim shafts of light from the streetlights that lined the waterfront. To the right were the closed offices of the tugboat line. Past the office was another open, corrugated iron door that led to a walkway along the water where several tugs were docked. It was quiet enough that they could hear the boats bumping against the pylons and the slap of the waves.

"I've been watching you," Aashif said, holding the gun at his side. "Obviously, you didn't give the encryption keys to Sam, so you must still have them with you, or you can tell me where you've hidden them. If you give them to me now, I can still let you walk away."

"You're not going to let me live."

"Maybe that's true," Aashif conceded. "But it's going to be much worse if you don't cooperate. My Russian friends tell me that a bullet in the knee is very painful." Aashif didn't sound as sure of himself as his words suggested. He kept raising the gun to point it at Will, then lowering it again to his side. He looked no more comfortable holding a gun than Will would have.

He guessed that Aashif was alone in San Francisco, separated from the other members of his cell. Why else would he come by himself, when he was so obviously a planner rather than a trained killer?

"What can you hope to accomplish by killing innocent people?" He figured that he could buy some time if he could get Aashif talking.

"I'm not here to engage in a dialogue with you. And why do you assume that those people are innocent? Look at the culture they've created, look at the leaders they've chosen."

"The world will only see you as murderers."

"Your world, maybe. But I don't live in your world." He raised the gun again. "Now, where are the keys?"

"I don't have them here. Why would I carry them around like that?"

Aashif lifted the gun and aimed at Will's knee. Although he was only six feet away, Aashif failed to hold the gun steady, and the bullet missed, ricocheting and striking metal somewhere above them in the rafters.

They were both startled, Will by the realization that his knee was still intact and Aashif by the incredible racket created by the gunshot reverberating off aluminum in the empty space. Unaccustomed to the noise of the shot, Aashif stupidly stared at the gun for a moment as if that were the problem.

Will recognized the opportunity and charged at Aashif, grabbing the hand that was holding the pistol. His momentum knocked them down, with Will on top and still gripping the hand that held the gun.

Will slammed Aashif's fist repeatedly against the concrete floor, but he wouldn't release the gun. With his other hand, Aashif punched at Will's head, but he couldn't get much force behind it.

Will managed to get his finger over the trigger as they struggled. Will squeezed, and a series of shots struck a concrete wall until there were no more bullets and the firing pin just clicked.

Aashif finally managed to get his right hand free and struck Will in the forehead with the barrel of the gun. With his left hand, he punched Will in the windpipe.

Will coughed and struggled to breathe as Aashif got to his feet. Before he could recover, Aashif kicked him hard in the ribs. Then he stepped back and kicked him again in the stomach.

Realizing that he wouldn't be able to remain conscious if he absorbed another blow, Will managed to throw himself forward, tackling Aashif at the knees. Aashif fell backward, and the back of his head struck the concrete hard.

Aashif kicked out to keep Will off him, and his shoe struck him a glancing blow on the cheek. Aashif got up and staggered to the other side of the warehouse.

When Will stood up, Aashif was nowhere to be seen.

Will remained motionless, listening for movement, but there was no sound. He walked slowly toward the opposite end of the warehouse and stepped outside onto the narrow walkway lined with crates where the tugs were docked.

Will still didn't see Aashif. It was hard to hear small movements now over the sound of the wind, the lapping waves, and the creaking of the tugs straining against their moorings. He took one step, then another, until he was halfway down the walkway.

Will leaned over to see if Aashif was crouched on the deck of a tug.

Suddenly, he felt a sharp pain in the front of his left shoulder and a tearing sensation. He was pulled backward and spun around. Will saw that Aashif had been hiding behind a crate and had speared his shoulder with the single curved point of a grappling hook used to secure tugs to the dock.

The pain was paralyzing, and his left arm no longer seemed able to move the way he wanted it to.

Aashif punched Will in the face, and he fell backward onto the wooden walkway. Will lay sprawled, the grappling hook still embedded in the front of his shoulder with the handle resting on his chest.

Standing over Will, Aashif placed his foot on the hook, then slowly put his weight into it. Will felt the hook sink deeper into the flesh of his shoulder. Explosions of red and white filled his vision.

"Tell me," Aashif said. "Tell me and you can live."

Groaning, Will sat up a bit, as if he were about to speak. Aashif took a step back. Then Will aimed a kick at Aashif's knee, landing the heel of his shoe squarely on the kneecap. Aashif cried out and dropped to one knee.

While Aashif held his knee in pain, Will managed to stand up. By the time Will was firmly on his feet, Aashif was also standing. Will rushed at him, hoping to shove him off the pier into the water.

Aashif and Will struggled at the edge of the walkway for a moment, and then they both pitched into the dark waters of the bay.

They dropped a few feet, and then the frigid waters closed over them. The shock of the cold and the pull of the current were familiar to Will from his windsurfing days. It allowed him to focus more quickly on what he needed to do.

He kicked to propel himself to the surface, gasping for air as the waves struck him. Aashif was several feet away, still coughing and sputtering.

The grappling hook was still buried in his chest. As

carefully as he could under the circumstances, Will removed the long steel hook from his shoulder. A cloud of red appeared around him in the water. He felt like he was about to pass out. Then he saw Aashif swimming toward him, almost upon him.

Aashif reached Will just as he was recovering his breath and placed both hands around his neck, choking him and forcing him down. Even in his weakened state, Will was a strong swimmer, and he managed to push Aashif upward until his back was against a pylon.

They were face-to-face now as Aashif tried to strangle him and stay afloat. Will still had no use of his left hand, but he managed to throw punches with his right, slamming Aashif's head backward into the barnacled pylon. After three blows, Aashif released his grip on Will's throat.

With a useless left arm and dizzy from blood loss, Will knew that he couldn't swim for very much longer, much less fight. While Aashif was still stunned, Will swam away from him and climbed a wooden ladder, hauling himself dripping and exhausted onto the pier.

Will staggered back into the building, hoping to find a weapon. He wasn't going to win a fight with one good arm. Behind him, he heard a wet thud and knew that Aashif had also climbed back onto the pier.

When Will looked behind him, he saw that Aashif was inside the building now. He was frantically examining the contents of a tool bench, also searching for a weapon.

When Aashif turned to face him, he held a hammer. Will scanned the room and saw another tool bench on the wall closest to him.

He thrashed through fast-food bags and old newspapers that littered the workspace. He could hear Aashif's footsteps advancing quickly behind him.

Will's fingers closed around a long Phillips screwdriver. It would have to do.

When he spun around, brandishing the screwdriver, Aashif was only a few feet away. Aashif stopped, and they circled each other looking for an opening, both breathing heavily and dripping wet.

Aashif was not more physically imposing than Will. And he didn't seem to be any more experienced when it came to fighting. The one thing about Aashif that unnerved him was the look in his eye that indicated that he had absolutely no qualms about killing. Will thought that he could kill Aashif if it was a matter of self-defense, but that wasn't the same thing.

Aashif swung the hammer at Will's head, but came up short. Will lunged ineffectually with the screwdriver. He quickly realized that the screwdriver was going to work as a weapon only if he could get in close.

Aashif jabbed at Will with a left. Will blocked the blow easily, but then realized it was a feint and that Aashif was swinging the hammer at him with his right hand.

The hammer struck below Will's damaged left shoulder. He heard ribs crack with a sound like dry branches snapping underfoot. Will didn't feel the pain in his side so much. It was more systemic than that, like a rolling blackout. He felt his knees starting to buckle.

The near-blackout must have lasted no more than a second because when Will regained his senses, Aashif still hadn't managed to pull the hammer back into position for a final blow. He lurched forward into Aashif like a struggling boxer going for a clinch.

They danced about awkwardly for a moment as Aashif tried to push him away and retain his grip on the hammer. With his one good hand, Will landed a punch to Aashif's face, the screwdriver facing away in his fist.

Aashif's eyes widened as he saw Will turn his fist around so that the point of the screwdriver was aimed at him. With the strength he had left, Will plunged it down into Aashif's throat, so that little more than the yellow plastic handle showed.

Blood began to spurt from Aashif's neck. Aashif reached up to gingerly touch the handle of the screwdriver, perhaps hoping that the injury wasn't as grave as it seemed. Then he slowly sat down with his back against an iron support column as the blood continued to flow, but more slowly now. Within two minutes his eyes closed, and he was gone.

Will sat down on the concrete floor, woozy from the adrenaline, blood loss, and exhaustion. He wasn't sure how long he remained like that, but he hoped it wasn't long. He wasn't safe yet, and he needed to remain conscious.

Will wanted to call Jon and tell him everything that had happened, and perhaps come clean to the authorities as well. After all, he had killed Aashif in self-defense. Wouldn't he be considered a hero for stopping the man who was about to launch a massive terrorist attack, including the murder of hundreds of BART commuters?

Will wasn't so sure. If he told the authorities the entire story, several different agencies would all have to accept his claim that he wasn't a willing participant in the Russians' schemes. At best, they would force him to testify against the *mafiya* and enter the witness protection program. His legal career would be over, and the Russians would be trying even harder to find him and kill him before he could take the stand. Will knew what happened to witnesses against the *mafiya*.

Will's calculations were interrupted by a police siren outside. Someone had called in the gunshots. From the sound of the siren, the patrol car was still a block or two away. The police probably didn't know which building the shots had come from.

There was no more time to deliberate.

Will walked onto the pier and threw the gun and the screwdriver far out into the bay. Then he ran out of the building, climbed into his car, and pulled out onto the Embarcadero, careful not to accelerate. Will drove slowly for a couple hundred yards, his eyes glued to the rearview mirror, but the police car was not following him.

Will rolled down the windows, letting the cold, damp air in. It cleared his head but seemed to make the pain in his shoulder and ribs worse. As he drove away, he felt an overpoweringly acute awareness of the simple fact that he was alive.

THIRTY-FIVE

Will threaded his way among the pedestrians on the sidewalk. It was eight A.M. on a mild Tuesday morning, with blue skies and clouds dispensed in roughly equal portions. As he passed a market, he inhaled the extravagant scent of mangoes from a sidewalk table. He had been at his new job for only two weeks, and nothing was routine yet, not even the walk to work. Will passed the ornate, pink stucco wedding cake that was once the El Capitan Theater.

Will walked briskly and felt good to be able to swing his left arm at his side. He'd only recently been able to remove the sling that he had worn for two months.

He turned into the Ixtlán Taquería and ordered a breakfast burrito and a large black coffee. He was greeted by a few cries of "Hey, *abogado*" from behind the kitchen counter, followed by a stream of Spanish spoken far too quickly for him to follow. After one week, they'd identified him as a regular. After two weeks, they'd started teasing him about his crude Spanish.

Bearing a cardboard cup of coffee and a brown paper bag with a rapidly expanding grease stain, Will climbed the stairs next door to the *taquería*. He could hear a Mexican tenor singing a *norteño* folk song from the Spanish-language record company on the first floor. When he entered the Law Offices of Coulter and Connelly, the usual gathering of soft-tissue injuries and neck sprains swiveled stiffly to greet him with expressions that, at least on that day, he interpreted as gratitude.

Ingrid presided contentedly over her domain from the reception desk. Apparently, her waiting room charges were still too sleepy and disorganized to mount any serious challenges to her authority.

"What's on my calendar?"

"You have Mr. Díaz at nine thirty." Will was drafting a partnership agreement for Roberto Díaz, a successful auto parts dealer who was taking on investors and opening new locations in Sacramento and Diamond Bar.

"Is that it?"

"There's also Mr. Heard at eleven." Steve Heard, whom he had represented at Reynolds Fincher, was that rarity in the current economy: a high-tech startup entrepreneur. Will was incorporating his new social networking website, which was actually still operating out of a garage. Like faster microchips, hope was a perennial in Silicon Valley.

Will was not as busy as he had been working at Reynolds Fincher, but he found that the slower pace suited him. He had been retained by a few of the clients that he had worked with at his former firm, and almost every day someone new walked in the door with an agreement to be negotiated or a small business to be formed.

He was only earning a fraction of the salary he'd made at Reynolds Fincher. By the standard of success he'd measured himself against over the past ten years, he was now an abject failure. His prospects of climbing back up to a position at an Am Law 100 law firm were slim. By selling his condo and his BMW and liquidating some of his savings, he had managed to pay down enough of his oppressive student loan debt so that he could actually live on his newly reduced income. He jokingly referred to it as The New Austerity. Somehow, though, it didn't seem to bother him nearly as much as he had expected. He'd even gotten used to seeing the photos of Dana in the *Chronicle* with the mayor-elect.

The first door on the right was Jon's office. His elbow was on his desk, propping up his head about two inches above a file. Jon was preparing for an afternoon hearing on a summary judgment motion in a construction defect case. He was representing the plaintiffs, a Sunset District family whose roof had collapsed.

Jon looked up and clucked under his breath, "Fuck fuck fuck fuck fuck fuck."

"Everything okay in there?" Will asked.

"You know, we could actually lose this summary judgment motion. Fuck fuck fuck."

"Sounds like you're fucked," Will said, who had learned to take Jon's daily laments in stride.

"Yeah, maybe," he responded, his eyes fixed somewhere over Will's head, assembling his counterarguments.

Will entered his office and adjusted the blinds to cast sunlight on his desk. He cleared away client files and unwrapped his breakfast burrito.

Claire Rowland entered his office, picked up his burrito, and took a large bite out of it. Claire had declined another

job at a big financial district law firm to go to work for Will
as his sole associate.

"What was that?"

"You don't pay me enough. You should at least feed me."

"I think this whole dating thing is undermining the chain
of authority around here."

"Yeah," she acknowledged. "But what are you gonna
do?" She dropped a stack of paper on his desk. "Here's a
draft of that partnership agreement for Díaz."

"Thanks. Why don't you drop back by at ten, and you
can sit in on the meeting when we review the agreement."

As she circled around behind his desk to leave, she
brushed her fingers across the back of his shoulders.

"Hey, don't think that those little incidents of sexual harassment go unnoticed," he said as she left.

Will ate his burrito, drank his coffee, and examined the
stone lions in the façade of the building next door. It was a
1940s movie palace that was now a teeming garage sale of a
store where everything was ninety-nine cents or less. Will had
purchased his first new desk accessory there: a plastic action
figure of a masked Mexican wrestler known as "El Guapo." El
Guapo glared at him over the half-eaten burrito, legs planted
firmly apart and hands extended with fingers spread in a grap-
pler's stance. As he stared at a patch of sunshine on his desk,
he realized that he was smiling, although he wasn't sure why.

Will's face-off with El Guapo was interrupted by the
ringing phone. A sunny voice answered, "Haaah Will! This
is Mary Boudreaux of the DOJ!"

"Hello, Mary."

"I hear you've started your own firm. Congratulations!"

"Well, I joined a friend's practice. But thanks."

"I guess you've heard about Sam's Bowen's death. Such
a tragedy."

"Yes, it is."

"You worked with him, didn't you?"

"Yes, I did."

"Wasn't he your mentor at the firm?"

"I wouldn't go that far."

"You must be upset. When was the last time you saw him?"

"Mary, you know I'm represented by counsel, so if you have questions that you would like to ask me, you really should go through him. He's right next door, and I can transfer you over to him if you like."

"No, no, that won't be necessary. I just wanted you to know that Dennis and I were thinking about you. About how lucky you are."

"Lucky?" Will asked, nonchalantly. "How so?"

"Think about it. Out of the blue, we receive an e-mail from Bowen containing some very incriminating evidence. A smart lawyer like him, you'd think he would have at least held back on delivering the goods until he had cut a deal for himself."

"Maybe he just wanted to do the right thing."

"Uh-huh. And then Sam makes an appointment with us, which puts us in exactly the right place at the right time to witness his murder and take down those Russians. Now, you have to admit, Will, that was . . . serendipitous."

"When you put it that way, I guess you're right."

"And look where that puts you. Now that we know about Sam, you're no longer the focus of an insider trading investigation. And, in another stroke of luck, one of the tracksuits that we shot at Justin Herman Plaza is going to live, and he's decided to testify against Boka."

"Isn't that breaking their code of silence or something?"

"When you murder someone with four federal agents

as witnesses, your options narrow down quite a bit. Boka
has already been taken into custody based on Tracksuit's
statements, and the city's Russian *mafiya* are facing their
first credible prosecution in years. And all of this is going
forward without you having to testify." There was a long
pause.

Will still worried that Boka might choose to come after
him one day, but he figured that the Russians still had no
idea of the role that he had played in blocking their plans.
And since Boka was probably busy preparing his defense
to the federal case against him, Will guessed that he was
the least of Boka's concerns.

Mary continued, "And then the next day, we find the
body of Aashif Agha inside a pier building, less than a mile
away from where Sam was murdered. It looked like he had
been in quite a fight."

"You have any idea who did it?"

"I have a theory, but it's not fully developed. Probably
never will be. But you've got to be pleased to see that
another associate of the Russians has been eliminated,
someone who might have come after you. As far as I'm
concerned, whoever killed Agha deserves a medal."

"I couldn't agree more."

"Now, Will, as the beneficiary of all that amazing, incredible luck, I wanted to know if you have anything that
you'd like to tell me. Something that might complete the
picture here?"

"I'm afraid I don't, Mary."

Another pause. "Of course you don't. Just thought I'd
ask. I had to ask, right? And as long as I'm beating my head
against the wall, I was wondering if you had anything to do
with the Senate's investigation into Jupiter's connections to
the NSA and its surveillance activities?"

"I'm following that story in the press just like you," Will said.

Claire's conversations with her former colleagues at the Electronic Privacy Information Center had led to a flurry of Freedom of Information Act requests, front-page press coverage, and, ultimately, Senate hearings regarding how the NSA had used the Clipper Chip, and its relationship with Jupiter, to secretly spy on U.S. citizens. The president had held a press conference berating the *New York Times* for its role in breaking the story, charging that it was "giving comfort to the enemy." In the wake of the scandal, Jupiter's stock price had plummeted, and the company was hit with class-action lawsuits brought by the company's investors and users of the Paragon encryption program.

"I thought it was interesting that EPIC led the way in bringing the story to light, since Claire was a former employee there."

"Quite a series of coincidences," Will said.

"You're probably wondering why I bothered to make this call, aren't you?" Mary asked. "Well, I just wanted you to know that Dennis and I are going to be keeping an eye on you, checking in from time to time. Just to see how you're doing."

Will's pager began beeping. Cradling the receiver against his shoulder, he searched his satchel for the device. "Thanks for calling, Mary, but I'm afraid I've got an important call coming in."

As he hung up the phone, he examined the text message on his pager, which read, BERKELEY MARINA WINDS AT 12.8 KNOTS. A PERFECT DAY FOR WINDSURFING!

Checking his schedule, he figured that he could be on the water by one.

Will paddled his board out over the lightly choppy waters of the bay, which were brownish-green from the sediment kicked up by the waves. When he was about twenty yards out from the Berkeley Marina, he uphauled his sail and adjusted the boom until the vinyl caught the wind and filled with a snap. The board jerked forward and he was in motion.

Settling into position, with his feet on the centerline of the board and leaning back against the tension in the sail, he quickly picked up speed. The board bounced over each swell, sending him airborne for one still second before he hit the water with a jolt. With his backhand, he spilled some wind from the sail to regulate his speed. Racing into open waters, he gazed at the towers of downtown San Francisco across the dappled expanse of the bay, which gleamed in the afternoon sun like hammered silver. He spotted Four Embarcadero Center, where he had once worked. His time at Reynolds Fincher already seemed as distant as the tower itself.

Will reached into a pocket of his wetsuit and produced the memory stick. He tossed it into the bay and watched its silver surface glint for a moment like a minnow as the sunlight struck it before it disappeared into the depths.

Skimming across the bay, no longer struggling with the sail, no longer even trying to slow down, he experienced the feeling that was the reason why he windsurfed. It was a moment of perfect, trembling equilibrium between the stillness of his stance and the rushing water beneath the board. He felt the weight of his body counterpoised against the wind in the sail, the cold water of the bay, and the warmth of the afternoon sun on his shoulders through the wetsuit. He let the wind fill the sail, and the dark green water lost its softness and became hard like glass. The boom shivered in his hand, channeling the force of the wind.

As he tacked to remain flush with the wind, he was led farther and farther across the bay until the marina was only a green bump in the distance. Just when he thought he couldn't go any faster, a southerly gust sent him rocketing. As he reacted to the shifting wind currents, hurtling forward through the spray and glare, he realized, not unhappily, that he had drifted far from his carefully plotted course.

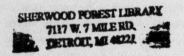